"Why should St
you, after what you did?"

Chase hadn't meant to ask himself the question out loud, and the surprising way the quiet words broke the stillness startled him. Stevie wouldn't care. She would get over him. Someday she'd find someone else. He tried not to think about it.

Stevie needed to find someone who would slip into her life without a ripple, bringing no shadows, no ghosts. Someone who'd wave to Mrs. Trimble in the mornings, who'd eat Leo's chicken soup...

Chase shook his head at the sudden, unexpected sense of longing that filled him. Who would have thought he would miss something as simple as the gentle companionship of his neighbors, the people who'd made room for a withdrawn loner like him in their lives?

Because of Stevie. She had brought him into their fold. But whether she cared or not, hated him or not, he knew she would be with him forever....

Dear Reader,

When two people fall in love, the world is suddenly new and exciting, and it's that same excitement we bring to you in Silhouette Intimate Moments. These are stories with scope and grandeur. The characters lead lives we all dream of, and everything they do reflects the wonder of being in love.

Longer and more sensuous than most romances, Silhouette Intimate Moments novels take you away from everyday life and let you share the magic of love. Adventure, glamour, drama, even suspense— these are the passwords that let you into a world where love has a power beyond the ordinary, where the best authors in the field today create stories of love and commitment that will stay with you always.

In coming months, look for novels by your favorite authors: Kathleen Eagle, Marilyn Pappano, Emilie Richards, Heather Graham Pozzessere and Kathleen Korbel, to name only a few. And whenever—and wherever—you buy books, look for all the Silhouette Intimate Moments, love stories with that extra something, books written especially for you by today's top authors.

Leslie J. Wainger
Senior Editor and Editorial Coordinator

JUSTINE DAVIS

Stevie's Chase

SILHOUETTE·INTIMATE·MOMENTS®

Published by Silhouette Books New York

America's Publisher of Contemporary Romance

SILHOUETTE BOOKS
300 East 42nd St., New York, N.Y. 10017

STEVIE'S CHASE

ISBN: 0-373-07402-6

First Silhouette Books printing October 1991

Printed in the U.S.A.

JUSTINE DAVIS

lives in San Clemente, California. Her interests outside of writing are sailing, doing needlework, riding and driving her restored 1967 Corvette roadster—top down, of course.

A policewoman, Justine says that years ago, a young man she worked with encouraged her to try for a promotion to a position that was, at that time, occupied only by men. "I succeeded, became wrapped up in my new job, and that man moved away, never, I thought, to be heard from again. Ten years later he appeared out of the woods of Washington state, saying he'd never forgotten me and would I please marry him. With that history, how could I write anything but romance?"

To the Olamendi's party crowd—thank you all.

Chapter 1

As soon as she heard the sound, Stevie knew without looking that it was the mystery man. As she dodged under the cover of the carport to get out of the rain, she glanced at her watch; he was later tonight than usual.

She pulled open the door of her car and leaned in for the book she'd left on the seat. The sound of the motorcycle was closer, yet markedly restrained now compared to the screaming howl she knew it was capable of. At least he was considerate enough to keep the beast leashed when he got close, she thought as she spotted the book that had fallen onto the floorboard.

She heard the whir of tires on wet pavement as he pulled into the end of the alley and wondered once more what on earth "C. Sullivan" did that required his presence seven days a week, beginning at dawn and ending well after dark.

In her thoughts she used the name she'd seen on his mailbox, right next to her own "S. Holt." It was the only name she knew. Although he'd lived in the apartment next to hers for six months, no one seemed to know any more than that, not even Dan Bartlett, the irrepressible intern who seemed

to know everything about everyone within five minutes of
meeting them.

"He's tight-lipped as a clam," Dan had told her. "He
leaves early, comes home late and doesn't talk to anyone."

"Maybe he likes it that way."

Stevie had had to smother a grin at Dan's bemusement;
the idea of keeping to oneself was totally foreign to the
young doctor. But Stevie, having a great respect for privacy, understood. And she could hardly complain; except
for the motorcycle, he was exceptionally quiet. The perfect, if peculiar, neighbor.

The beam of the single headlight caught the falling rain
in a shaft of brightness, making the drops look eerily suspended. She wondered if he had, even in this unusual
weather for San Diego, gone through the odd routine she
had noticed before, that of stopping at the entrance to the
parking area and looking around in all directions before he
pulled in, as if he were watching for someone, or something.

If he had, she doubted if he could have seen whatever it
was if it—or they—had been five feet away. Not in this rain.
Her eyes instinctively went to him as the bike came to a halt
in the spot next to hers.

That he was soaked was obvious. Water ran off him in
small rivulets, puddling on the relatively dry asphalt beneath the carport roof. His jeans were so wet it was impossible to tell if they were blue or black, and from the knees
down they were spattered with mud. The mask of his full-
face helmet was so wet with rain she wondered how he could
see anything. Then something about his very stillness caught
her full attention. She turned toward him, watching.

He did nothing. He didn't shut the bike off, didn't take his
helmet off, didn't put the kickstand down . . . nothing. He
just sat there, the big cycle balanced by his feet on either
side, his head bent slightly downward, his gloved hands still
gripping the handlebars, as if now that he was here, he
wasn't sure what to do. The light in the carport wasn't that
good, but she could have sworn she saw a shudder ripple

through the tall, lean body. Then he straightened suddenly, tugging at the heavy gloves.

Galvanized by his movement, she sat down in the front seat of her car, leaning over to reach for the thick paperback. She remembered the first time she had seen him, the day after he had moved in. She had had an early meeting with a client in Los Angeles and had been stifling a yawn as she walked to her car. It wasn't until she had set her portfolio and the layouts for the meeting in the back seat that she had realized someone was kneeling beside the spotless motorcycle that had appeared in the next space.

When he stood up, she'd wondered how on earth she could have missed him. He had to be at least six feet, probably more; he seemed to tower over her own five foot six. Her second thought had been how incredibly he would photograph.

Lord, she'd breathed silently, I could sell anything from ice cubes to matches with this guy. Icy cold and fiery hot, it was all there, physical beauty with just the right touch of rough edges.

She'd tried to laugh at herself, at the habit she'd developed of looking at everything in relation to her work, of converting everyday scenes into ad campaigns in her head, but she'd been too rapt in her appraisal to stop.

Long, lean legs were encased in snug, worn, faded jeans, bunched slightly at the bottom where they slid over heavy black boots. The jeans rode low on his narrow hips, emphasizing the flat belly beneath the simple white T-shirt. His hair was dark, thick and a little long, just long enough to add to the slightly menacing look of him.

The jacket he wore was—inevitably, it seemed—black leather, but its battered condition, the unmistakable product of long usage as opposed to the current, factory-produced "old" look, banished any thought that it was worn to advance an image. And if it hadn't, one look at his face would have.

Stevie had never seen eyes like his. While he had the chiseled features that were traditionally called handsome, and the firm set of his beard-shadowed jaw was gentled attrac-

tively by the softer line of his mouth, all of those faded
away, as did any thought of menace, the moment she looked
into those eyes. They were vivid green, fringed with thick,
dark, beautiful lashes, and they were the most haunted eyes
she had ever seen.

The image of those eyes, piercing yet strangely hollow,
had stayed with her. She had seen them looking different
since, as they met briefly in passing, or on the odd occasions when she seemed to feel someone's gaze and had
turned in time to see him avert his head abruptly. She had
seen them flat and expressionless, shadowed with weariness
or a touch of something vaguely resembling a bitter longing, but never had she been able to erase the memory of that
first look.

They had exchanged the bare minimum of words that day,
just an acknowledgment of mutual existence, and Stevie had
sensed that, for him, that was a veritable talking jag. Nothing had happened since then to change her mind. Including
now.

By the time she climbed back out of the car with her book
in hand, he was off the bike and had shed the gloves and
helmet. He was running a hand through his thick, dark hair.
He had long, supple fingers, she noticed, strong fingers.
Fingers that were, at the moment, shaking.

Even as she realized it, so did he, and he clamped them
around the rim of his helmet and stuffed the gloves inside
with a short, angry motion. As if he felt her staring at him,
he turned his head, and the beam of light from the single
bulb in the carport caught those incredible eyes and made
them gleam, fever-bright, in the chill air.

Before she could speak he nodded abruptly, turned on the
heel of his scuffed boot and walked away. Stevie stared after him, her eyebrows raised; that was rude, even for him.
Although they'd never progressed beyond the occasional
hello in passing, he at least generally made an effort at a
smile. Not much of one, it was true, but it was an effort.

Something about the way he was moving held her eyes as
he strode across the wet parking area. Although she only
realized it now, when it had changed, he usually moved with

a smooth, tightly coiled grace, which put her in mind of some jungle cat, all lean muscle under sleek skin.

"Good Lord, Holt," she chided herself, chuckling inwardly, rolling her eyes at her own vivid imagery. Really pushing that bad-boy notion, aren't you? Tigers in black leather? But, she thought as she closed the car door, there was definitely something different tonight. He was walking rigidly, carefully, as if over broken glass.

"Stevie!"

She turned at the call and saw Dan Bartlett heading for his car. She waved and waited under the shelter of the carport.

"Talk to Sheila, will you?" the young doctor said, referring to his wife. "She wants to change the next picnic to Sunday."

Stevie shrugged. "Fine with me." She grinned. "I'm a lady of leisure for three weeks."

"And about time," Dan said sternly. "You need a vacation."

"Yes, Doctor," she said formally, but her grin widened. "I have absolutely nothing to do except this—" she held up the book "—and Beth's baby shower tomorrow."

"Good." Dan used his best severe, doctor's tone, then laughed. "Anyway, Mr. Henry can't get here Saturday, and he'd hate to miss it."

Stevie nodded. The genial, portly little man who was the owner of the small five-unit building that sat a few blocks from the beach in the San Diego suburb of Pacific Beach always attended the monthly potluck gatherings on the small lawn in the center of the U-shaped building. They all liked Mr. Henry immensely; he was a kindly old man who kept the older building in good repair, the rent reasonable, and had such a genuine liking for people it seemed almost contagious.

Contagious except for Mr. C. Sullivan, who appeared immune, she thought as she raced through the rain to her door, after promising Dan she would talk to Sheila.

Maybe not quite immune, she thought. Although he had never come to the picnic, which was the sum total of the social calendar of the building, she had seen him stop and watch once or twice when the gathering had run long enough to go past his late arrival home. He had lingered in his doorway, but when she had turned to look, planning to wave an invitation, he'd turned away hastily, as if he'd been caught staring illicitly.

She glanced at his door as she opened her own; his was already shut tight, and there was no sign of lights or life. Whatever he does, those hours must wear him out, she thought as she shook what water she could from her now sopping jacket. She shivered as she stepped inside and kicked off her equally soaked tennis shoes.

"Lord, he must have been freezing!" she exclaimed as she scurried for dry clothes.

She tugged on some thick wool socks and curled up with the afghan it had taken her nearly a year to finish in her limited spare time, her book and a cup of of hot apple cider. Within minutes she was raptly involved in the fast-paced thriller.

Stevie stifled a yawn as she pulled into the alley behind the apartments. Beth Walker's baby shower had been a lengthy, if fun, affair, and it was approaching midnight. She was smiling softly, glad that her gifts had been such a success. Her boss at Walker and Dunn had loved the soft, stuffed dinosaur that played a lilting nursery tune when you squeezed it and had blushed becomingly over the sexy nightgown Stevie had selected. "So you don't get forgotten in the rush," she'd said.

"Leave it to you, Stevie," Beth had responded as she planted a kiss on her cheek. "You always think of what no one else does."

Her words had warmed Stevie; Beth had been a good friend *and* a good boss. She had taken a chance on a young beginner, then used her considerable influence to get Stevie the account that had changed her career and her life. She had—

Stevie put the brakes on abruptly as her headlights lit the carports, thankful in that moment that the rain had stopped and she didn't skid sideways. Then she edged the car for-

ward, parking it carefully before she got out to stare at the
adjacent stall.

"What on earth?"

"C. Sullivan" took care of that bike scrupulously; it was
always sparkling and running smooth, although she had no
idea when he worked on it. She had heard him leave at the
customary time this morning, and he hadn't been back before she had left for Beth's at seven, so he'd come back, as
usual, after that. Tired, no doubt. Even so, he wouldn't have
been that careless with his sole means of transportation. So
why, she wondered, was it on its side, handlebars digging
into the asphalt?

She touched it tentatively, having no illusions about being able to pick it up herself; the machine was huge. Had it
fallen, the kickstand giving way? She glanced downward.
The stand was still in the upright position for riding, but she
noticed it was spring-loaded, so it could have snapped up by
itself. Then an odd gleam caught her eye, a crescent of reflected light from a smooth, curved surface, and she realized with surprise that the black helmet he always wore was
on the ground beside the toppled motorcycle.

She shook her head slowly. She might not know anything else about him, but she knew the way he looked after
that bike, and this wasn't it. After a moment's pondering
she picked up the helmet. She would knock once, she decided, and if he answered, she would tell him about the bike.
If not, she would leave the helmet on his step; it would be
safer there than out in the carport.

A few minutes later she was tucking it under the bush next
to his door, where he couldn't miss it, but it would be invis-
ible from a few feet away. He hadn't answered the door, but
she hadn't really expected him to. He must be exhausted all
the time, she thought sympathetically. She'd never seen
anyone work so long without a single day off. Or maybe he
was just not answering on purpose; he certainly wasn't
overly sociable with his neighbors.

As she walked away, she glanced back over her shoulder
at the bright brass circle of the obviously new dead bolt he'd
added to the one already on the door. She wondered for a

brief second if it was to keep the world out or himself in, then laughed at her own thoughts.

It was, she reminded herself as she opened her own door, his own business. She slid out of the short tweed skirt and soft angora sweater she'd worn and kicked off her high heels gratefully. No heels for the rest of your vacation, she promised herself with a yawn as she flipped off the light, slipped between the smooth sheets and tugged the thick, colorful patchwork quilt up over her shoulders.

She wasn't sure what had awakened her, and she sat bolt upright, waiting. As if her mind had recorded it, she heard the sound again—the unmistakable tinkle of broken glass followed by a heavy thud, both muffled by the wall between her apartment and her mysterious neighbor's. She held her breath, but nothing else happened, and the racing beat of her heart gradually slowed.

Probably stubborn about turning the lights on in the middle of the night, she thought. Just like Sean had been, insisting that he knew the house, he didn't need the lights. She smiled, remembering how she'd always told him to tell his toes, not her. The smile faded as she remembered that she would never say that to him again. It took a long time to go back to sleep.

When she awoke again, she was startled by the brilliant sunshine streaming in the window. A quick glance at the clock startled her further; it was 10:00 a.m. She pulled on some comfortable sweats and the tennis shoes that were only now dry after her excursion into the rain.

She went through the sliding door that led out to her verdant patio, stretched expansively as she breathed in the fresh, rain-washed air.

"You guys have grown a foot already," she teasingly said to the surrounding plants, refusing to feel foolish about talking to them. They grew better than anyone else's in the building, so she wasn't about to change her tactics now.

She leaned over the patio railing to let the spring sun warm her face, but her motion stopped abruptly when she glimpsed the carport area. She stared in puzzlement. She had assumed that she had, for once, slept through her neighbor's predawn departure, but the motorcycle lay where it had been last night, looking awkward and ungainly sprawled on its side.

"This is getting weird," she muttered.

She glanced over at the door to his apartment; it was blankly unhelpful. She could just make out the shape of the black helmet where she had left it last night. She told herself to mind her own business, but a nagging sense of unease stayed with her the rest of the morning.

She was trotting back to her apartment after a trip to the building's laundry room when she saw the man. He was tall, lean except for a slight paunch, clad in khaki pants and matching shirt, with gray hair showing under a yellow hard hat. He was also standing at that blank, uncooperative door next to hers, knocking loudly and getting no answer.

She slowed to a walk, watching him curiously. He turned as she approached and looked her up and down with a gaze that held only a cheerful appreciation of her face and figure, and was pleasantly devoid of the sense of the lurid sexual assessment she observed so frequently. She smiled tentatively. He smiled back, with an open, friendly expression. She relaxed a little.

"Can I help you?" she asked.

He shoved the hard hat back from his forehead. His eyes were a warm brown, with lines at the corners that spoke of a life of sunshine and laughter. She liked him immediately.

"Do you live here?" he asked in a voice that matched his eyes.

She nodded, gesturing at her door. "Next door."

"Then maybe you've seen Chase?"

"Chase?"

"Chase Sullivan." He looked at her a little oddly. "He does live here, doesn't he?"

"Yes, he does," she hastened to say. "I just didn't know his first name."

The smile came back. "As talkative at home as he is at work, huh?"

She grinned; she couldn't help it. "I haven't seen him since the night before last. You work with him?" She looked past him to the truck parked at the curb, labeled Starr Construction.

"You could say that," the older man returned, then held out a tough, calloused hand. "I'm Charles Starr. I'm...sort of Chase's boss."

"Stevie Holt," she said, her hand dwarfed in his big, calloused one. "You're 'sort of' his boss?"

"Yeah. Sometimes I think he's more the boss than I am. I've been in the business thirty years, but that boy can run circles around me. Don't know why he doesn't start his own business—" He broke off suddenly, looking a little sheepish. "Sorry, don't mind me."

Stevie smiled up at him. "I don't." Well, at least she knew know what he put in those ridiculous hours doing. "I think it's nice that you care. A lot of bosses wouldn't."

"He's my best man. I've got a tough bunch of guys, but when he talks, they listen. He could go anywhere he wants in this business, but he won't even take the foreman's job I tried to give him, even though he's already doing the work."

"Does that job have weekends off?" Stevie asked a little dryly.

"Working weekends is his idea," Starr said hastily. "I've tried to get him to back off, but he says he'd rather work."

"One man's labor is another man's solace," Stevie paraphrased softly, not sure where the idea had come from.

Charles Starr raised an eyebrow at her. "You know that, but you don't know his first name?"

She flushed. "I... It was just a feeling." She hastily changed the subject. "Why are you—" She stopped as the answer became obvious. "He didn't come to work?"

Starr nodded. "First time in six months."

It was Stevie's turn to raise an eyebrow. "Why didn't you just call?"

"He doesn't have a phone."

That startled her into silence. No phone. By choice? Or should she suggest that Charles give his best man, a man who worked every weekend on his own initiative, a raise? Or did Chase Sullivan also have some private drain on his finances, unknown to the rest of the world? Some quiet, secret problem that put that hollow, shadowed look in those green eyes that should be sparkling and clear?

She came out of her musing with a start as Starr held out a business card, slightly bent at the corners. "If you see him, tell him to call me, will you? My home number's on the back. I've got to get back to my crew. Things just aren't going right today."

Without Mr. C. Sullivan, Stevie thought as she watched Charles Starr drive off, liking him for being concerned enough to come here in person.

Chase, she thought, trying it out in her mind. Unusual. I wonder if it's a family name? And I wonder where he is? She had entered her apartment and was mechanically folding the last of her clean laundry, her mind not really on the routine task as she wondered where the mystery man had disappeared to since she had seen him last.

Her folding stopped as a vision of that wet, cold night replayed in her head. She remembered that long, odd moment when he had just sat there on the big bike, unmoving except for the shiver that rippled through him. She remembered the shaking of those long, strong fingers, and the glitter in those piercing green eyes, a glitter that now, in retrospect, seemed much too bright to have been caused by the dim light of the single weak bulb in the carpet. And the way he had moved, too tightly under control.

She dropped the towel she held. Her mind leapt ahead to last night, to a heavy thud and breaking glass. Oh, Lord, she breathed. She spun around and was out her door in seconds.

It was no use, she thought, after another fruitless session of pounding on his door. She had checked every window, as well, and been unable to find even the merest sliver of open drapes to peer through. She sat on the front step, staring at the shiny helmet still beneath the bush, as if she could find the answer in its gleaming surface.

Well, Holt, she said to herself, you've got two choices. You can go away and worry about it all day, or you can do something. Like call the police.

"Oh, great thought," she muttered. That ought to really please him if he's just ignoring the world and taking a day off for a change. But surely he would have told his boss...?

Her eyes strayed to the spot she had been pointedly trying to ignore. As in her place, there was a tall, narrow strip of glass louvers that ran floor to ceiling beside the front door. She had had hers welded shut when, after Mrs. Trimble's visiting grandson had managed to lock himself in her apartment, it had taken all of thirteen seconds to remove the screen and enough of the glass to slip inside.

Three possibilities, she recited silently, as if reading a checklist. He's gone, in which case you scoot right back out and immediately end your career as a snoop and burglar. Or he's there and fine, and you're going to have a hell of a lot of explaining to do. Or...

She finally had to admit it. That third possibility outweighed all the rest. That crash in the night echoed in her mind. He could be hurt, or sick, and with no phone to call for help. And if he was, it was bad enough that he couldn't even get to the door. And bad enough that he had left his precious motorcycle ignominiously on its side all night.

She could call Mr. Henry, who would have a passkey, but the hour it would take him to get here suddenly seemed interminable. She glanced at the window once more and then, disgusted with her own vacillation, got to her feet. She sucked in a deep breath and reached for the screen.

It took her only ten seconds this time. Practice makes perfect, she thought ruefully as she set the last of the glass panes down carefully. She waited, holding her breath, for some sound, for the outraged shout she half expected. Nothing came. Gingerly, she crawled through the small opening she had made.

It took a moment for her eyes to adjust from the bright sunlight to the shadowed dimness inside, and she stood unmoving until she could see. The floor plan was exactly the reverse of hers, so she knew immediately where everything was. This, she knew, was one of the two units Mr. Henry rented furnished, and while it didn't have the comfortable feel of home, it was a lot nicer than some she had seen.

Her first step was nearly her undoing; her foot caught on the heavy weight of the leather jacket that lay on the floor just inside the front door. It seemed odd; the rest of the room was carefully tidy. She bent to pick it up, then had to reach down again to pick up the heavy gloves that had been hidden beneath it.

She laid them on the nearest chair, wondering if she should turn on a light. She tugged the drape back instead, and the shaft of sunlight showed her that the room was empty. Not only of its tenant but of virtually any personal touches at all. Other than a few magazines—one of them, she noticed with surprise, the glossy journal containing her own most recent work—and several books, there didn't seem to be any sign that the place was occupied.

"Come on, Holt, you've come this far," she muttered, berating herself in the effort to fight down the sudden desire to go right back out the way she had come in. She crossed the room, taking a second to peer into the kitchen. One lone cup sat on the counter; the rest was as neatly barren as the living room.

Well, here goes, she muttered silently, eyes fixed on the almost-closed door that she knew led to the bedroom. Steeling herself, she tapped on the door.

"Chase?" she called lightly, tentatively, the name she had only just learned feeling strange on her lips.

She was met with silence. She tapped again. More silence. She let out a frustrated sigh, and her lips twisted ruefully. Then, with a shrug, she slowly eased the door open.

He was there. Sprawled at an awkward angle on the big bed, half on his side, half on his stomach, with his feet and most of his legs off the bed, he had one arm held close to his ribs, the other flung outward, tangled in what looked to be a white T-shirt. He seemed oblivious to her presence. She stared, her eyes following the sleek muscles of his bare back involuntarily. Lean and well defined rather than bulky, they were muscles gained from hard work, not from workouts at some expensive gym. What she saw quickly told her that he worked hard, and frequently outside with his shirt off; even in the dim room she could see the golden color of skin that looked so smooth her fingers itched to touch it.

She shook her head sharply. Grow up, Holt, you came in here to see if he was alive, not drool over his bod. She leaned over.

"Chase?"

Not even a flicker of movement. She knew he was breathing; she could see the rise and fall of his ribs. She took a step closer. It was only then that she noticed the jeans he wore looked oddly uneven in color; it took her a moment to realize they were damp from about midthigh down.

Lord, she thought, had he been here since he'd gotten home last night? It looked like it, as if he had dropped the jacket right inside the door and only made it this far before collapsing. Was he just exhausted? Biting her lip, she reached out, thinking briefly that she was going to find out what that skin felt like after all. She touched his shoulder gently.

She drew back her hand instantly, with a muffled cry. His skin had nearly singed her fingers; he was burning up. In disbelief she took the last step to the edge of the bed, leaned over and laid the backs of her fingers on his forehead.

She hadn't been wrong. She had never felt anyone so hot before; he must have a raging fever. He never even stirred at her touch, and that scared her nearly as much as the heat that seemed to come off him in waves.

All she could think of for a moment was that he looked so uncomfortable, but when she moved to swing his feet up on the bed she saw he still wore his boots, and they were less than clean from the rain and mud. The absurdity of worrying about dirtying the bed when he was so obviously ill shook her out of the fog she seemed to be in.

She wheeled around and raced out of the apartment, barely pausing to unlock the heavily secured front door on her way. She spared a brief moment to wonder again at the extra lock; while crime in this quiet neighborhood was not unheard of, it was hardly usual. She'd always felt quite secure with the lock and the dead bolt that had been on the door originally, but obviously that was not enough for Chase Sullivan. Paranoid? she wondered as she ran across the courtyard.

She came to a skidding halt at the Bartletts' front door; she knew Dan was doing his residency on the night shift at Scripps Memorial Hospital, and that, although probably asleep, he would be home.

Sheila answered the door at the first knock. The plump blonde—"I like her that way, something to hold on to," Dan always said—took one look at Stevie's face and went for her husband.

"Can I help?" Sheila asked after Stevie had explained to the slightly groggy young doctor what was wrong.

"No, hon," Dan said. "Go ahead to work. We can handle it." He gave her a quick kiss, then went for his bag.

Sheila left with a hasty goodbye to Stevie, clearly feeling not the slightest qualm at leaving her husband with her lovely neighbor. Dan had known Stevie long before he'd known Sheila, and they had both lived here for over three years. Stevie knew that Sheila figured if they hadn't begun anything in that time, they weren't about to now. It was a refreshing change for Stevie, especially since she liked them both.

Dan noticed the stack of glass louvers and glanced at Stevie questioningly.

"I'll explain later," she said as she led him into the bedroom. She flipped on the light this time and immediately realized what she had heard last night; a lamp that had been on the dresser lay in shards on the dark brown carpet. So he had gotten up at least once, she realized. And probably immediately collapsed again. At least he'd made it to the bed. Almost.

Dan let out a low whistle at his first touch as he began to examine what was now clearly a patient.

"You were right, Dr. Holt. He's hurting. Looks like a nasty cut there, too. Probably from that lamp. He must have fallen on it."

Stevie swallowed tightly at the sight of the blood on the side of his head that had been pressed against his outflung arm. It looked terrible.

"It probably looks worse than it is," Dan said as if reading her thoughts. "Head wounds bleed a lot. He's lucky it missed his eye. I'll check it for glass in a minute." He wrestled with the limp figure, trying to shift him up on the bed. "Whew! He's pretty lean, but it must be solid muscle—he's heavy!"

Stevie moved to swing the unconscious man's legs up on the bed, tugging off his boots as she did.

"Dan? His jeans are still wet."

"I'll get 'em off him. You want to help?" Dan grinned crookedly at her, then chuckled. "Why, Stevie Holt, I do believe that's the first time I've ever seen you blush!"

"Knock it off, Dr. Bartlett." Stevie grimaced; it seemed cruel to be joking over Chase Sullivan's limp body.

Dan gave in with good grace. "Okay, okay. Go see if there are any extra blankets around, will you?"

She nodded. "I've got a couple of he doesn't."

He didn't, and by the time she got back from her place with two thermal blankets under her arm, Dan had his patient tucked neatly under the covers. Still, she couldn't help but notice that Chase Sullivan's chest was as nicely muscled as his back and just as smooth and golden, except for a slight dusting of dark hair over his breastbone.

Stevie watched while Dan did a quick but thorough examination; the patient never even blinked. She held a light while he examined the cut for any bits of glass, then closed the wound with several small butterfly bandages.

He looks younger than I thought, she mused as she set the lamp back down. She had thought he was in his middle or late thirties when she'd first seen him; now she wondered if perhaps it was just his eyes that made him look older.

Dan leaned back and inspected his work. "It's long, but not too deep. He shouldn't need stitches. His breathing's a little rough, and his temperature's a hair over 103, but the other vitals are good. I don't think it's pneumonia yet, but he was headed there in a rush. If you hadn't found him..."

He left the unnecessary unspoken.

"Does he need to go to the hospital?" she asked hesitantly; somehow, she didn't think Chase would like that idea at all.

"He should. Hospital care is what he needs—"

"No."

It was low, harsh and startling, because it rose from the man in the bed. His eyes were open, though still glazed with fever, but there was no doubting the fervency of the words.

"No hosp..."

The rest faded away as the dark lashes fluttered down again. Stevie looked at Dan.

The young doctor sighed. "Well, I suppose I could treat him with antibiotics and probably beat it off. But he's exhausted. That's probably why it nailed him. He needs rest and, once the fever's broken, food. I wouldn't trust him to handle either, from what I've seen, if he's left alone."

Stevie could only nod in agreement. "He...pushes himself awfully hard."

"Yes. I should call an ambulance right now."

"You heard him...." She trailed off, shaking her head.

"Yes." Dan eyed her thoughtfully. "Stevie...?" he began slowly, and she didn't like the look in his eyes at all.

Chapter 2

This was the craziest dream he'd ever had. He'd had nightmares before, more than he cared to remember, but this was something completely off-the-wall. First the broiling sun, then a blizzard with snow so thick he couldn't see or feel anything but cold. But the oddest part was the soft, gentle hands that seemed to cool him in the heat and warm him in the freezing cold. They gave him cool, sweet water for his parched throat and were accompanied by a soft, soothing whisper that reassured him, even though the words came from a long way off.

He tried to open his eyes, to see who belonged to the wonderful hands, to the husky voice, but the only image that rose before him was the same, lovely image that had haunted his nights for months now. The same red-gold hair, the same glowing, clear blue eyes, the same sassy, upturned nose with its sprinkling of freckles that saved delicate features from cold perfection.

"Go 'way," he mumbled thickly. "Too damn beautiful...look like Stevie."

He heard a small gasp, the merest breath of sound. It was too much. He fought to go back to the darkness, the welcoming, blank darkness, and when it reached out to enfold him, he surrendered thankfully.

The darkness faded to gray, and he heard the murmur of voices. It disturbed him, made him restless, until one of the voices settled into that now-familiar, soothing tone, and he felt the hands put something wonderfully cool on his forehead, easing the ache. He tried to say thank you, but all he could see was that tousled, gamine mane of red-gold hair and those sky-blue eyes, and he knew he must still be asleep.

"Dreamin' again," he muttered, not at all sure he wanted to give up this dream that was lasting so long. When compared to the grimness of his reality, the slightly foggy fantasy was a beautiful alternative. Maybe he'd just stay.

When he opened his eyes again, Chase had no doubts that he was awake. Every aching part of him screamed it; the sense of incredible weakness that seemed to fill him underlined it. But when at last, carefully, he moved his head, it seemed impossible that he wasn't still dreaming. For there, in the big armchair from his living room, sitting with her legs curled up under her and her head pillowed on her arm, was Stevie Holt.

Stevie. His beautiful, talented, sassy, so-near-and-yet-so-far neighbor, with the legs that wouldn't quit and the body to match. With that hair that caught the light and sent it flying in red-gold sparks, making you want to warm your hands in the thick silk of it. With those eyes the color of the summer sky, eyes that gave you the feeling she was seeing the best and the worst in you, and made you wish that there was more of the first and less of the second. With that mouth that made you feel hot and cold at the same time, made you want to—

Made you want what could never be, he said to himself suddenly, harshly. And you'd damn well better remember that.

What the hell was she doing here, anyway? He tried to move, but his body let him know in a hurry what it thought of that idea; a small groan escaped despite his efforts.

She opened her eyes, her gaze flying to him instantly, telling him it had been her first action long enough to become automatic. He didn't like the idea.

"Hi."

It was the voice. The one that had been in and out of his fevered dreams. Had it been real, had she been here, or was it the product of whatever had left him feeling like an empty burlap bag? Why couldn't he remember?

"Welcome back. Frown and all."

He hadn't meant to frown. At least, not until he found out what the hell had happened. He opened his mouth to ask, but all he could seem to manage was a croaked, "Wha...?"

"Take it easy," she said, and his body responded to the soothing tone as it had before, relaxing despite his mind's protest. God, had she been here? Why? It was crazy, she wouldn't...

He closed his eyes for a moment, certain that when he opened them again everything would be back to normal. This had to be part of one of those damn dreams. But even as he thought it, he knew it wasn't true; his dreams about the lovely sprite who lived next door had a decidedly more erotic tone. Since he'd known nothing would ever really happen, he'd let his imagination have free rein in the dark hours of night. And it had helped him stay away from her; he was usually too intensely aware of what he'd dreamed to be able to face her for long in the light of day.

He opened his eyes again; she was still there. Still looking at him with those eyes, made huge by the shadows thrown by the bedside lamp. Eyes that were warm with concern and brightened by a touch of relief.

Then he saw the things on the nightstand—the bottle of capsules of some kind, the pitcher of water and a glass and the small bowl with what looked like a damp towel hanging over the edge.

Those, along with the slightly rumpled, sleepy look that made the girl in the chair not less but even more attractive, made the truth inescapable. She'd been here, caring for him, and he'd been too out of it to know. He tried to move again and found his muscles were no more cooperative than his mouth had been.

"Relax," she said softly, putting a hand on his arm.

If he'd been able to, he would have jumped, would have pulled away sharply, to escape from that wonderful, tempting touch on his bare skin. The danger signals were going off in his head, and he was helpless to do anything about them. He'd been helpless before, trapped in a hospital bed, but then he'd only had to fight the pain of his battered body, not the frustrated longings of his mind and heart. His mouth opened automatically to snap at her not to touch him, but his throat was so dry it came out as merely a raspy croak of sound.

"Here, maybe this will help."

She picked up the glass beside the pitcher, filled it, and, with a smooth, practiced motion that spoke volumes about how often she'd done it, she slipped one slender arm behind his head and held the glass to his lips. The feel of her skin, softer and smoother than even his wildest dreams had conjured up, and the light, spicy scent of her, made his throat close up tight. He half expected to choke on the welcome wetness. But his need for the water overcame his reaction to her closeness, and he managed two or three swallows. Even that small effort seemed to exhaust him, and his brow furrowed in frustration.

"Damn." It was barely a whisper, but it was intelligible this time. "I feel like..." He trailed off, unable to think of anything that sounded as weak as he felt.

"Wet spaghetti?" she suggested drolly.

His brow cleared abruptly, and he let out a rueful sigh. He would have smiled at her apt simile if he'd had the strength.

"Yeah," he muttered after a moment, closing his eyes tiredly.

"I'm not surprised. You've had a rough couple of days."

"Mmm." His eyes snapped open as the sense of her words penetrated the fog in his brain. "What?"

"What?" she echoed, not sure what she'd said that had caused this sudden reaction.

"What day...?"

"Wednesday." She glanced at her watch. "Oops, make that Thursday. It's one-fifteen."

"Thursday?" It was a groan. He'd been out for two days? "What happened?"

"You don't remember?"

He started to lift a hand to rub his aching head, but when he realized how unsteady it was, he let it drop back to the bed. "I remember...Monday? Work. Hurt to breathe, and it was hot." His brows furrowed. "That's crazy. It was cold out. Raining. Wasn't it?" He looked at her, puzzled.

Stevie nodded, looking at him with such warm sympathy that it eased his confusion even as it set the danger signals to clamoring again. "You were pretty sick."

"I guess so," he said slowly. "Two days..." Sudden awareness flooded his brain once more, banishing for the moment the dull flatness of pain and fatigue. "Damn," he said again. "Charlie'll have my a—" He broke off, but Stevie just smiled at him.

"If you mean Mr. Starr, don't worry. I called him. He said to take as much time as you need to get well."

"You...called him?"

She nodded. "He came by looking for you and left me his card."

"He...came here?" Chase wondered if his mind had been affected; nothing seemed to be making any sense.

"He's a nice man. He was worried about you."

That was silly, he thought. Why would his boss worry about him enough to come out here? He never talked to him except about work. "When?" he asked, sure she must have been mistaken.

"Tuesday morning, when you didn't show up. That was before I found you."

"You...found me?"

He gaped at her, wishing he had the strength to shake his head. Maybe if he rattled his brain a bit, he could catch up.

"Look," she began in a rush, "I know it was wrong, but I was worried. I mean, I heard the crash of the lamp, and you looked so ill the night before, and you've never not left on time before, and I knew you would never leave your motorcycle that way on purpose, and your place is like mine, so it was easy..."

At last she trailed off. He gave up trying to figure out why she sounded so uneasy and grabbed at the only thing that made sense to him.

"My motorcycle?"

She nodded. "I knew you couldn't have meant to leave it lying down like that."

"Down? On its side?" He hadn't, had he? He tried to rise and could have yelled in frustration.

"Don't worry. It's up now." She pushed him back down gently. She saw the odd look on his face and hastened to reassure him. "It's fine. The gearshift is a little bent, but other than that..." His expression didn't change, and she trailed off.

"You...did that?"

He was stunned. He'd never said more than three words to her at a time. In fact, he had more than once been nearly rude to her, so why on earth would she have gone to all this trouble?

"Me? Are you kidding? That thing weighs a ton! I had to have Dan help me. I don't know how you do it alone."

Despite himself, his mouth quirked into a wry smile. "I try not to drop it."

She stared at him for a second, startled, and then she laughed. It was a lovely, silvery sound, a sound he had heard before, a sound that always made him stop whatever he was doing just for the sheer joy of listening to it. He'd heard it from her apartment and sometimes from the small square of grass in the courtyard, when everybody was gathered for their monthly picnic.

It washed over him now, and a myriad of thoughts raced through his mind. Why had she, from all appearances, nursed him through whatever it was that had hit him like a freight train? And who was Dan? Her boyfriend? He'd never seen anyone at her place, never seen a strange car around, and Lord knew he was always watching for anything the least bit unusual. But then, he wasn't here much, either, he thought.

She'd said she had found him. Did that mean she had put him to bed? He was suddenly aware of his nearly nude state under the covers, and a heat that had nothing to do with his recent fever began to rise in him.

"Who's Dan?" It seemed the safest of all the questions whirling in his head.

"Dan Bartlett. Dr. Dan Bartlett," she amended. "You know, he and Sheila live right across the courtyard."

"Oh." He placed the couple, the hyper, cheerful young man from across the way and his equally cheerful blond wife. The realization made him feel oddly pleased, for a reason he didn't have the energy to analyze right now.

"He's been treating you. In fact—" she lifted a slim wrist to look at her watch again "—he should be here any minute."

"Now?"

She nodded. "He works the night shift at Scripps. He usually gets home right about now. He's come by the last two nights to see how you're doing."

As she spoke, she reached out to touch his temple; only then did he realize that it was bandaged. She read the question in his eyes.

"You cut it when you fell. On a piece of the lamp, I think. At least, that's what it looked like. Dan said you didn't need stitches...." She lowered her eyes, catching her full lower lip worriedly between even, white teeth. The simple movement made him swallow tightly.

"What?" he managed to ask. "I'll pay him, if that's what you're worried about." It came out harsher than he'd intended, but he had to do something to get his mind off her mouth.

Her head came up sharply, hurt flaring briefly in her clear blue eyes, but it was nothing compared to the pain that suddenly flared in the pit of his stomach. He hadn't meant to do that.

"I'm sure Dan doesn't expect anything," she said coolly. "He came as a favor to a neighbor." There was no hint in her voice that she knew perfectly well that he hadn't been much of a neighbor to anyone, but he knew she knew it as well as he did.

"I'm . . . I'm sorry. I didn't mean it like that."

She studied him for a moment, then nodded. She seemed about to say something more when there was a soft tap on the door. She got up, and as she left the room, Chase closed his eyes tightly. It didn't work. He could still see her, long legs clad in snug jeans that hugged her tight bottom, and wearing a soft blue sweater that made her eyes stand out vividly and clung subtly to the full curves beneath it. She was trim, taut, yet feminine—all long lines and lush curves. She made his heart hammer in his chest, and made him, for the moment, glad he was too weak to do anything about the hot, heavy pulse that was rippling through him.

When Stevie returned with Dan Bartlett in tow, he managed a tight smile in the face of the man's unfailing cheer.

"Well, you're back among the living, I see."

Short, stocky and with medium brown hair already receding, Chase could picture him in thirty years: the stereotypical picture of the family doctor. Stevie left them alone, and Chase submitted to the indignity of being helped to the bathroom only because he knew he couldn't face having Stevie doing it. Then he bore the quick examination with as much grace as he could muster.

"Fever's down," Dan announced unnecessarily as he stood up. "And the cut's healing up nicely. Still hurt to breathe?"

"Not too bad."

"Any coughing?"

Chase looked puzzled; he didn't remember coughing, but his ribs were a little sore. Dan glanced over his shoulder at Stevie, who had slipped quietly back into the room when she'd heard Dan begin to talk.

"Not since he woke up," she said quietly. "Or for the last few hours before that."

Chase flushed. Had she slept here? "What are you, a nurse or something?" he grated, knowing perfectly well that she wasn't. He knew all too well what his feisty neighbor did for a living; he kept track through the business section of the

paper of what accounts had been given to Walker and
Dunn, and he could spot her style in the resulting ads with
ease.

Dan looked a little startled at his tone. "She's enough of
a nurse to have kept you out of the hospital," he said with
mild reproof, aware of his patient's weakened state.

"Hospital?"

Surprise, and something else that was there and gone so
fast Stevie couldn't name it, flashed in the green eyes. He
obviously didn't remember his own feverish protest.

"That's where you would have been if Stevie hadn't
agreed to stay with you."

His jaw tight, Chase's eyes flickered to the woman standing in the shadows behind the chair.

"It seemed to upset you, so I just thought it would be
easier if I stayed," she said softly.

He stared at her intensely. She met his gaze steadily, a
wealth of understanding and compassion in those blue eyes.
Suddenly he knew that that was what she had been going to
say when he had snapped at her, that she had been going to
apologize for making a decision for him when he had been
unconscious. A decision that she couldn't have known the
importance of to him. Even after all this time, just the
thought of those sterile, green corridors...

"No," he said, his voice tight. "I wouldn't have wanted
to go. Thank you."

She didn't dissemble, didn't modestly say it was nothing,
just nodded and quietly accepted his thanks. He found her
honesty refreshing.

"You were about that far—" Dan measured a small space
with his thumb and forefinger "—from pneumonia, son."

Son. What was it about doctors? Chase wondered, judg-
ing that Dan was at least a year or two younger than his own
thirty. And a thousand years younger than his old, battered
soul. He sighed, knowing he was indeed weak when he
started feeling sorry for himself. He was glad when the out-
going young doctor launched into a lengthy dissertation on
what had happened.

As the man talked, the rushed, rather frantic explanation Stevie had given him began to make sense. What didn't make sense was why she had bothered. He knew the few people who lived here were as close as they were varied. He had known that before he had ever moved in, even as he had known he could never become a part of the group.

Elderly Mrs. Trimble, the very image of everyone's favorite grandmother, the doctor and his wife, getting by on his intern's salary, and Leo Rubin, who ran the little deli on Mission Boulevard—they were all here for the friendly atmosphere, the quiet and the reasonable rent for the nice, spacious but older apartments.

Stevie Holt, he didn't know about. It seemed that her job with a successful advertising firm would have enabled her to live in a bigger, newer place. Perhaps she just liked it here; she seemed content enough.

He was here because it was an unremarkable, inconspicuous neighborhood, a place that was mostly unnoticed, where it was easy to fade into the background. Which he had managed to do, he thought. Until now.

"...even worse shape if she hadn't found you when she did." Dan was winding down now. "So, we put you to bed—"

"We?" Chase asked, speaking for the first time during the long story.

Dan grinned, accurately reading his patient's thoughts and guessing at the reason for his unease. "Sorry, pal, I did the undressing honors. Stevie suddenly went shy on me."

"Dan!" Stevie blushed furiously.

"C'mon, girl," Dan teased. "Any man in his right mind would rather have someone who looks like you take his clothes off than me!" He threw a sly wink at Chase. "If he's awake to enjoy it, of course."

"Well, he wasn't," she said shortly, "so I'm sure he wouldn't have appreciated it."

"Academic, actually," Dan said with a shrug, then looked at the man in the bed rather pointedly. "By the time she got back with the extra blankets, you were all tucked in and covered up."

Something passed between the two men, a look of understanding given and received that Stevie saw but couldn't fathom.

"And I'm not shy," she said with irritation. "I already broke into his home, for crying out loud. Wasn't that enough of an invasion of privacy without ripping his clothes off, too?"

Chase went suddenly still. "You . . . broke in?"

Stevie's cheeks flamed. "I know it was presumptuous, but I—"

"How?"

It was sharp, short, and she paled at the look in his eyes. Lord, he was truly angry. She swallowed tightly.

"How?" he snapped.

"I . . ." She paused. What did it matter how? But his eyes, those searing green eyes, were fastened on her unwaveringly; it obviously mattered a great deal to him. "The windows in front. The louvered ones." She lowered her eyes nervously. "They slide right out. It's easy. I had mine welded shut."

"Damn," he muttered. "I never thought about those. Everything else, but not those. Stupid."

For a moment something so empty, so bleak, showed in his eyes that Stevie felt a sharp, barbed pain that drove her to say in a rush, "I'm sorry, I know I shouldn't have done it—"

"No." The hollow, grim look faded as he interrupted her. He hadn't meant to make her feel like that. It wasn't her fault he was so touchy about security. "It's all right. Don't feel guilty about it."

She looked relieved, and Chase knew she had been feeling guilty. That was why she'd sounded so funny before, he thought, even though Dan Bartlett had made it clear what would have happened to him if she hadn't broken in. He'd never known a woman with such a healthy respect for privacy; most he'd known were too busy prying into everyone else's business, it seemed. It was why he never took chances with them. He raised an eyebrow at her.

"I wouldn't have minded if you'd helped," he said mildly; he owed it to her to ease that guilt, he thought. "Of course, I would rather have been awake...."

It took her a moment to catch the barely perceptible twinkle in the depths of his green eyes, to realize he was teasing her about taking off his clothes. At first her already high color deepened, but then, despite her embarrassment, she laughed.

He let himself soak it in this time. That lovely sound. It couldn't hurt, not just this once, could it? Besides, he was too weak to fight it right now. Sure, he told himself ruefully. Even when you're not sick, it's all you can do to fight yourself; no way in hell could you fight her, too. Distance, he reminded himself fiercely. A buffer zone was the only answer. Wearily he closed his eyes.

"Keep him taking those pills, and as much liquid as he can. And food as soon as possible." Dan's voice had changed to the efficient tone of a doctor giving instruction.

Chase opened his eyes once more. "I'll be fine," he said, looking at them both. "Thanks for everything, but I'll be fine."

Neither Stevie nor Dan missed the implication that he would rather be left alone. "Sorry, I never abandon a patient until he's on his feet again. And for you, that's going to be awhile." Dan turned back to Stevie. "You'll stay until he can take care of himself, won't you?"

Stevie nodded.

"I can do that now," Chase interrupted, an edge in his voice. I can't take this, he thought desperately. I can't have her here....

"You," Dan said succinctly, "couldn't even feed yourself at the moment. So just resign yourself to having the prettiest strawberry blonde in town for a nurse for a while. Enjoy it while you can." After a promise to check back the next day, he left.

Stevie idly straightened the clutter on the nightstand, then turned to face the bed. "Look, it won't be that bad—"

"Won't it?" Lady, you don't know the half of it.

"You heard what Dan said—"

"Doctors are a pain in the butt."

She eyed him disgustedly. "Patients are apparently worse."

"Damn it, I don't need you to nursemaid me!" Why the hell did I have to get sick? he thought angrily. And why the hell did she have to be the one...?

"I see." Stevie stared at him for a long moment. "Well, since you have a problem with me, perhaps Mrs. Trimble might come over for a while."

"I don't—" He broke off, closing his eyes and taking a long, harsh breath. She's giving you an out, fool, he told himself. Take it. He didn't. "I didn't mean it that way," he said, his voice quiet now. "I just hate... fussing."

"Definitely no Mrs. Trimble, then," she said, as if he hadn't just been yelling at her. "You're in luck, though. The Holt School of Nursing is right next door. No frills, no fuss. Just whip 'em into shape and leave 'em on their own."

Chase sighed. "I don't suppose you could just leave me to die in peace?"

"Not a chance. But I'll make a deal with you. First time you can stand up long enough to heat up a bowl of Leo's chicken soup yourself, I'm outta here."

In spite of himself, he chuckled. Weakly. "I give," he said, shaking his head wearily.

"Good. We'll start with the first bowl now. Leo sent some over yesterday." She turned to head for the kitchen.

"Why?" he asked, astonished.

"He's a good neighbor," she said simply, then left.

I don't get it, Chase thought. I don't do anything to be friendly with these people, and they do this. A wry smile twisted his lips. I go out of my way *not* to be friendly with that little firebrand, and I wind up with her practically moving in. So much for well-laid plans.

It's only a couple of days, he told himself. I can handle that. I sure as hell can't do anything else, lying here limp as...as wet spaghetti. "Enjoy it while you can," Bartlett had said. Did he dare? Could he just enjoy her being here, being with her, without looking beyond these few hours? Just take a break from the dreariness and bask in her vivid presence? It would be safe, wouldn't it? She'd be gone soon. It was only for a little while. Nothing would happen.

He felt suddenly as if a brief, shining moment had been handed to him on a silver platter, for him to take or leave. If he took it, it meant the risk of burning himself on its very brightness, of deepening the aching, empty part of him that he knew he could never fill. But he couldn't pass up the unexpected gift of these days. The temptation was too much. It was only for a moment, after all.

"Just take it and quit acting like a two-year-old who doesn't want his vegetables, all right?"

Chase set his jaw, his lips firming into a thin line as he let out a disgusted breath.

"Look, you can't eat by yourself until you get your strength back, and you can't do that if you don't eat!"

"Catch-22," he muttered.

"But a fact of life, nevertheless," Stevie insisted. "Now eat."

He sighed resignedly and opened his mouth for the spoon she held.

"That's more like it. I mean, if you don't eat you won't get better, and then you'll never get rid of me."

Don't tempt me, he thought bitterly, but he said nothing, just swallowed the hot soup. It did taste good, and he was surprised at how the first touch of hot food woke up his stomach; it growled loudly.

Stevie cocked her head, listening. "About a three-day growl, I'd say."

She grinned at him, and in spite of himself, he grinned back. She stopped, staring at him. My Lord, she thought. No wonder he never smiles. It's too dangerous. He could melt a city block with that grin; it's lethal. And the way it lights up those green eyes....

"What's wrong?"

She shook her head. "You got a license for that smile, mister?" He looked startled. "Never mind," she said quickly, scooping up another spoonful of soup. "Just eat."

He let her feed him the whole bowlful, not that he had much choice. He was so weak, he couldn't have held an empty spoon, let alone a full one. And after the initial adjustment to the indignity of being fed like a baby, he hadn't minded that much. It gave him a chance to look at her.

Not that he hadn't long ago committed her to memory. He'd never forgotten the first time he'd seen her, the first time he'd come here to look at the apartment. She'd been to the beach, and her hair was windblown and tousled, glowing in the sun with that unusual, beautiful, red-gold color. She'd been too far away for him to see her clearly, but he'd gotten a glimpse of that saucy little nose, and of long, lithe legs below the ragged sweatshirt she wore over her bathing suit.

The loquacious landlord had volunteered her name and her career proudly, as if she were a loved daughter; Chase wished the man had kept the information to himself. When Chase had realized she was heading for the apartment right next to the one he was standing in, he hadn't known whether to run or grab the keys from Mr. Henry right away, so the man couldn't give them to anyone else. Chase had known a month after he'd moved in that he should have run.

But he had stayed, although he hadn't dared to exchange more than a few words with her when they passed. He knew he had more than once bordered on rudeness, but he didn't dare let down his guard. That way lay danger, to him and anyone around him. He had to remember that. And he would, he thought. Later. After she was gone, when he was alone again. But right now he would savor what little he could get.

She said nothing more when he finished the soup, merely left with the bowl and spoon and headed for the kitchen. She went through the motions of cleaning the utensils automatically, her mind intent on the enigmatic man in the other room. What was it that made him look so ghastly at times? What had put that dreadful, haunted look in his eyes? And what had that odd exchange of glances between him and Dan meant?

Immersed in her thoughts, she instinctively pulled open the drawer that, in her own apartment, held her silverware. Her fingers tightened convulsively around the spoon she'd been about to put away as she stared downward. Hastily she shut the drawer, but nothing could erase the image. The sight of the small but deadly-looking blue-steel revolver was etched irrevocably in her mind. She stared at the closed drawer for a long time before she was able to find the right one.

Stevie couldn't believe this was the same man who had gone six months with barely a civil word to her. Any resemblance between the man who had snapped at her so vehemently and the man who awakened the next day was difficult to find.

He had made no complaint when, after Dan had stopped in before going into work and pronounced him progressing well, she had appeared with another bowl of soup. He merely asked her to thank Leo when she saw him.

"Do it yourself," she said, not harshly at all, as she had begun to feed him. "He doesn't bite."

"Unlike some people?" he suggested wryly between mouthfuls.

"Some people just bark a lot," she said airily, ignoring his sudden flush.

To her amazement, they spent the rest of the afternoon in lively and varied conversation, and she found herself telling him about growing up in San Diego, and her days at San Diego State University. She thought at first he was just being polite, but he seemed genuinely interested, asking a lot of questions.

And he laughed. When she told him about the time her high school senior class had dismantled the vice-principal's Volkswagen and then reassembled it—in his office—he had burst into delighted laughter that made her smile widely and gave her an oddly warm feeling somewhere deep inside.

That warmth changed to an oddly disconcerting pang when she saw how laughter had erased that haunted look from his eyes; they were sparkling and clear, as she had thought they should be the first time she'd ever seen him. She wished she could keep him laughing forever, just to keep that look away.

That thought startled her, even scared her, and she busied herself with dispensing the antibiotic capsule he was supposed to take. He swallowed it obediently, grimacing only slightly when he couldn't quite hold the glass steady by himself.

"Soon," she promised. "Dan said you could have something a little more substantial for dinner. That should help."

"Like a steak?" he asked, so wistfully she had to laugh.

"I think we could manage that. I've got a couple in my freezer. How about a baked potato?"

"I can smell it already." He grinned at her.

She'd gotten more accustomed to it now, that thousand-watt grin, but it still ranked in the lethal category. It was such a startling change from the taciturn, unsmiling man she had seen until now that she had to remind herself occasionally that they were one and the same. She suddenly became aware she was staring at him and hastened to speak the first thing that popped into her head.

"Where did your name come from?"

"What?"

She gave a little start, taken aback by his sharp tone. "I... It's unusual. I just wondered."

He let out a long breath, closing his eyes for a second. "It seemed appropriate at the time," he muttered, and before she could wonder at that cryptic remark, he asked her how long she'd been at Walker and Dunn. She was startled that he knew where she worked, and he read her look.

"Mr. Henry mentioned it when I rented this place," he explained.

"Oh." She smiled at the friendly landlord's name. "I've been there four years now. I started right after I finished college. Beth Walker—she's the daughter of the original Mr. Walker—visits all the local schools, scouting, I guess. She recruited me. I started as just a gofer, but eventually I made it into layout and design. And finally they let me do some complete ad campaigns. It's hard work, but I love it."

"It shows." She looked at him quizzically, and he lowered his eyes sheepishly. "Er... he also mentioned the store you were doing ads for, so... I kind of watched for them."

She stared in shock. She remembered the magazine she had found in his living room; she never would have guessed why he had the glossy society rag.

"Why?" she asked, amazed.

"Just curious. Mr. Henry said you were really good."

"He's prejudiced." She didn't know what else to say. The thought that this silent man had followed her work when he would barely even say hello astonished her.

"No. You are good. I like the new one, on the beach."

It was the ad in that newest magazine, the last of the series of five ads she had done for the exclusive Pirate's Cove jewelry store. It was set on one of San Diego's lovely white beaches, with a trail of glittering gold and jewels strewn in a wavering line across the sand, as if dropped in haste from overflowing hands. The tracks beside the dazzling path were a whimsical touch; the booted foot and the peg-leg imprint of an old-time pirate.

"Thank you." She was proud of the work, yet all too aware that it had been a fluke that she had gotten it. "I never expected to get the job. It's such a big account. I only did because Beth—my boss—pushed for it, and Joe Bradford broke his leg skiing. He's the head of the department. It should have been his account."

"No," he said again. "It's perfect."

She flushed. "Mr. Dunn didn't think so. I was his absolute last choice." She gave a short little laugh. "I was scared to death I'd blow it."

"But you didn't."

"Almost. Lord, I was terrified! I sat up all night in front of that drawing board, wishing I'd listened to my mother and learned how to type." She rolled her eyes. "It was nearly morning before I thought of something, and by then I was so scared and tired, I had no idea if it was any good."

But they'd loved it. The striking image of the ebony bird, the forbidding countenance of Poe's raven perched ominously below an equally dark Jolly Roger, its gleaming feathers the only hint of its shape against the black background, made a dramatic counterpoint to the brilliant spill of emeralds and gold from its beak. It was bold, eye-catching and effective, and the store had signed the contract on the spot. That ad had launched Stevie Holt into a two-year whirlwind she was only now slowing down from.

Only when she went to fix the steak he was so hungry for, did she realize she'd done nothing but talk about herself all afternoon. Never once had he met one of her stories with one of his own, and the one time when she'd asked him about his name, his reaction had been startling. She turned the thought over in her mind as she fixed the meal, but she couldn't come up with an answer. ''Mystery man,'' she muttered as she prepared the meal.

The memory of the cold, killing steel of the gun in the drawer rose from the corner of her mind where she had hidden it. She pushed it back, telling herself that a lot of people had weapons for protection. Just because she'd never met any before didn't mean anything. She fought the instinct that wanted to tie this to all the other odd things about him, the instinct that told her to run while she had the chance. She couldn't run, not yet, not until he was on his feet again. Then she would...

Would what? Walk away and not look back? The little shiver of distress that rippled through her at the thought made her nearly as uneasy as the image of that cold, metal weapon.

Chapter 3

Stevie carried the plates into the bedroom, along with a serving tray she'd brought from her place. Chase insisted on trying to feed himself and she didn't argue, but first she cut the meat into bite-sized pieces and handed him the fork. It was slow and hard to watch, because he was still shaky, but he did it. The milk he'd asked for was another matter; full, the glass was too heavy, and he had to ask her when he wanted it.

As she finished her own meal, she glanced once more at the drawing on the wall opposite the bed. It was the only personal touch she could find in the whole place, but it was a fascinating one. Perched on a cliff that soared above a restless ocean was a house, a dramatic blend of wood, brick and glass that seemed a part of the landscape. In fact, it seemed to emphasize the stark beauty of its setting.

It was drawn in a style that seemed to show the very bones of the house, as if whoever had done it had known exactly how the place was built. Or would be built, if it hadn't been. And it should be built, Stevie thought. It was too beautiful to exist only on paper.

"Chase?"

"Hmm?" He looked up from the now half-empty, almost manageable glass he was carefully setting down.

"Where's that house?"

The glass hit the tray with a clank. It wobbled, but she knew better than to try to help. He steadied it with a hand that was none too steady itself.

"It is real, isn't it?"

"Why do you say that?"

If his voice seemed a little odd, she didn't comment. "I guess because it's wonderful. It should be real."

"It's not," he said flatly. "Look, thanks for the food, but I'm a little tired."

Whew, Stevie thought. You just knocked on another wrong door, Holt. He sure seems to have a lot of them. But she merely nodded and picked up the dishes. He'd finished the steak and done a creditable job on the potato, more than she had expected. She guessed he would be feeling better in the morning.

After she'd cleaned up the plates, she went back for the tray, to find him waiting for her with a contrite expression.

"I didn't mean to snap at you. I'm just edgy, I guess. I'm not used to being cooped up."

"Cabin fever?"

"Something like that. I'm sorry." He gave her a crooked grin. "I guess I shouldn't bite the hand that feeds me, huh?"

Stevie looked at him ruefully. So he *did* know how to use that grin to advantage. Rat, she thought, with an inward grin of her own. She reached for the tray on his lap, careful to avoid touching him. Just looking at that smooth, muscular expanse of naked chest had been doing funny things to her all day; she didn't dare think of what touching it, even accidentally, would do. Just as she didn't dare wonder if Dan had really taken all his clothes off....

"I'll get this out of your way," she said hastily as she picked up the tray. "So you can sleep."

"Stevie?"

She turned back to look at him.

"I'm not really sleepy." Her gave her a half apologetic, half wistful look. "Would you stay...and talk for a while?"

She set the tray down in the doorway. "Meaning I talk and you listen?"

He winced. Then he lowered his eyes, but not before Stevie had seen a flash of that old, shadowed look haunting the green depths. She winced herself; she felt as if she'd been punched in the stomach. Without another word she went back to the big chair and sat down, curling her legs up under her as she had when she'd been keeping vigil over the unconscious, feverish figure in the bed.

After a long moment he looked up. "You were right. Sick people are a pain."

"Mostly because they're *in* pain," she said gently.

"I'm fine," he said in denial of any hurt, "only tired of being so damn weak. It's just that I seem to have...forgotten how to just talk to somebody." Especially somebody who looks like you, he added silently.

Stevie searched for a topic that seemed safe. "How about your job? I know you work for Mr. Starr, but doing what?"

He shrugged. "A little of everything."

"I thought in construction everyone had a specialty. You know, carpenters, electricians, like that."

"Normally, yes. But Charlie's nonunion, so he gets away from that. I'm a decent cement man, and a passable electrician, but I do carpentry, mostly."

"Mr. Starr said you know more than he does after thirty years."

"He said that?" Chase stared at her.

She nodded. "He said sometimes he felt like he was working for you. And so did the rest of the crew."

"He must have been kidding. I'm just one of his men, worse than some, better than others." He gave her a a sideways look. "Nothing fancy, just plain old blue-collar construction work."

She met that look levelly. "If that's my cue to stick my nose in the air, you can forget it." He looked startled that she had read him so easily. "I have a great deal of respect for 'plain old blue-collar construction work.' If the men who built this place hadn't cared about their work, it would have tumbled down long ago, and I like this place."

"Sorry. I thought, with you working with all those swanky people..." He had the grace to look abashed. "Why do you stay here? It seems kind of off the beaten track for a big-time advertising type."

"Because it *is* off the beaten track. And I'm not a 'big-time advertising type,' I'm a graphic artist. Just a plain old ordinary graphic artist."

"Touché." He grinned at her use of his words, taking no offense. Then he shook his head. "Nothing plain or old about you, Ms. Holt." She looked startled. "Or ordinary," he added softly, and smiled in wonder as she blushed. When was the last time he'd seen a woman blush at such a small compliment?

He didn't know that his words had called to her mind the memory of other words, mumbled with feverish intensity, words telling her that her silent, slightly intimidating neighbor had more than just noticed her. She'd convinced herself that she had misunderstood him then; now she wasn't sure.

"You're rather unusual yourself, Mr. Sullivan."

She saw that look flash in his eyes again and wondered why. It was quickly gone, but when he spoke there was a note in his voice that made her think of it again.

"Your folks must be very proud of you," Chase said.

"It's not exactly what they had pictured for me, but they know I love what I do, so they try to accept it."

"What did they have pictured for you?"

"The usual affliction of middle-aged parents. Happily married, the little house with the white picket fence and a half dozen grandchildren."

"You don't...want that?"

"I hate white picket fences."

He smiled at her diversionary effort, but couldn't help asking one more question. "So you haven't married?"

"No. I came close once, but it didn't work out."

"I'm sorry." Only if it hurt you, he added silently.

"I'm not. He had a little problem with monogamy. Better before than after." She shrugged. "You?"

He shook his head. "One near miss. She had a problem with...problems, I guess." And took off running at the first sign of trouble, he thought.

Stevie's lips twisted into a wry smile. "Know where she is? Maybe we could introduce them."

He laughed, and that odd note was gone from his voice once more. He asked her about her family, and she told him, not quite able to shake the feeling that he was drinking it in like someone long thirsty for the routine of ordinary life. She told him about her parents and their small printing business— "Printer's ink is in your blood," he teased—and then, before she even thought about it, she mentioned Sean.

"You never said you had a brother," he said curiously.

"No," she said shortly, "I didn't."

She seemed so open about everything else, he couldn't help wondering. "Why?"

Her eyes went frosty. "You think you're the only one who has things you don't talk about?"

He recoiled from that icy look. God, of all people, he should know better. She seemed so joyous, so blithely content, but he knew better than anyone how appearances could hide a multitude of burdens. He should have guessed, he said to himself accusingly. Happiness hadn't put that look of quiet wisdom in her eyes, hadn't given her that knack of insightful perception.

He let out a short breath. "You're right. I didn't mean to pry."

She sighed. "No. I'm the one who mentioned him, I shouldn't take it out on you." She slid him a sideways look. "But you are the original clam, aren't you?"

He lowered his eyes. "Not by choice," he said, so quietly it was almost a whisper.

She didn't have to see his eyes to know that that look was back. She tried for a lighter note. "Okay, no questions about your family. If I don't ask, you don't have to not answer."

Her tone made it clear she was kidding, but he answered her as if she'd been serious. "I'm...not sure I have a family anymore. I've been...out of touch."

There was so much pain in his voice, and he was trying so desperately to hide it, that it clawed at something deep inside her.

"I'm sorry, Chase," she whispered. "I know how it feels to want to talk and want to keep things inside at the same time. I wish I could help, but all I can do is listen if you want to let it out."

I can't, he thought wretchedly, but he couldn't seem to stop the words. "My parents are in—" He caught himself; he had to be at least that careful. "Up north. At least, I think they are. With my little sister." He let out a harsh laugh. "Not so little anymore, I guess, she's...nineteen now. Maybe she's not there. Maybe she's out on her own."

He raised one arm to cradle his head in a hand that had grown steadier after his first solid food in several days. "Hell," he said huskily, "the only one I'm really sure of is my brother. My big brother, the hero."

"You know where he is?" she asked softly when he stopped.

"Exactly," he said flatly. "Arlington."

She knew even before she said it. "Cemetery?"

His arm dropped to the bed, and she saw his hand clench. "And on the twelfth panel of names on the Vietnam Veterans Memorial."

Instinctively she reached for that tightened hand. She was surprised when he didn't pull away; whenever she'd touched him before, inadvertently or in the course of helping him, he'd seemed to draw back. "I'm sorry," she whispered. "You must miss him."

He was too aware of her cool, gentle hand on his. His mind ordered his arm to move away; instead, as if of their own volition, his fist unclenched and his fingers grasped hers.

"I was twelve when he left. He was nineteen. I'd spent my whole life being Ja—being his little brother. I didn't mind it a bit. He could do anything, be anything. I idolized him. And he always put up with me, something I didn't really appreciate until I got older and had a little sister hanging around."

Stevie squeezed his hand, a small smile curving her lips. He saw it, and something turned over inside him. He swallowed heavily and went on.

"The last time he was home, we went for a walk. He was...different. He talked about how hard it was sometimes to do what you thought you had to do, what you thought was right, but that you had to do it anyway. I never understood that, either. Until later." He gave a short, harsh laugh that grated on her ears. "So we both did what we thought was right. It got him killed, and me—"

He broke off suddenly. The danger signals were suddenly shrilling too loudly to be ignored. He'd nearly lost himself in the release of communicating with another person, in the pleasure of that person being Stevie. He felt the soft, smooth warmth of her hand in his, and the hot, heavy beat of his pulse shifted somehow, as if it were centered under her slender fingers.

He had to put some distance between them. He knew it, but somehow he couldn't seem to move. Then she spoke, just his name, a soft, vibrant note in her husky voice that sent tiny ripples of sensation down his spine. Only jaw-clenching restraint enabled him to slowly release her hand rather than jerk away as if he'd been burned. He closed his eyes, effectively shutting her out.

"I really am a little tired now, if you don't mind."

Stevie knew by the flat, dull tone of his voice that there would be no more talking tonight. She left the room silently, wondering what he had been about to say. What right thing had he done? And what had it gotten him? Had it put that look in his eyes, that pain in his voice? No matter what it was, she found it hard to believe it had been worth it.

Stevie juggled her soda, her book and the sweater she'd grabbed as she wrestled with Chase's front door. She nearly dropped them all, only saving the soda from spilling by wedging it against the door with a quiet thud. She winced; Chase had been sound asleep when she left to run home, but if she kept this up, he wouldn't be for long.

"Sit with him one more night, just in case," Dan had advised her. "Then he should be okay alone."

At last she nudged the door open with her foot, steadied her grip on the soda and stepped inside. And nearly dropped it again.

He was a shadowy, robe-clad figure near the door to the kitchen, and it was with a little shock that she realized he was reaching for the drawer that held the gun. She made a little sound and he jerked upright, swaying slightly. His hand fell back to his side.

"Stevie," he breathed, staring at her.

"Of course," she said, her voice a little tight. "Who were you expecting?"

"I thought . . . I didn't . . . I just heard a noise. . . ."

And immediately went for a gun, she thought as he trailed off. Even though he could hardly stand. On the thought he swayed again, one hand coming up to search almost blindly for the wall for support.

"You'd better get back to bed."

She expected an argument, but he said nothing. He just turned away, and by the time she got the door shut and followed him, he had discarded the robe and was back in bed. His eyes were closed, and he didn't open them when she came in and sat down. Although she sensed he was still awake, she didn't press it. The image of him reaching for that drawer was still too fresh, and it took a long time before she was able to put it from her mind. And it was still longer before she was able to stop wondering what had made him feel so threatened that even his debilitating illness hadn't stopped him from going for that deadly weapon.

"Three weeks! Are you crazy? I can't be off for three weeks!"

Dan Bartlett watched Chase silently; he'd expected that reaction. What he hadn't expected was the scene he'd walked in on.

His eyes told him that the man sitting up in the bed was the same one who had been so sullenly quiet when he'd stopped by last night, but he couldn't quite believe it. He had thought then that there was more to his morose mood than just the indignity of his own current weakness, a particular strain for someone as obviously private as Chase Sullivan. Whatever it had been, it was clearly gone now; any resemblance between that man and the one who sat there now, carrying on a lively conversation with Stevie about baseball, was fleeting.

"Ah-ha!" Dan had exclaimed when he'd come in on his own after no answer had come to his knock. "You've discovered Stevie's secret passion!"

Chase froze, staring at Dan Bartlett as if he'd never seen him before. "I didn't hear you at the door," he said tightly, hoping his tone would be put down to being startled, not to the crazy places his mind had flown at the words "Stevie's secret passion."

"It's not a secret," Stevie said, glaring in mock anger at Dan. "You just haven't recovered from the Cubs losing the pennant to the Padres in '84."

"A fluke." Dan waved a hand breezily. "A mere fluke. Now, how's the patient?" he had asked, beginning the examination that had brought on Chase's incredulous exclamation.

"It should be longer than three weeks," Dan said sternly, "the kind of hours you keep. Don't you ever take a day off?"

"What for?" Chase said defensively.

"To rest! You do know what the word means, don't you?"

"I'm learning," Chase said, looking at the bed in disgust as he scratched at his whiskered chin.

"That's not what I meant. I meant relax, take a break, give yourself a chance to unwind."

"That's what I keep telling him."

Chase's head jerked toward the door, and his jaw dropped as his boss walked into the room. He swiveled his head around to look at Stevie.

"You send out invitations?" he asked dryly.

"You quit harrassin' that little girl," Charlie ordered, "and listen to the doc. He's right. You work too damn hard."

"That from my boss?"

"Don't get me wrong. You do more in a weekend than most of the guys do all week, but—" Charlie eyed him sternly "—you aren't doing any work now, are you?"

"I—"

Dan cut him off. "Don't argue with your boss. If you'd taken a little time off now and then, you might not be flat on your back now. Working fifteen hours a day, seven days a week, will knock down your resistance real fast."

Chase looked from one man to the other, then at Stevie. "Don't you want to put in your two cents?" he asked grumpily.

"Nope. I'm saving all my money. To go relax and have some fun." Chase rolled his eyes and let out a disgusted sigh. "Maybe I'll go watch the Padres trounce the Cubbies this Sunday," she said, with a grin aimed at Dan.

"Good idea," the young doctor said expansively, not rising to her jibe about his beloved Chicago team. "Take him with you," he said, inclining his head toward Chase.

If Stevie was surprised, she hid it well. "Sure," she said easily.

Chase's eyes flicked from Dan to Stevie and back, startled. "What?" he said, a little weakly.

"You heard me," Dan said. "I'll make you a deal. You spend the time resting—go to a ball game, a movie, whatever. In short, doing absolutely nothing resembling work, and I'll let you go back in two weeks instead of three."

"You'll *let* me?" Chase glowered ominously. "Just how do you propose to stop me from going back sooner?"

"He won't have to," Charlie cut in. "You're not working for me until he says you can."

Chase glared at the older man and opened his mouth to retort angrily, then controlled himself with an effort. "What is this, a conspiracy?"

"Certainly," Dan said cheerfully. "We're going to teach you how to relax whether you like it or not. You take him to that game Sunday, Stevie, get him out in the sun, soak up some vitamin-D rays. Be good for him.''

"Would you mind not talking about me like I'm a five-year-old?''

Stevie giggled; she couldn't help it. Chase's gaze flew to her; green eyes met blue, and he knew exactly what she was thinking.

"Damn,'' he muttered under his breath. Maybe he *was* acting like that five-year-old, but he was sick of being so helpless. And he was touched by the concern of these people he'd tried so hard to keep at arm's length. He was being drawn to them, and he didn't dare let it happen. But most of all he didn't dare let himself be pulled any closer to the powerful, relentless magnet that was Stevie Holt.

"I'll pick up the game tickets for you on my way in today,'' Dan said brightly, then was gone before Chase could protest.

"See you in two weeks,'' Charlie added and, sensing an explosion coming on, beat a quick retreat himself.

Chase stared at the door, then at Stevie. Her expression was carefully even, and she kept her eyes lowered, as if she didn't dare look at him. Realization hit.

"Two weeks was what he wanted all along, wasn't it?'' he asked wryly.

Stevie raised her head; the teasing glint in her clear blue eyes was unmistakable. A soft smile curved her lips.

His resistance melted, and his anger followed it. His mouth twisted into a rueful, crooked grin as he rubbed his whiskered jaw. "I think I've been set up.''

"Dan has a unique approach to getting what he wants. Besides, he's right, you know.''

"Let's not start that again,'' he grumbled, scratching his chin again. "I've had enough of everybody telling me what to do, for one day.''

Stevie watched him for a moment, suddenly seized with the desire to see that strong, firm jaw clean-shaven again. "I could do that for you,'' she said tentatively.

He blinked. "What?''

"If you want a shave, I mean. I...I used to do it for Sean."

"Your brother?" he asked, surprised she had mentioned him again. She nodded. "I thought he was younger than you."

"He is, but he's still old enough to shave, silly. I am twenty-six, you know."

"No. I didn't." He had thought she was younger. Except for those moments when something infinitely old and wise changed those sky-blue eyes, she looked barely out of her teens.

"I promise not to cut your throat," she said, thinking his silence was hesitation.

He lowered his eyes suddenly. "I'm not sure I'd blame you if you did," he muttered. And he meant it. She'd been so open, so giving, and he'd done nothing, given her nothing, in return, only snapped at her when she probed too close to the wound that never healed.

"Don't be so hard on yourself. It's tough being sick."

I wish that was all it was, he thought grimly.

Moments later, when she returned with a towel, razor and shaving cream, he wished he'd said no. He could have tolerated the itch of his growing beard better than her closeness as she sat on the edge of the bed and leaned over him. His nose was full of the light, spicy scent she wore, and the feel of her smooth, slender fingers on his face was torture.

She had obviously told the truth; she moved with quick efficiency, sliding the razor over his face with smooth, even strokes. She turned his head, first one way, then the other, and he gritted his teeth in his effort to control the heat that was building in him at her touch.

"Relax," she said, laughing. "I'll be careful. Wouldn't want to mess up this gorgeous jaw of yours."

He couldn't breathe. The thought that, even jokingly, she found any part of him attractive was more than he could handle. Then she moved to shave under his chin, tilting his head back and bracing herself with her free hand at the base of his throat, palm flat against his heated skin, fingers lying outstretched in a feather-light caress. His heart began to slam in his chest.

How could she not feel it? He was burning up; the blood was pounding through his veins. He couldn't believe she didn't feel it beneath her hand. She turned his head again, her fingers brushing against his ear as she worked on the side of his face. The hot, heavy beat slowed, centered somewhere low in his body, and he felt himself begin to tighten. Damn, it had been so long, too long....

He knew that wasn't quite it. True, his life had been barely short of celibate for a long time, with only a brief, no-strings diversion to break his self-imposed isolation when the need became unbearable. But never had anyone—not even Victoria, when he'd supposed himself madly in love with her—been able to do this to him. No one had ever been able to send his blood racing with the merest of innocent touches, been able to stop his breath with the slightest smile.

The phantom sprite who had haunted his dreams since the first day he'd seen her, the woman he'd watched from afar with longing and quiet resignation, faded away beside the fiery, sassy reality. Stevie Holt was all too real, and if he'd hoped that she would somehow make it easier to stay away by not living up to his imagination, that hope had died a quick, blazing death. She was more than even his wildest dreams had ever conjured up.

Finished at last, she sat back and inspected her work. Chase shifted uncomfortably, grateful for the thickness of the bedcovers, which at least hid his body's response to her touch. Great, he told himself scathingly. *She nursemaids you around the clock out of the kindness of her heart, and you react like a teenager in heat. She was only shaving you, for God's sake. It's not like she was touching you to . . .*

He nearly groaned aloud at the thought of Stevie touching him for other reasons. Of her running those lovely, gentle hands over him, over his naked skin, of how it would feel to have her cradle his aching flesh in her palm. With all his depleted strength he tried to rein in his surging senses, cursing his rebellious body for wanting something it wasn't going to get. For making him once more have to burn the reminder into his soul that such sweetness, such heaven, was not for him.

"Hey, no frowning now, you haven't seen it yet. I did a fine job, I'll have you know!"

"I...I know." At the taut, husky sound of his voice, she stared at him. He tried again, managing to sound faintly lighthearted. "Not even any bleeding."

She laughed, and at the caress of that sound he had to redouble his efforts to ignore the shaft of heat that shot through him to once again stab his aching, wanting flesh. Desperate, he crossed the line she had drawn before, thinking that even if he made her angry, he had to put some space between them. Fast.

"Why did you have to do this for—"

He stopped. He couldn't do it. Not when she had so easily accepted his own vast silences. Not even when it was to save himself from his own inability to fight the spell she seemed to have cast over him.

"He was...hurt. In a car accident." Chase's eyes widened, not at what she'd said, but because she was answering him at all. "He was laid up for a long time."

The underlying pain in her voice helped him to do what his own will had been unable to accomplish; he beat back the urgent ache and steadied himself. "Is he all right now?"

She sighed, a small, sad little sound that tore at him. "They've done as much as they can for him. The rest is up to him." He caught the undertone of a heavy load carried in silent resignation. It was a tone he was very familiar with.

He wanted to pull her into his arms, to hold her, to soothe her and make all the pain go away. He wanted to protect her, to make sure she was never hurt again, that her fiery spirit would never be smothered under that kind of burden again.

He laughed bitterly at himself as she began to wipe the remnants of shaving cream from his face. He couldn't even protect himself, couldn't even promise himself tomorrow, let alone anyone else.

"There. They might even let you into the ballpark now."

"Stevie... I know you kind of got roped into that—"

"If anybody got maneuvered, it was you," she said with a little laugh. "If you don't want to go, I understand."

Not want to go? Not want to spend an entire day with her, not as patient and nurse but as . . . As what? he wondered grimly. She had been the victim of Dr. Bartlett's organization, that was all. It was part of his treatment. Take the patient for an outing.

"You've already spent too much of your vacation on me. You don't have to do this, too."

"I don't mind. I was planning on going anyway. I haven't been to a game since opening day. Besides, it would be a good chance to get out, see how you feel. We can always leave early if it's too much."

If he had an ounce of brains he would say no. He would be up and around on his own by then; he wouldn't need her anymore. . . .

Something cold and hard knotted up inside him. He couldn't think of anything he needed, anything he wanted, more than the warmth and light of her presence.

It was only for a couple of days more. Surely he could handle that. He could control these adolescent urges that seemed to have taken him over; he was sure it was only his weakened state. And he'd lost them, hadn't he? There had been no sign of anyone for months now. It would be safe, just for a while, wouldn't it? He swallowed heavily. Could he steal these few precious hours more? Could he stay in the sun just a little longer?

His lips twisted wryly. The question was, could he cast himself back into the darkness so soon after this shining being had come into his life? That he must, soon, he couldn't deny; whether he could right now was another question. He felt as if the sun was rapidly retreating behind a grim, hovering cloud.

"I'd like to go." He hadn't meant to say it; it seemed like some hidden part of his mind had taken the decision away from his rational intellect.

"Good," Stevie said, smiling, and the sun came out again.

* * *

"Don't fall. I'd never be able to pick you up."

Chase wheeled around, grabbing at the doorjamb just in case; his balance had improved, but he'd only been back on his feet for two days. His first thought was surprise that she hadn't chastised him for getting up alone, as he would have expected from most women. His second thought was ruefully directed at himself for thinking that Stevie Holt would ever do what he expected.

Then he got a look at her, and all other thoughts fled. She was an impossible combination of sexy woman and adorable tomboy. The shiny, tousled mane of red-gold hair was pulled back in a bouncy ponytail that made her look about sixteen, especially with the baseball cap she wore at a jaunty angle. But the pale blue T-shirt she wore highlighted the full curves beneath it, and the trim white shorts bared a tantalizing length of lithe, shapely legs.

He supposed her fair complexion prevented her from getting the deep, dark, eventually hazardous tan favored by so many in this sun-worshiping state, but she had a lovely, golden color that he found infinitely more appealing. He swallowed tightly.

"Hi," he finally managed, wondering why she was looking at him so oddly. Probably waiting for you to fall on your face, he told himself dryly. "Figuring you're going to have to carry me today?" he asked when she didn't say any more.

Stevie shook her head, suddenly devoid of the ability to speak. He was standing in the doorway of the bathroom, leaning against the doorjamb. Something about the angle of his body, the sight of him on his feet and obviously regaining his strength, did odd things to her. It had, she told herself firmly, nothing to do with the bare expanse of muscled chest she was looking at, or the way the sweatpants he wore rode low on his lean hips, baring the tip of the trail of dark hair that began below his navel and arrowed downward.

"I was just going to take a shower," he said. "I'll be ready in a few minutes."

"I... That's fine," Stevie said, having found her voice at last. "I'm a little early."

After a moment she heard the water start, and an odd little shiver went through her at the thought of him naked beneath the streaming shower. What is wrong with you? she asked herself fiercely. You're acting like you've never seen an attractive man before. You work with dozens of them.

So why didn't any of those high-powered junior executives, who looked as if they'd all been stamped out with the same cookie cutter, do these weird things to her blood pressure? She turned away from the sound of the water, trying to shut out the images in her head of that bare chest she knew by heart now, gleaming slick and wet, the scattering of dark hair between his flat, brown nipples clinging to his skin.

With an odd little sound she crossed the room, coming to a stop in front of the framed drawing on the wall. She stared at it for a while, fighting her own thoughts. After a few minutes she managed to chalk it all up to the fact that, since Sean's accident two years ago, she'd had no time for a man in her life. Or, in truth, since she'd begun work at Walker and Dunn. She'd been determined to make a success of her chosen field, and, except for her family, everything else had fallen by the wayside.

She put those errant thoughts out of her mind, telling herself that Chase Sullivan was merely a neighbor who had, for a time, needed her help. When he was completely well again, he would go back to his own very private life, and she to hers.

The picture she was staring at gradually came into focus as the chaos of her thoughts about Chase receded. It was truly a marvelous house, she thought. She could imagine the spectacular view from the soaring walls of glass that faced the expanse of sea and sky. She could see the starkness of those walls warmed by the softness of wood and brick. She could even picture the interior, all light and air, not trapped by the walls of the house but rather free to move and change, as free as the people who lived in it.

"Stevie?"

The query came unexpectedly from close beside her, but his voice was so soft, so quiet, she wasn't startled; it seemed

to blend perfectly with the mood brought on by her con-
templation of the house.

"It's beautiful," she murmured. "You could be safe
there, and free at the same time."

"Is that . . . how it makes you feel?"

She nodded slowly. "Like you could do anything, take
anything, if you had that to come home to." She looked at
it again. "I'd like to know . . ."

"What?" His voice was barely above a whisper.

"I was going to say the person who designed it," she said
softly, "but I think I mean the person who dreamed it."

She came abruptly out of her reverie at his sudden stiff-
ening; she'd forgotten his reaction when she'd asked about
it before. But he wasn't glaring at her, he was looking at her
with an expression she couldn't read.

"Let's go," he said abruptly.

She turned to follow him, sighing inwardly at the shattering of that quietly intimate moment. You should be
grateful, she told herself. He obviously doesn't want anyone intruding on his life, and you certainly don't need another moody male in yours.

He was waiting, leaning against his open front door, and
Stevie's breath caught in her throat as she got her first real
look at him. He'd put on a pair of jeans that were less faded
and worn than those he worked in, but they clung to his lean
body just as lovingly, from the long, smooth muscles of his
legs to the taut swell of his buttocks. His pullover shirt was
a lightweight cotton, its loose fit somehow emphasizing the
broad expanse of his chest as much as the mint-green color
lit up his eyes. Instead of the black boots, he wore a pair of
white, high-topped tennis shoes, an oddly innocent touch
that made the image of the slightly menacing figure in black
leather blur a little.

His hair, still damp from the shower, curved against his
neck, although she knew it would dry dark and straight and
thick. Although brushed back now, she knew that it would
fall forward, softening the firm, sculpted lines of his head.
It was odd, after years spent with countless businessmen
with their short, carefully styled hair, that this slightly
shaggy, longer mane made her fingers itch to run through it.

He had removed the bandage from his temple; the cut beneath was still slightly red, curving from the hairline down to stop an inch or so above his right eye. She wondered if it would leave a scar, then decided it wouldn't matter; nothing could detract from those looks. It would probably only add to the aura that seemed to cling to him, that sense of secrecy, of danger, of mystery.

He was looking at her quizzically, and she pulled herself together quickly and walked past him out the door. He blinked a little as they stepped out into the bright spring sunshine; he hadn't been outside yet, and it took a moment for his eyes to adjust.

Stevie let out a startled little cry when he grabbed her arm and thrust her behind him.

"Wha—?"

"Shh," he hissed, moving swiftly to block her when she began to step to one side, to see what had happened.

"Chase, what—"

"Hush!"

Stung, she backed away from him and stared at his broad back. Talk about moody males, she thought, this one takes the cake. And why was he retreating, edging her back toward the door of his apartment? She reached out with one hand to touch his arm, then withdrew it in alarm; he was rigidly tense, every muscle taut and strained.

"My God, Ch—"

"Get back inside." He snapped the words, and something in his voice sent a little pulse of fear racing down her spine. She went; somehow it was impossible not to obey that sharp command.

He backed through the still-open door after her, then shut it solidly. Stevie felt that little ripple of fear again when she saw him throw home the dead bolt with a vicious jerk. He stood there for a moment, the quickened rise and fall of his chest visible as his still weakened body caught its breath. Then he swallowed heavily and took one long stride over to the window to stare out through the gap in the thick drapes.

At last Stevie found her voice. "What *is* it?"

"I'm not sure." He never looked away from the window.

"Then what is this all about?"

"There's somebody out there. In a car."

A sharp retort rose to her lips, but she bit it back with patience learned the hard way, after Sean had been hurt.

"Of course there is," she said carefully. "It's the middle of the day, on a weekend, and we're within walking distance of the beach."

He turned his gaze on her then, and Stevie's stomach knotted. His eyes looked as they had the first time she'd seen him, haunted, hollow.

She tried again. "There are always people around, waiting for a parking place to open up."

"Then why is he looking this way instead of toward the beach?" His voice was harsh.

Stevie leaned forward to look around him, to peer through the window, feeling a little silly. When she pulled back, she looked up at him curiously.

"What car?"

He jerked sharply and looked out once more. The car was gone. He slowly straightened up. Doubt still showed in the lean planes of his face, but the hammer blows of his heart slowed, as did the pace of his breathing.

"They do it all the time, Chase." She studied him for a moment before asking softly, "Who did you think it was?"

He stiffened, his face becoming the impassive mask that she'd come to know meant the conversation was over. "Never mind," he said flatly. "It doesn't matter. I was mistaken. Let's go."

Stevie sighed inwardly. Lord rescue me from temperamental males, she muttered to herself as she once more went out the door. Even ones with green eyes that made your heart skip, and grins that could light up a city block.

But as they headed toward her car, she knew that wasn't really what she wanted. What she wanted was for Chase to be rescued from whatever had the power to put that look in his eyes. And to know who on earth he had thought was out there, and why it had sparked that incredible reaction. And, most of all, she wanted to believe it had nothing to do with that gun in his drawer.

Chapter 4

He took the passenger seat in her car without comment, sliding the seat back to accommodate his long legs. She was glad he didn't have any ego problem with letting her drive. He caught her glance as she settled in behind the wheel.

"I know I'm in no shape to drive," he said a little testily. "I may be stubborn, but I'm not stupid."

"I know that," she said evenly. "I just wasn't sure where the stubborn stopped."

Her quiet answer to his bad-tempered words did more to chasten him than any sharp response would have done. He let out a disgusted breath, shaking his head ruefully.

"I've apologized more in the last week than I have in my entire life, so what's one more? I'm sorry."

She shrugged. "All right."

He studied her as she backed easily out of the carport. He was embarrassed by his earlier overreaction to the strange car, and more than a little ashamed of snapping at her. "You're pretty...tolerant, aren't you?"

"Experience." She kept her eyes on the traffic as she eased out onto the street.

Experience? Her words about her brother came back to him, banishing his puzzlement. That was what he was to her—another patient whose crankiness and quirks were to be put up with. For the first time it occurred to him that perhaps his personal inability to restrain the incredible effect she had on him might be a moot point; she suddenly seemed as remote as the stars.

What did you expect? his inner voice asked, bitingly acid. She's a high-class lady, for all that she lives in that apartment and drives a car that's beginning to show its age. To her, you're just a—

He broke off his own thoughts, knowing even as they formed that they were unfair. Stevie Holt wasn't like that at all, not like so many of the other women he'd come across, looking down their noses at the men who built the houses they lived in, the stores in which they purchased their chic clothes. While he had seen her on her way to work looking as though she belonged completely to that haughty group, he knew that, beneath the elegant facade, she was one of the most unpretentious people he'd ever met.

He stared out the window as she maneuvered the car quickly and smoothly onto the freeway that would take them to Jack Murphy Stadium, his thoughts having effectively driven his instinctive response to the strange car out of his mind.

No, he couldn't use snobbery as an excuse; there wasn't an ounce of it in her. But it seemed now it didn't matter. His chaotic reaction to her wasn't going to be a problem after all, he thought glumly. Whatever her effect on him, it was clear it was one-way. He wondered why he wasn't relieved. But at least, instead of treating him like a burden, a patient who had to be humored, she tried to be friendly. If she seems distant now, it's your own damn fault, he told himself. You've been a jerk ever since she hit a nerve about the house. Again.

It was a beautiful May morning, warm with the promise of summer, and they were cruising along nicely. In dead silence.

''Stevie?'' he said at last, tentatively.

"What?" She seemed more intent than necessary on keeping her eyes on the road.

"I ... Look, I don't want to mess up your day. I'm sorry I've been such a jerk."

"Don't worry about it. I could enjoy a baseball game with King Kong."

Ouch, he thought. It seemed he'd finally found the limits of her extensive patience.

"I guess I deserved that," he said wryly, studying the slightly worn armrest of the passenger door. "But King Kong?"

"Oh, I didn't mean you. You're more along the lines of Attila the Hun."

He winced, but when he glanced at her, he saw the barely perceptible twitch at the corners of her mouth. "Thanks," he said wryly.

"They say," she said mildly, "that he wasn't as bad as he was painted."

"Bad press," Chase said solemnly. "It's hard to overcome a bad reputation."

"But not impossible." The teasing note in her voice was clear now. She glanced sideways at him, her eyes alive with that glint he'd come to recognize, and he knew he was forgiven.

He promised himself right then that it wasn't going to happen again. If he was going to have this time with her, these moments snatched from a brighter life, he'd better enjoy them to the fullest, because soon the memory of them would be all he would have. Just for now, he would put aside the dark, would pretend that there was no danger, no shadow hovering, and savor every golden minute.

Stevie was amazed. Once again he had startled her with the completeness of his turnabout. It was as if those astonishing moments this morning had never happened. They had a brief, teasing argument about who would pay for the parking in the huge stadium lot, ending when Chase forced a promise from her that he would buy the requisite ballpark hot dogs with all the extras.

"Let me salvage at least that much of my male pride, will you?"

"Okay, but I warn you, at this place I become a shark in a feeding frenzy!"

"Have at it," he told her, grinning crookedly. "I have a lot of overtime money saved up."

He got an inkling of how serious she was about the sport when she bought a scorecard and carefully filled in the starting lineups from the scoreboard information. She caught his glance, and, after swallowing a bite of the hot dog—the first hot dog, she had cheerfully warned him again—she grinned.

"I always start out with good intentions, but by the seventh-inning stretch, I'm usually too into the game to keep track anymore."

He couldn't remember, even in the happier times he labeled in his mind as "before," having this much fun. The crowd was enthusiastic, as only the champions of perennial underdogs who have had a taste of glory can be; the winning season of 1984 had fired this city to baseball like never before.

But for Chase, his enjoyment came from the unrestricted, unembarrassed, sheer exuberance of the woman beside him. She cheered and booed with all the carefree abandon of the true fan, and she also had the true fan's ability to appreciate good plays, even when made by the opposition.

He found her knowledge of the game amazing. He could hear the local announcers from several radios in the vicinity tuned to the broadcast of the game, and often, after Stevie had mentioned some obscure fact about a play or a player, he heard it echoed by the men in the booth on the press box level. When she casually suggested that the team might try a double steal two seconds before the runners took off from first and second to do just that, he shook his head in awe. "You really are something."

Stevie grinned at him. She didn't know what had brought on this latest change in him, this switch to lighthearted affability, but she wasn't about to question it.

"What I am," she said, "is ready for another hot dog."

She hadn't exaggerated that, either, he thought. "Where do you put it?" he asked in wonder after the second hot dog was followed by a box of Cracker Jack and a frozen chocolate malt.

"Ballpark food," she said happily. "It doesn't count."

Along about the seventh inning break, when the slightly off-key crowd was singing "Take Me Out to the Ball Game," he realized she was watching him rather speculatively.

"I'm fine," he assured her when he saw the look in her eyes. "Really. I feel great. And I could have gotten that last hot dog for you."

"Why should you walk all the way up there when I'm the one eating it?" she said simply, then grinned. "I let you pay for it, didn't I?"

"That makes me feel much better," he said dryly, but the smile on his face belied his tone.

He meant what he'd said; he felt great. What would have been fatigue under other circumstances had melted into a sense of complete relaxation he'd never felt before. The sheer release of letting down his constant guard, of not thinking beyond this day, this time with her, had flooded him with a tranquil peace that buoyed a spirit too long shoved behind the barred door of his mind. It overrode everything, even the gnawing edginess that had been so much a part of him for so long.

It had long passed warm in the crowded stands; hot was the only word for it. Chase watched Stevie fan herself with the program and smiled. "Want another beer?"

She shook her head. "One's my limit, even here. What about you?" He'd had a soda earlier, saying a beer would probably put him to sleep.

"Uh-uh," he said. "I'm not much of a drinker." I don't dare, he thought grimly, not when staying alive depends on staying alert. "How about a soda, then?" he said abruptly, slamming the door on the thoughts he had banned for the day.

She nodded, then watched him thoughtfully as he made his way up the steps to the refreshment stand. If this was the real Chase Sullivan, she wished he'd hang around for a while.

She was fuming through an intentional walk of the Padres' best hitter when a flutter of high-pitched female voices whispering furiously from behind caught her ear. Turning to see what had caught the attention of the giggly teenagers this time, she saw the eyes of all three sixteen-year-olds, who had been unabashedly boy-watching most of the game, fastened on someone coming down the stairs.

They were quiet for once, staring raptly at the lean figure with the tousled dark hair and the vivid green eyes. At Chase. Who, she noticed with a sense of satisfaction she didn't quite understand, ignored them completely.

Can you blame them? she thought suddenly. And if they ever saw him as she had, in his boots and leather jacket, she was sure the giggles would become squeals of slightly apprehensive delight.

Suddenly she was more aware than ever of the feeling she'd always had that there was some dreadful, heavy sorrow clinging to him, some bitter hopelessness that had battered his soul and put that haunted look in his eyes, that look she'd never been able to forget. And now that she had seen him without it, her heart ached at the thought of him slipping back into that shrouded gloom.

Chase didn't know what had brought such a look to her face, what had put that soft, tender warmth in those clear blue eyes; he only knew that somehow it was directed at him, and that its strength stunned him. "Stevie?"

A roar from the crowd turned everyone's attention to the field, and the ensuing ruckus over an umpire's call destroyed the moment; Chase wasn't sure if he was disappointed or relieved.

The game that should have been over in nine innings went on for twelve, until even Stevie was ready to join the hundreds who had left in disgust; four hours of baseball punctuated by errors and lost chances was not exactly exhilarating. And she was worried about Chase, although he seemed to be doing fine.

In fact, he seemed so relaxed and at ease that he was bordering on lethargic, and if it hadn't been for the small smile that curved the corners of his mouth and the way he tilted his head back to absorb the afternoon sun with such obvious enjoyment, she would have been afraid he was sick again. It was hard for her to believe that this was the same man who had been strung as taut as a bowstring this morning.

Finally, on a humdrum little pop-up to the second baseman, it was over.

"I thought you loved it, no matter what?" Chase teased her as they joined what was left of the crowd exiting the stadium. As he had been coming in, he was grateful for the escalator that carried them from the loge level; walking was one thing, climbing multiple flights of stairs another.

"I do," she said, "but that doesn't mean I'm blind. That was a sloppy game, even if they did finally win it."

He smiled inwardly. She was such an intriguing mix. She was the stylish, sophisticated woman he'd seen dressed for business, self-assured and aware of her own talent and worth. She was the sassy, lively sprite who whooped at the top of her lungs at a home run. She was the gentle, caring nurse who managed to take care of you and yet somehow leave your pride intact. She was the pensive, thoughtful woman with that ancient wisdom in her sky-blue eyes. She was incredible, and with every passing minute the thought of wrenching her out of his life was more painful.

Once more he shoved that thought back into the recesses of his mind. He'd promised himself this day, and it wasn't over yet.

By the time they got to the exit of the crowded parking lot, it was nearing six o'clock. Stevie looked at Chase, her lower lip caught between her teeth. It was a gesture he'd come to know, indicating there was something she wasn't quite sure how to bring up. Familiarity with the sight of that full lip being nibbled on did nothing to ease its effect on him.

"What?" he asked after a moment, pretending an interest in the pickup truck full of slightly inebriated baseball fans that was determined to cut in front of them as they exited the lot.

"I didn't think it would go this late," she began hesitantly. "I need to drop something off at my parents', but I could take you home first."

"Where do they live?"

"In La Mesa."

He raised an eyebrow at her. "That's the other direction," he observed unnecessarily.

"I know."

He gave a low chuckle. "I'm fine, Stevie. In fact, I can't remember when I've felt this good. Another ten miles won't kill me."

"My mother might," she said ruefully. "She has definite fussbudget tendencies."

"You must not take after her, then."

"Nope. I'm Daddy's girl, all right. And Daddy, bless him, is a stubborn, independent, no-fuss type."

"I never would have guessed."

She gave him a sideways look. "Okay, pot."

It took him a split second. "As in calling the kettle black?" he said with a grin. "I confess. Guilty as charged." He was suddenly serious. "I'm thankful you take after your father. I couldn't have handled a ... fussbudget."

"You don't have to keep thanking me, you know. Anybody would have done the same."

"I doubt that," he said softly, thinking that very few people would have gone to the lengths she had for a complete and unsociable stranger.

Even though she had carefully given them more than enough room, Stevie kept her eyes on the reckless pickup truck ahead. She winced as another car had to jam on the brakes to avoid a collision. There was a swift movement as a young boy jumped hastily out of the way, and an ear-splitting screech of tires on asphalt. Stevie sensed rather than saw Chase go suddenly rigid. She glanced at him.

He wasn't looking at the near collision. He was pressed back in the seat, his eyes tightly closed. His face was pale, not as it had been during the worst of his illness, but with the ashen tinge of shocked reaction. His jaw was clenched, muscles standing out along his neck, and his hands were gripping the edges of the seat so tightly his knuckles were white.

"Chase? What's wrong?"

He let out a short, compressed breath. The tension drained out of stiff muscles. Then the touch of color he'd gained this afternoon slowly returned. At last he shrugged.

"I'm fine."

"But—"

"I'm fine," he repeated. "I just thought . . . he was going to get hit, that's all."

Stevie hesitated; his response seemed disproportionate for what had, or rather hadn't, happened. But she had come to know that flat, masked expression; it meant he would say no more. She turned her attention back to driving, to getting them onto the freeway.

She was aware that he was watching her, as if waiting. Then he seemed to relax. After a few moments of silence, she pointed out the buildings of San Diego State University, visible from the freeway below it as they headed east toward La Mesa.

"You liked going there?"

"Loved it. It's a good school. An old school. It's got an incredible range of buildings, from old halls to the most modern style. It's like a living history of architecture, from 1897, when it was begun, to now. Even the modern buildings fit in with the old adobe and tile, because they didn't go for some out-of-place Doric columns."

"You sound like you don't care for that style." His voice was oddly intent.

She shrugged. "It's fine, when it works. But I've always felt so many of the people who use it now are trying to imitate something else, instead of doing what the site and the buildings' function call for. It's like those old bank buildings you see, trying to look like the Acropolis at street level when they're twenty stories of steel and concrete. They just wind up looking silly.''

She glanced over at him when he didn't speak. He was wearing that expression she couldn't fathom again, that same look he'd worn when they'd stood in front of the picture on his wall. She didn't know what she'd said this time.

"Sorry. Don't mind me," she said lightly. "The oddest things offend my sense of design. Occupational hazard, I suppose.''

"Don't apologize," he said, his voice oddly harsh. "Not many people see what you see. Or understand it.''

Stevie had to concentrate on heading for the upcoming exit and couldn't look at him. She wanted to, wanted to see his face, to know if the underlying pain she'd heard in his words was reflected on his face. By the time she could look, there was nothing there to give him away, and she had a feeling she would never know what had made him sound that way.

She wondered about his words as she headed for the residential area where her parents lived. He had sounded so definite, as if what she'd said was something he'd long ago accepted as fact. And as if he spoke from experience. Perhaps he'd worked on one too many of those kinds of buildings, she thought. She'd always wondered what the people who built some of the monstrosities of the world had thought about them.

When she pulled to a stop in front of her parents' small house, he looked at it with interest. "Is this where you grew up?''

"No. The old house is a little farther out. My folks sold it after my brother moved out. Business wasn't real good for a while, but they're okay now. They get by on what the print shop brings in, and they can work together.''

She paused with one hand on the door latch, the other holding a manila envelope she'd retrieved from the back seat. "You're welcome to come in, but if you'd rather not, I understand. I'll make it quick.''

He shrugged. It was a casual gesture, concealing the fact that he was intensely curious about her family. Did she take after her father in looks, as well? Or her mother? Or neither? Then he heard a deep male voice call out her name, and when he looked in that direction, his question was answered.

He was graying and a little thick in the waist, but there was no doubt that the man coming toward them was Stevie's father. It wasn't just the color of his hair or his fair complexion, it was the set of his jaw and the easy stride, the flashing blue eyes and the smile that lit them.

Chase felt strange just sitting there while the pair embraced warmly, so he got out of the car, standing beside it hesitantly, eyeing the smaller, dark-haired figure who was bustling down the driveway from the little house.

"Hello, Mother. Dad, here's the layout you wanted for the ad." She handed him the envelope, then paused until the woman had joined him. "This is Chase Sullivan. He's my next-door neighbor, and be gentle, please. He just put up with me through a twelve-inning ball game."

"You have my sympathy, son," the older man said, extending his hand. Chase shook it, grinning in spite of himself at the twinkle in those blue eyes that were so like Stevie's. "I'm Steven Holt. Yes," he added in answer to Chase's look, "I'm the reason this girl of mine is saddled with that name. A temporary aberration I've never regretted for a minute."

Chase, still grinning, glanced at Stevie, who rolled her eyes with the fond exasperation of someone who'd been through this time and again.

"And this is my wife, Margaret," the older man went on, and before Chase could respond, the tiny woman broke into a torrent of words.

"Call me Maggie. Margaret makes me feel much too old." She was looking at him with open curiosity; he couldn't blame her, he supposed. "You're Stevie's neighbor? That's nice. Although I don't know why she stays there in that little place, even if it is close to the beach. You young people, I don't know."

Chase risked a glance at Stevie; her mouth was twisted into a grimace, and he read the words "I warned you" as clearly as if she'd spoken them.

Maggie's eyes flickered to her daughter. "You've been to a ball game? And I suppose you filled up on all sorts of junk," she said reprovingly.

"It's my only vice," Stevie said mildly, "so I try to do it right."

"Hmph. And how about you, young man, did she coerce you into eating all that terrible food?" Startled, Chase gaped at her. "You look a little pale. And tired. Not that I'm surprised. This girl doesn't have a lick of sense when it comes to that silly game. I—"

"Mother," Stevie cut in, sensing Chase's unease. "He's been sick, that's all. Today's his first day out in a while."

"And you drag him to a ball game and fill him full of junk food?" She gave Stevie a reproachful look. "Well, it's a good thing you're just in time for a solid, healthy meal. Come along now, there's plenty to go around. You both could use it, too. You're much too thin." She turned and hastened up the drive before they could answer.

"It's an old trick of hers," Stevie said wryly at Chase's stunned expression. "She steamrollers you, then leaves before you have a chance to argue."

"She means well," Steven Holt said indulgently, his arm still around his daughter, "but she is a little hard to slow down sometimes. So you're both quite welcome, and we'd love to have you, but don't feel you have to stay."

Stevie looked at Chase questioningly. "It's up to you."

"I..."

No. The word was on the tip of his tongue. He couldn't take this, not an entire evening with her family. It would only make it worse when he had to turn his back on her. Then he looked at Stevie, and he knew nothing could make it any worse. With the sense of a drowning man surrendering his last grasp on the life preserver, he shrugged.

"Okay." He managed a smile. "But I don't know where you're going to put any more food."

"Be grateful," Stevie said as they headed for the house. "Nagging me for not eating will keep my mother off your back."

There was a touch of strain in her voice, and Chase's gaze sharpened, but then they were inside and he had no chance to pursue the thought.

The first part of the meal was much more pleasant than he'd expected. It was a traditional dinner of roast beef, potatoes and green vegetables; Maggie Holt was old school in more than one area, it seemed. The meal was hot and filling, and it did seem healthy after the afternoon of fast food.

What he enjoyed most, though, were the tales of Stevie's childhood, told with loving fondness by her father. Chase stole an occasional glance at her and had to smother a smile at the look she wore, that age-old expression of the child embarrassed by the foibles of the parent.

"Enough," Stevie finally proclaimed, her previous, more subtle attempts at changing the subject having failed miserably. "Talk about something else, even nag me about my car, but no more 'she was so cute when' stories!"

"Well," Maggie said, "now that you've brought it up, when are you going to buy a new car?"

"My car is fine. I keep it up, and it has a lot of miles left in it."

"But when you got that nice big promotion and raise, I thought you'd at least think about a new car. And what about that bonus Mr. Dunn gave you for the jewelry account?"

"I . . . had some bills to pay."

"Really, dear, you should be more prudent about spending your money."

"Yes, Mother," Stevie said in the weary tone of one who had heard this all before.

Chase looked at her curiously; she had certainly never impressed him as a spendthrift.

They talked then about other things, until Steven Holt decided Chase had been too silent and asked him about his work. He answered awkwardly, sounding strained to his own ears, realizing just how far he had withdrawn from the world when answering such a simple question seemed beyond him.

"So what job are you on now?" Steven asked patiently.

"Remodeling a small shopping center in Clairemont," he answered, trying to curb his uneasiness. "We were lucky and were down to the interior work before the rain started."

Chase caught Stevie's small movement out of the corner of his eye and lifted his gaze to hers. "Okay," he admitted, "so I wasn't so lucky."

"Did I say something?" she asked innocently.

"Volumes," he said dryly.

"What's this?" Steven asked.

"Oh," Stevie said airily, "just a comment on people who don't know when to rest."

"I'm resting, I'm resting." Chase tried unsuccessfully to sound irritated. Without even realizing it, he had relaxed under her gentle teasing.

"Just remember where working a hundred hours a week got you."

"A hundred hours?" Maggie piped up in disbelief. "Oh, that's much too much! Steven was doing that when we first opened the shop, and he almost wound up in the hospital. Why, he worked himself to a frazzle, got sick—" She stopped on her own for once, looking at Chase as she remembered her daughter's words. "And you did get sick, didn't you? You men, you just don't know how to take care of yourselves. And when we try to tell you, you just say we're nagging."

Stevie barely stifled a giggle, and Chase threw up his hands and surrendered with a laugh. "Okay, okay, I'll be good, I promise." He gave Stevie a wry grin. "Besides, I don't have much choice. My boss says the next time I show up on Sunday, I'm fired."

"Good for Charlie," Stevie said cheerfully.

Maggie Holt then seemed to launch herself on a one-woman campaign to get Chase to eat as much as possible. He was sitting there wondering how he was possibly going to finish the piece of pie buried in ice cream sitting in front of him when Maggie said to Stevie, "We talked to Sean today."

"How is he? I haven't talked to him for a week."

"About the same. He's not happy about being away at that camp for so long."

Stevie shrugged. "I didn't expect him to be. He's not happy about much of anything these days."

"He'll get over that," Steven said with a confidence Chase thought sounded a little forced.

"Of course he will," Maggie said briskly. "They'll teach him so many things he needs to learn. I'm so glad you found that place, dear."

Stevie glanced at Chase, who was quietly poking at the pie she knew he was too full to eat. He clearly wasn't going to pry, and she knew he was remembering her first outburst on the subject of her brother. He felt her gaze and raised his head.

"Sean . . . lost a leg in that accident. He's at a rehabilitation camp to teach him how to get around and use a prosthesis."

She didn't try to hide the pain that tinged her voice, and Chase closed his eyes against the answering pain that twisted in his gut.

"I'm sorry, Stevie," he said softly. His eyes flickered to her parents, marveling that they could talk about it so calmly.

"It's been nearly two years now," Steven explained. "We're used to the idea."

"We are," Stevie said with a touch of weariness, "but Sean isn't."

"But he will be," Maggie insisted. "After all, he did finally decide to go to the camp, didn't he?" Chase saw Stevie open her mouth and then abruptly shut it again. "It's just a good thing your insurance company is so helpful. I know that's part of the reason he was so stubborn about it. He knew how expensive it is."

Stevie became suddenly entranced by the dessert on her plate.

"You know, he was really worried about that," Maggie chattered on, oblivious to her daughter's withdrawal, "and our insurance was used up on just the accident. And with him only working part-time while he's in school—"

"He hasn't been in school for two years," Stevie said, her voice tight.

Chase watched her, saw her jaw clench, felt the tension suddenly radiating from her.

"He'll go back," Steven said brusquely, again with that forced note.

"Sure, Dad. He will."

Chase saw her knuckles whiten as her hand tightened around her fork. Then she set it down with exaggerated care. She seemed to slump wearily, and Chase felt a sharp pang at the defeated set of her normally straight shoulders.

"Stevie?" he asked softly. When she lifted her head and he saw that weariness echoed in her eyes, he suddenly knew he had to get her out of here. He wasn't exactly sure what had happened, but he knew instinctively that she'd had about as much as she could take. He cleared his throat. "Uh, I don't want to be rude, but I'm…a little tired. I guess I'm not as recovered as I thought."

"Typical man," Maggie chided. "You should go home and go straight to bed. Here, I'll wrap up the rest of that, and you can take it with you. Stevie, you barely touched your pie. You take yours, too." She was off and bustling.

Stevie didn't know what had possessed the normally stubborn Chase to admit he wasn't quite one hundred percent yet, but she was thankful for it; nothing else could have facilitated their escape quite so quickly as giving her mother a chance to fuss. Then she met that green gaze and knew suddenly that he felt fine; this was for her.

How had he known? Had she somehow betrayed her tension, her need to get away? I must have, she thought. I just hope Dad didn't notice; Mother is oblivious, as usual.

By dint of pure concentration, she managed civil goodbyes, aware of her own stiffness as they walked to the car. Chase quietly, out of earshot of her parents, volunteered to drive, but she said she was fine and slid behind the wheel.

By the time she'd gone two blocks she wished she'd let him. She was grateful it was dark now, hiding the death grip she had on the wheel as she tried to keep her hands from shaking. It was then that his voice cut through the strained silence.

"Pull over."

Stevie nearly jumped at the quiet command. "What?"

Chase pointed to a spot near the curb lit by the golden halo of a streetlight. "Pull over."

Numbly she obeyed, not having the strength at the moment to argue. When she had pulled up next to the curb, he leaned over and switched off the ignition. She stared at him, not at all sure what was happening, only sure that if he was going to dump something else on her, she was going to fly apart into a million pieces.

She was startled when he reached up and pried her cramped hands from the wheel. He held them in his own and turned her around to face him. She didn't fight him, just stared at him as if even a token protest was beyond her.

Chase sat there for a long moment, aware of the trembling of the slender hands clasped in his. He swallowed heavily. "Stevie, please. Don't let it tear you up like this."

She shuddered slightly, a small ripple of movement that sent a similar shudder down his spine. "I... I'm sorry. I know I shouldn't let it get to me, not after all this time. But it's so hard when they..." She trailed off, shaking her head.

"When they won't see the truth?" he asked gently. She lifted her eyes to his, then nodded shakily; he saw the glistening moisture in her eyes.

"Sean... has given up. He only went to this camp because I wouldn't drop it. I badgered him into it. He has no intention of ever learning to walk again, let alone going back to school. They just won't admit it."

"Parents generally see what they want to see," he said softly, holding her hands tightly.

"They love him so much." The tremble became a shudder.

"So do you."

She nodded, sucking in a deep breath as she tried to control herself. "I do. I really do. That's why it's so hard to see him like this. He was so alive, so physical. He was on the football team at San Diego State. The Aztecs. He was good, really good. He might have made the pros. Now he won't even try to walk on crutches. He just sits in that damn wheelchair and stares into space. If this camp doesn't turn him around, I don't know what will happen."

"You'll go on. You can't live his life for him."

"I know. But sometimes I wish it could have..." She trailed off again.

Chase sat up sharply, staring into her eyes. The words she hadn't spoken were there, as clear to him as if she'd said them.

"Stop it," he said harshly. "Don't you dare wish it had been you!"

"I can't help it," she whispered. "My mother...she had such plans for him, she loved him so much...."

"She loves you, too."

Stevie shrugged, a jerky little movement that told him of her doubts. "Sure. I just can't seem to do anything right. I don't drive a good enough car or have a good enough job. I don't live in a nice enough place. I drag sick people to baseball games. I—"

"Why haven't you bought a new car?"

"What?" She was startled by how intently he was watching her, waiting for an answer to his incongruous question.

"Why?" he repeated. He'd dealt with big advertising firms; he knew what kind of money their top people got paid. That kind of salary didn't fit with her modest rent and aging car.

She avoided his gaze. "Like I said, I have bills to pay."

Chase lifted her chin, looking at her in the shadowy light from the street lamp. "There is no insurance, is there?" he said softly. "You're paying his bills." Her eyes widened in shock, and he knew he'd guessed right. "God, Stevie, why don't you tell them? Why do you let them think—"

"Because it would be worse for them to think that they can't afford to take care of their only son."

Her voice was low and tight, and it clawed at Chase's emotions, ripping through the years of control. He couldn't stop himself; he reached out and pulled her into his arms.

"So you let them think you're some kind of bubblehead about money and talk to you like they did just now, while you do without so your brother gets what he needs. And you don't tell them so they won't be burdened." He smoothed her hair with a gentle hand. "And I suppose Sean doesn't know, either?"

"I . . . couldn't tell him. He never would have gone to the rehab camp, or to any therapy." He felt the tremor ripple through her, and knew she was on the verge of breaking down.

"So you carry it all alone." He held her tightly, his face pressed against her hair. "Oh, Stevie. None of us is worth what you do to yourself," he whispered. "Not your brother, not your mother, and sure as hell not me."

She made a small sound of protest, and he wasn't sure if it was over what he'd said, or the fact that, in spite of her gallant efforts to stop them, the tears had begun to fall.

"Let it out," he encouraged softly, tightening his arms around her as she clung to him, the wrenching sobs beginning. They were choked and awkward, and if he hadn't known already, the sound would have told him that she did not cry easily or often. At least, not for herself.

How long had she carried this burden? he wondered as she shuddered in his embrace. How long had she let her family berate her while she protected them with her own sacrifices? Had she truly done this for two years, since her brother's accident? No wonder the tension had built up so much; he knew her well enough by now to know that self-pity was not in her vocabulary. He felt a pang of guilt. He had spent so much time wrapped up in his own problems that he hadn't given much thought to anyone else's.

It was a long time before she finally managed to get herself in check again. She gulped a couple of times, sniffed; then, becoming suddenly aware of being so close in his arms, she pulled away and sat up.

"I'm sorry," she said, wiping at her tearstained cheeks with impatience. "I don't usually do that."

"I know that," he told her, feeling strangely cold now that she'd moved away. "But you needed to now."

She studied him for a moment, embarrassment warring with gratitude on her face. "I...got your shoulder all wet," she said tentatively, shyly.

He spoke lightly, trying to ease the strain she was feeling. "If it hadn't been for you, that shoulder might be in a hospital somewhere. I'd say that gives you shoulder rights."

She smiled—a small one, and none too steady, but a smile nevertheless. "I really don't think of it that way, you know, as a sacrifice. I love my brother. I want to help him."

"As long as you know you can't do it for him, or make him want to do it. He has to do that for himself."

"I know." She sighed. "That was the hardest thing to accept. He's my little brother, and I wanted to make it all right for him."

"Sometimes the best thing you can do is nothing at all."

She met his gaze, saw the green eyes warm with sympathy and understanding, and the tight knot in her chest loosened a little more.

"And that's the hardest thing of all to do," he added quietly.

She stared at him for a long moment. He even understood that, she thought. He saw so much...,

"How did you guess?"

He shrugged. "I knew you had to be making more money than you were using to live on, but I knew you weren't blowing it, either."

Stevie stared at him, an odd warmth spreading inside her. He knew that, when her own parents couldn't see it?

"And I know you'd do damn near anything to help your brother. Besides, I don't think there's an insurance plan in the world that would cover an adult brother unless he was carried on it in advance, and who would think to put a healthy young football player on it, anyway?" He hesitated a moment. "I suppose he didn't have any insurance of his own?"

"Not enough. There was a small policy from the school, but it was mainly for injuries during games. This was on the way home the day after an away game, so they sidestepped a lot of it."

"How much has it cost you?"

"It doesn't matter," she said, some of her battered pride resurfacing. "It's getting paid."

He hadn't really needed an answer; he knew from unpleasant experience just how high the bills could run for a major injury and a lengthy hospital stay. He just wondered how much of it she had taken onto her slender shoulders.

Stevie wiped her cheeks once more, then moved back behind the wheel, her control returning. After a moment, she reached for the ignition.

"We'd better get back. It's been a long day for your first time out."

"It's been a long day for both of us."

"Yes," she agreed softly; she owed him that much at least, she thought as she started the car.

Chapter 5

Stevie pulled into the carport carefully, a smile curving her lips as her headlights lit up the gleaming motorcycle in the next space. Who'da thunk it? she mused, remembering once more that first day she'd seen Chase. She glanced over at him. Somewhere between repassing the stadium and home, he had slipped into a weary sleep, head pillowed on the arm he had braced against the window of the passenger door.

She shut off the engine and flipped off the lights; he never stirred. Even when she got out and closed her door, he didn't move. She walked around and carefully opened his door, afraid he'd fall over, he was so soundly asleep. He didn't. He just ignored her and shifted his head to the other side.

"C'mon," she said with a little laugh. "You've got to wake up enough to walk. I sure can't carry you."

"Mmmmph."

"Chase," she pleaded, tugging at his arm.

"Mmm-hmm." He still didn't awaken, just shifted so he was a dead weight against her hands.

"You're going to be awfully stiff if you end up sleeping in this dumb car all night," she warned.

"'kay."

Well, it was a word, at least. Almost. She shook him again. "Let's go, Sullivan. Up and at 'em." She reached up and tugged at his ear, and was rewarded with a fleeting glimpse of one green eye.

"Wha—?"

"Come on. A hundred feet. You can do it."

"Sureican."

It came out as one slurred word. She pulled his arm over her shoulder and managed to lever him out of the car. He came to a bit more and somehow found his feet. She knew he had the best of intentions, but by the time they got to the corner of the building, he was leaning on her heavily.

It's your own fault, Holt, she told herself sternly. You're the one who kept him out all day when he should have been home resting. She staggered, trying to guide him up the two steps to the courtyard.

"Sorry," he mumbled. "Li'l wobbly."

The extra twenty feet from her door to his seemed like the Sahara desert: unconquerable. With a sigh she propped him up next to her door, barely getting it unlocked before he started to slide down the wall. She grabbed him, thinking that she would be laughing at this if it wasn't for the fact that she wasn't at all sure she could even get him inside. When she at last released him and he flopped down on her couch like a puppet with the strings cut, she felt as if she'd carried him every step of the way.

She glanced at her watch. It was nearly nine, and she doubted if he would wake up until morning, and late morning at that. She went and got one of the blankets she'd brought for him that first day, and a pillow from her bed. She knelt beside the couch and gently untied the laces of the white tennis shoes, tugging them off and setting them out of the way. She eased his shoulders down on the couch, his head onto the pillow, then lifted his feet up and spread the blanket over him. He never even blinked, nor did he stir when she locked the door and turned out the lights.

* * *

Crazy, he thought. Am I sick again? That time I dreamed I was seeing her. Now I can smell her perfume, that spicy—wait, I didn't dream her before. She was really there....

Slowly, unwillingly, his mind rose up from the groggy depths of sleep. Something was out of kilter. He was turned around, his bed pointing the wrong way. No, not his bed. And that taunting, teasing scent was rising from his pillow. No, not his pillow. He lifted his head, prying one eyelid open gingerly.

Absolutely nothing looked familiar, and for a split second he wondered if this was an especially vivid dream. Or had he slipped back into that fevered fantasy?

Then he realized he was on a sofa, still dressed except for his shoes, covered with a patterned blanket that looked vaguely familiar. At last something about the size and the layout of the room he was in began to register. He lifted himself to one elbow and opened the other eye.

"Morning, sleepyhead."

He rolled over onto his side, running a hand through his sleep-tousled hair as he looked at her. She looked marvelous in a pair of clinging nylon running shorts and a royal blue tank top that turned her eyes the same color. She had a sweatband around her head, holding back the strands of hair that were curling damply on her forehead. She had obviously been out for a run; her cheeks were flushed and glowing.

"Hi," he said as he worked his way up to a sitting position, looking around. "How'd I get here?"

"It was the best I could do. I wasn't getting much cooperation."

He rubbed at his bleary eyes. "I...guess I crashed, huh?"

"And burned," she said cheerfully.

"What time is it?"

"A little after eight. You slept about eleven hours." And she remembered so well how he had looked, younger, vulnerable somehow, the thick, long lashes resting in dark semicircles on his cheeks, his hand curled under his head as he slept.

He yawned, then shook his head to clear it. "You've been up awhile," he said, eyeing her attire.

"Just long enough for a run to the beach and back." She grinned a little sheepishly. "I always go into these paroxysms of guilt after I pig out at a ball game."

"Hasn't hurt you any." He looked her trimly curved figure up and down.

"Flattery will get you everywhere. In this case, breakfast, if you're interested. Let me take a shower, and then I'll throw together an omelet or something."

He rubbed a hand over his beard-shadowed face. "I'd better do that, too. As soon as I remember how to walk."

"You needed that last night," she said, tossing a teasing grin over her shoulder as she headed for the bathroom.

He sat on the edge of the couch for a few minutes, fighting the lingering grogginess left after his lengthy sleep. He looked around the room curiously, enjoying the warmth of the deep, rich colors and the coziness she had managed to achieve. Knowing now how limited her funds must be after her brother's expenses, he was even more amazed at what she'd accomplished.

Blowups of two of her first ads—the one with the raven and another with the improbable juxtaposition of a glittering ruby necklace hanging in a gym locker along with a pair of questionable socks and what were clearly a pirate's eye patch and cutlass—were framed and hung over the couch. He smiled; it pleased him both to look at them and appreciate her talent and to know that she knew she was good. Here, at least, she had no doubts.

He liked the comfortable couch, combining the rich, jewel colors of the rest of the room. And the multitude of pillows, some plain, others patterned, that seemed to pull the whole room together. He noticed the antique-looking pieces and remembered having seen them on her patio, where she had apparently been stripping them down and refinishing them herself.

Of course herself. Not for Stevie Holt the luxury of having someone else do it. The memories of last night came rushing back, and their painful poignance made the bright, animated picture she had presented this morning even more precious. Suddenly seized with the need to move so he could hurry back, he got to his feet, picked up his shoes and dug in his pocket for his own keys.

He was halfway through the delicious omelet she'd fixed, laughing with her over the story she'd told him of how much trouble they'd had getting the raven to cooperate for that ad, before he remembered that he had had every intention last night of saying goodbye to her for good.

Stevie hung up the phone and stared at it for a moment, then went back into the kitchen, where Chase was cleaning up the last of the dishes from the last pancake breakfast they'd had. He glanced up, saw her expression and stopped, dish towel in hand.

"Something wrong? That call—"

"Was my mother. That was . . . very nice of you."

He looked blank for a moment, then flushed slightly and shrugged. "It seemed like a good idea at the time."

"Isn't a half-dozen roses a little extravagant for a simple dinner?"

He gave her the lopsided smile that did such funny things to her heart rate. "A dozen is extravagant. A half dozen is just right."

"You truly surprise me sometimes."

"Why? A construction worker can't have manners?" There was the barest hint of an edge in his voice.

Stevie shrugged that off impatiently. "Maybe I'm just surprised that you bothered to use them. Other people don't seem to . . . matter much to you sometimes."

He winced inwardly; she saw too damn much. He wished he could tell her, make her understand. "Maybe I just wanted her to feel a little bit guilty over how she talked to you."

Stevie grinned suddenly, unexpectedly. "Well, you accomplished that, all right. She was nearly speechless, and for my mother, that's something!"

She went back to the dishwater-filled sink and reached for the last of the plates and silverware, her mind on what her mother *had* managed to say.

"You know, dear, at first I wasn't at all comfortable with that young man. He looks . . . oh, just the slightest bit disreputable, don't you think?"

Stevie knew exactly what she meant; her mother had been trying to hook her up with one of those carbon copy three-piece-suit types for years.

"But I must say, he does have a lovely smile, and such pretty eyes. And to send flowers . . . Why, I didn't think you young people ever thought of such politeness these days."

Right, Mom, Stevie thought as she rinsed a fork. Nobody can live up to your standards. But Chase's parents had clearly made him live up to theirs, she thought, reaching for the last knife. I wonder, she thought for the hundredth time, what happened between them. Whatever it was, it must have been on their side; she would never forget the pain in his voice when he'd told her that he wasn't even sure where they were.

"Hey, Blue Eyes, you in there?"

She came out of her reverie abruptly. "Sorry."

"Does talking to your mother always do that to you?"

"No." But thinking about you seems to, she thought. "When did you manage to send flowers?"

"Yesterday, while you were taking your shower." He looked at her apologetically. "I borrowed your phone, and the delivery man came by here for the money."

Odd, she thought. Why didn't he just use a credit card? Or was he one of those who didn't believe in the little plastic monsters? Then the memory of her mother's disconcerted voice made her grin. "Don't worry. It was worth it to hear my mother so flustered!"

They finished the dishes in laughter.

Maybe he wouldn't have to do it. Maybe, when he went back to work, it would just resolve itself. He wouldn't be around; he'd be removed from the temptation. He could just fade out of her life, he thought, a little ashamed at how relieved he felt at the idea.

"Coward," he muttered softly. But no matter how hard he'd tried, he hadn't been able to find the strength to make the break on his own. The darkness still hovered, but even that threat couldn't overcome the pull of a certain strawberry blonde.

So he had once again extended his personal deadline; he would give himself these last days, the two weeks ordered by Dan Bartlett. He would consider it part of the doctor's orders. A prescription you quit taking when its time ran out. When your time ran out.

It had been the fastest, sweetest two weeks he could ever remember. She was like a drug he couldn't get enough of and couldn't walk away from. They shared meals and trips to the store to refill his depleted refrigerator. She sat with him while he worked on the motorcycle, handing him tools and asking him questions that showed at least a basic knowledge of what he was doing; somehow, he wasn't surprised.

They barbecued hamburgers and steaks—no hot dogs, she'd explained with a grin, because they never tasted as good without a baseball game in front of them—on her patio, where he marveled at her green thumb.

She introduced him to Leo, who he thanked gravely for the soup, bringing a bright smile to the little man's face. And Mrs. Trimble, who embarrassed him by looking him pointedly up and down and declaring with a wistful twinkle in her eyes that she felt a sudden wish to be thirty years younger.

They went for walks, short at first, until his strength built back up, then longer. Aimless, cheerful treks along the beach, still pleasantly uncrowded in these last days before the onslaught of summer. They sometimes stopped for lunch in one of the small, quaint, oceanfront cafés, or just bought ice cream to eat as they walked. And sometimes he was even able to forget, to stop looking over his shoulder, at least for a while.

They talked about the things and people they saw, her work, his work, and even, on rare occasions when the need to share overwhelmed him, stories of his own life and childhood. They were carefully edited but still things he'd never thought he would be able to talk about again. It was wrong, it was dangerous, it was stupid, and he couldn't seem to stop.

Today, feeling too lazily relaxed to even walk the few blocks to the beach, they sat on the small lawn in the courtyard, concentrating, as Stevie said, on doing absolutely nothing.

"Doctor's orders," she reminded him with a lazy smile that made his heart turn over.

He wadded up the shirt he'd pulled off and used it as a pillow as he watched her lean back on her elbows, tilting her face to the sun. The freckles that faded away in the fall and winter were dusted liberally across her nose now, giving her even more of a pixie look. She was wearing a pair of shorts that made it hard work for him to keep his eyes off the golden length of her legs, and a halter top that didn't bear thinking about.

He'd tried, with varying degrees of success, to keep himself under wraps around her. But once in a while, like now, she looked so beautiful, so tempting, that the hunger that welled up inside him threatened to overwhelm him. She let her head loll back, baring her slender throat to the sun and his gaze, and he nearly groaned aloud. He thought that if he didn't relieve this pressure, this aching need for her, he was going to explode.

Abruptly he rolled over on the soft grass, letting out a muffled grunt when he found it wasn't quite soft enough on one uncooperative portion of his anatomy. She looked at him curiously.

"Are you all right?"

"Fine," he grated. Count backward from a hundred, he told himself. In Latin.

"Sure?"

"Positive." It wasn't working.

"It's pretty warm. Maybe you should change into some shorts if we're going to sit out here."

"No." The line of questions *that* would bring on was the last thing he needed.

"I just thought—"

"Stevie..."

"Fussing, huh?"

"Yes."

"Okay. Shutting up now."

"Thank you."

Stevie watched him from under lowered lashes. He had buried his head in the makeshift pillow of his shirt and arms, throwing the muscles of his back and shoulders into sharp relief. She could see the way they stretched over his ribs and shoulder blades, the taut, hard curves flowing one into the other from the width of his back to his narrow waist and hips.

She found herself thinking that if he hadn't already been so tan, she could have offered to apply suntan oil for him, then had to tear her eyes away at the thought of running her hands over that smooth, sleek back. She colored at her own thoughts, glad that he wasn't looking at her.

She'd nearly grown accustomed to them, these odd pangs that struck her at the strangest times. It took nothing complex, just a certain tilt of his head, the way his hair brushed the back of his neck, the set of his jaw when he was intent on something, or the lowered fringe of his lashes when he was avoiding her eyes.

Which, she had noticed, he did with some regularity. She assumed it was some sort of protective instinct, to keep safe that private self he couldn't, or wouldn't, share. She never pushed it; she had only to remember the silent, withdrawn man he had been to remain grateful for the change evident in him. And to be reminded that those urgent little darts of heat and feeling he aroused in her would certainly not be a welcome intrusion into his intensely private life.

She so hid them as best she could, and if occasionally she surrendered to that new and strange yearning when she thought of how he had held her the night he had guessed about Sean, she did it silently and alone. With a smothered sigh she dropped down beside him to doze in the sun.

As she drifted in and out, images formed mistily in her mind, disturbing images of the first time they had taken a walk together. It had been a beautiful, warm, peaceful day, with few people on the oceanfront walkways, and she'd been unable to understand what was wrong.

"Are you all right?" she had finally asked.

"Fine."

"You seem a bit . . . edgy."

"I'm fine."

It was a little sharp, and her brows furrowed. But he wouldn't look at her, and she had no choice but to accept his words. Still, she noticed that he was strung much too tightly for a man out for a quiet walk on the beach. He seemed to be looking in all directions at once. Not at anything in particular, just looking, watching.

The most disturbing moment had come when, after a quick glance back over his shoulder, he had suddenly hustled her through the doorway of a small shop. She had begun a protest at his nearly rough haste, but it had died unspoken as she looked around in surprise.

"I didn't know you smoked."

"I don't," he muttered, peering out the window toward the sidewalk.

"Well, that explains it, then," she said dryly.

He glanced at her, then looked around the interior of the smoke shop as if only now noticing it. He let out a long breath.

"I . . . didn't realize."

Her eyebrows shot up. Pointedly she sniffed; the air in the little store was heavy with the pungent smells of flavored tobacco.

"Is your fever back? Or do you always dive into stores without even looking—or smelling—first?"

"Forget it, all right?"

He snapped it out, and with a final glance through the window he yanked the door open and left as swiftly as he had entered.

He had seemed to make an effort to relax after that, and although he was never completely at ease, at least he wasn't so on edge that it made her nervous just to watch him. He never explained that first day, just as he never explained what had happened with the car on the morning of the ball game, and she sensed that if she asked, he would withdraw behind his considerable walls. She didn't understand, but her respect for the privacy he so clearly treasured kept her from probing. But now she wondered if perhaps she hadn't exaggerated his reactions that day. He certainly didn't seem edgy today, not lying lazily here in the sun.

The next day they resumed their walking, stopping to sit and watch an old man toss crumbs to the wheeling, dipping flock of sea gulls that surrounded him. It was a pleasant spot, so after the man and his birds had departed, they sat on the beach, Chase staring out at the ocean, Stevie drawing idle patterns in the sand.

"Did you ever wish you could...?" His voice had been barely a whisper at the start, and then it faded away without finishing the thought. Stevie looked up at him; he had that tight, rigid set to his jaw that she had come to associate with the haunted look in his eyes. She hadn't seen it for a while.

"I wish a lot of things," she said slowly, carefully. "That I could go back and do something I didn't, or undo something I did. I wish I could change things I think are wrong, or make things right for people who deserve it. I wish Sean was whole again." She hesitated, then took a deep breath and plunged ahead. "I wish you were whole again."

He sucked in a harsh breath, closing his eyes, the pain in his face echoed in his voice. "Don't waste your wishes on me, Stevie. I'm so empty I'll never be whole again."

She knew he'd fought against saying it, had tried to hold it inside as he always did; that he had failed was a measure of the hell he was enduring. She drew in a shaky breath. When she spoke, it was the voice he had heard in his fevered sleep.

"Someone once said that 'Hell is not in torture, hell is in an empty heart.'"

"Gibran," he said hoarsely, the words of the long-dead poet putting the name to what he was feeling; that Stevie sensed enough to choose those words frightened him. She was getting too close....

He rolled forward onto his knees, knowing he had to get up and away from her. But she had moved when he had, and they came face-to-face, scant inches between them. Green eyes locked onto blue ones, and for one long, frozen moment, he couldn't move. His mind was screaming, throwing up the defenses that had always worked before, but his body wasn't listening. All his efforts to pull away, out of that magnetic grip, resulted only in his eyes shifting down to focus with relentless clarity on the soft fullness of her mouth.

Her lips were parted slightly, as if she, too, were having trouble breathing. The cords of his neck stood out as he fought the urge to lower his head, to taste, just for the briefest second, the sweetness that was so close. Only the certain knowledge that he would no more be able to stop there than he'd been able to keep to his self-imposed deadlines for getting her out of his life gave him the strength to resist.

With a short, jerky motion and a gasping breath, he once more hammered into submission the fierce, hot ache that shot through him, aware of—but unable to change—the fact that the effort left him shaking. It was all he could do to get to his feet and walk away from her.

The atmosphere between them was strained on the walk back, and he wondered if this was the time, if he could find the will now to tell her simply to go away. He gave a rueful, inward chuckle. Haven't you figured it out yet? His own thoughts rang sarcastically in his head. You don't have a will when it comes to her. But keep this up and you won't have to worry about it. She'll tell you to take a hike.

"Stevie," he said at last as they turned off the beach and started toward home, "I'm—"

"Don't!" she nearly shouted, whirling on him. "If you apologize to me one more time, I'm going to scream!"

With that she turned and raced toward the small apartment building they called home, leaving him staring after her. He'd done it, he thought, feeling no triumph. He'd finally pushed her far enough. He wouldn't have to leave her. She'd left him.

By the time he got to the building, she was in the courtyard with Leo Rubin and Dan Bartlett. Dan waved him over, and he went reluctantly.

"How's my prize patient?"

"I don't know," Chase said, glancing at Stevie, "but I'm fine."

Stevie didn't look up; Dan chuckled. "Well, you look good. I might even be inclined to tell your boss you can go back to work. On one condition."

"Which is?"

"Join the picnic tomorrow. Ah—" he raised a hand to wave off the protest "—none of that. I need to check you over, but I'm not missing the picnic to do it. We're overdue. We canceled the last one because Stevie couldn't make it."

Dan grinned at him. "Your fault, really, since she was nursing you. So you owe us a picnic. Besides, if you can last through that, I figure you're well enough to go back to work. Although," he went on with a laugh, "you may not feel like it afterward."

Every part of his rational mind told him no; every emotion, stirred and shaken out of hiding these last two weeks, cried out yes. He liked this jovial young doctor and the little delicatessen owner and old Mrs. Trimble. They had been unanimously concerned over the health of the one sour apple in their midst, and it had made him feel things he didn't want to feel.

But he *had* felt them, felt drawn to this tight-knit little group, drawn in the way only an outsider could understand. And he would have to stay an outsider. For their sake, if nothing else. He knew that. But he could thank them, couldn't he? He owed them that much.

And Stevie. His stomach knotted, his chest suddenly tight. He couldn't. Not yet. He needed time. Just a little longer, to get used to the idea. And if it cost him that much more when he had to turn away, then he would just have to live with it.

"Well, since I don't dare say 'I'm sorry,' I guess I'd better show up."

Stevie's head shot up at that, and he would have paid a far higher price for the smile she gave him.

Chase sipped at the beer he held, the first he'd had in weeks. All in all, the picnic hadn't been as bad as he'd feared. He'd felt awkward at first, but they had all welcomed him so openly he had been able to relax. At least, as much as he could, knowing what was coming.

Sheila Bartlett had him cornered against the large tree that shaded half the courtyard and was chattering on about their expansive plans for the future.

"Of course, we'd miss this place, it's been home for so long, but I miss my family. You know how it is."

"Yes. I do." His voice was carefully even.

This afternoon he had spent a quiet hour alone in his own living room, searching for the strength he knew he was going to need tonight. He'd dragged out all the old, ugly memories, knowing he would need every vivid, horrible scene as armor to help him do what he had to.

Then he had summoned up a picture of Stevie, that soft, gentle smile curving her lips, that sparkle lighting her sky-blue eyes. He had told her everything he didn't dare say to her in reality. And in solemn, tight-lipped silence, he had told her goodbye.

He knew Stevie was watching him now, but he didn't react. He was coldly aware of how beautiful she looked in a bright blue sundress that, save for two narrow straps, bared her shoulders and her long, lovely legs. As if from a great distance, he felt himself responding to the sight of her, but he ignored the surging swell of his body.

He felt as if he'd finally found the switch to turn off the emotions she roused in him, to calm the turmoil she'd brought to his mind and body. The vivid, brutal memories had been the key, and now he was oddly removed from everything around him, as if he were on the other side of some unseen wall.

He talked to Leo, who wanted to know what he thought about remodeling his store, and to Mr. Henry, who inquired after his health and the condition of his apartment. And to Mrs. Trimble, who casually mentioned that she had a very pretty granddaughter who would love to meet him. Unless, of course, she inquired delicately, he and Stevie...?

"No," he said, flatly to the first question, as tactfully as he could to the other. At last he worked his way over to Dan, who took him aside for a few moments to ask him some questions of his own, thankfully solely professional.

Once he had secured Dan's assurance that he would okay his return to work in the morning, Chase retreated to the shadows of the big tree to down a second beer, then a third, as it gradually grew dark. He laughed at himself. There wasn't enough alcohol in the world to make this easy.

As he had guessed she would, Stevie noticed his absence and tracked him down. She sat beside him, letting out a long breath.

"I'd forgotten how much Sheila can talk, once she gets rolling."

He didn't say anything.

"I suppose Mrs. Trimble tried to set you up with her granddaughter? She's been trying to marry off that girl for years."

He shrugged.

"Has it been that bad?" She tried to see his face in the darkness.

Now, he thought. "Let's get out of here."

She looked startled. "To where?"

"Your place will do."

She followed him, wondering what on earth had made him sound so cold. When they stepped inside her apartment, he reached behind him to shut the door and, to her amazement, lock it. When she reached for the light switch, he said in that same flat, icy tone, "Leave it."

"Chase? What's wrong?"

"Nothing," he said flatly. "Except this."

Stevie let out a shocked little gasp as he grabbed her and pulled her roughly against him. His mouth came down on hers harshly, his teeth crushing her lips, forcing them apart for the angry thrust of his tongue. Her hands came up to his chest in an effort to push him away; he simply tightened his grasp on her arms until she stopped.

She made a small, smothered sound that held a touch of fright. It ripped at him, tore at his gut, but his mind was safe behind that icy wall, and he didn't waver. One hand slipped behind her head to hold her in the vise of his fingers; the other slipped up to roughly cup her breast.

The feel of that soft, warm flesh, firm and full against his palm, nearly shattered his cool control. He hated this, hated all of it. He wanted to caress her with loving softness, to kiss and touch every inch of her until she was as mindless with desire and need as he had been. He wanted to sink into her soft heat, to hear her moan with pleasure, to bury himself in her so deeply that she would hold him forever. He wanted—

The dark, grim, bloody pictures he had forced himself to remember this afternoon flashed once more through his mind, and with them returned the iron grip he'd had on himself all evening. The darkness was closing in on him again, and he knew he couldn't delay this any longer. He had to go back now, while he still could, for her sake. To stay near her meant danger for her. He couldn't—wouldn't—let it happen to Stevie. Not even if that meant she would hate him.

She was squirming, trying to twist away from him. He reached for the strap of the sundress and yanked it from her shoulder, hearing the fabric tear.

"Chase!" She gasped, tearing her mouth free at last.

"Shut up," he said harshly, taking her mouth in a bruising kiss once more. He tugged at the blue material again, pulling it down until all but the tips of her full, swelling breasts were bared. He lowered his head, trailing biting, stinging kisses down her throat to the rising curve of her breast. He bit hard enough to bruise, and with each hurtful motion the darkness surrounding him grew.

Fight me, he urged silently. Fight me, damn it. She didn't.

"Chase, no, not like th—"

He moved his mouth back to hers, crushing her lips until he tasted blood, not knowing if it was his or hers. Please, Stevie. Get mad. Let me know when I've gone too far. Please, I can't do this. I have to do it.

His fingers clamped on her upper arms, biting deep. Then he reached for the broken strap of the dress, yanking it fiercely. It peeled downward, baring her left breast, full and round and tipped with a delicate coral nipple.

Oh, God. Searing, scorching heat poured through him, careening down to settle low in his belly, sending a surging, irresistible signal to flesh that responded instantly. He was thick and hard and rigid with need, and if something didn't give soon, he was going to lose all control.

She had been gasping for breath; when he ripped the dress from her, she stopped breathing altogether. For one split second he relaxed his grip, and she raised her hands to his chest and pushed. Hard.

He backed up a step, jaw clenched, not caring that the hardening of his body had to be obvious to her, only caring that it was over. He didn't have to hurt her anymore. And he had already hurt her so much. It was there in her face, in her wounded blue eyes. She stared at him, gulping in air, not even reaching to cover her naked breast. She searched his face, and he put every bit of ice he could muster into his gaze.

"I told you I wasn't worth it," he said savagely.

A sudden stillness came over her, and something oddly speculative appeared in her eyes.

He couldn't stand it any longer. He turned sharply on his heel, and although it took every last ounce of his faltering will, he unlocked the door and yanked it open, stalking out with every appearance of anger.

The slamming of his own door took the last of his strength. He fell back against it, sliding to the floor in a shuddering heap, his face buried in his hands, muffling his low, anguished moan.

Stevie threw down her pencil in disgust. She'd been trying all afternoon to get the layout on this ad right, but no matter how she shifted things around, the proportions always looked wrong. And to add to her rotten mood, she'd gotten called to Mr. Dunn's office and politely had been asked what was bothering her so much that she'd been caught daydreaming twice in this morning's staff meeting.

She let out the long sigh she'd been repressing all day. She'd been back at work for three weeks, though it felt like three months, and she hadn't accomplished three days' worth of work. She picked up the pencil once more and tried to concentrate, but a pair of brilliant green eyes, agonized in the moment before they turned frosty cold, kept interfering.

She couldn't seem to let the image go. Although her mind kept replaying the viciousness of what had happened long after the bruises on her body at last faded away, her heart kept seeing that look in his eyes. And she kept coming back to the same conclusion. He had known what he was doing. It had not been some thoughtless, crazed moment of frenzied heat; it had been cold and calculated. Done for effect.

Wearily she cradled her forehead in her hands. She'd thrashed it out countless times since that night. It was as if he'd wanted to hurt her, wanted to make her angry. Why? Was he afraid that now that he was well, she wouldn't leave him alone? All he would have had to do was say thanks a lot, now get lost, she thought tiredly. Was this his heavy-handed way of telling her not to get any romantic ideas?

But if that were true, why the look of utter torture that she had seen before that frozen mask had slipped into place, as if his actions were hurting him even more than they were hurting her? And if that was what he wanted, to hurt, why use those words, words that only reminded her of the night when he had so tenderly held her as she wept in his arms?

Gradually she had come to accept the idea that his intent had been to drive her away; what she couldn't understand was his drastic method. It hadn't been necessary. It wasn't as if they had become lovers....

Her breath caught deep in her throat, and she remembered that moment on the beach, that sizzling, electric moment when she'd been sure he was going to kiss her. Not

only had he made certain that would never happen, he had
done a bang-up job of making sure they couldn't even be
friends. Had that been what he wanted? Was he that manic
about his privacy?

She hadn't seen him since they had both returned to work.
He seemed to have returned to his old habits—gone at dawn
and back after dark, even later than she came home—and
she had to admit to putting in some long hours of her own.
If he was truly taking Sundays off, as Charlie had ordered,
he certainly wasn't spending them at home; he was up and
gone as usual.

She jumped at a sudden sound and looked up to see Beth
Walker's extremely pregnant figure in her doorway.

"Easy, girl! It's only the resident hippo. A little edgy
lately, aren't you?"

"Vacation hangover. How's the mother-to-be?"

"You mean the *QE II?*" Beth said dryly, brushing a hand
over the crop of blond hair she'd cut short, when bending
over to dry it had become a physical impossibility. "Actually, I'm the bearer of good tidings."

"Oh? The Parkinson account?" The Los Angeles-based
company owned several record stores, and Walker and
Dunn were hot on the scent of their newly expanded advertising budget. And Stevie was doing a little hoping of her
own; she had some ideas she wanted to try if they landed the
account.

"No, although Joe says it's looking good. What I meant
was this. Congratulations." From behind her back she
pulled a short letter and a rather ornate certificate.

"What is it?" Stevie tried to read it upside down.

"You, my friend, have been nominated for a San Diego
Ad Council Award for the 'Pirate's Cove' campaign."

Stevie's jaw dropped. "What?" The Ad Council awards
were some of the most prestigious in the country, and highly
coveted. She'd never expected even to be considered, let
alone nominated.

"For 'Continuing Theme in a Single Campaign,'" Beth
quoted, smiling widely. "You've done yourself proud,

Stevie. Not to mention have proven my good judgment several times over."

Stevie was stunned. And when the rest of the staff, even old Mr. Dunn, crowded into her small office with congratulations, balloons, streamers and a bottle of champagne, she was utterly speechless. Especially when Mr. Dunn, a twinkle in his pale gray eyes, teasingly asked her if she had felt sufficiently chastised this morning.

"That . . . that was on purpose?"

"Of course, my dear. How else could we have smuggled all this in here without you knowing?"

She didn't know whether to laugh or cry.

"We're awfully proud of you, Stevie."

"You've worked hard."

"You deserve it."

It was coming at her from all sides, and she felt the stinging of tears building up behind her eyelids. They were bittersweet tears. If only Sean were here. If only he still cared. He'd always been the one to support her, to encourage her, to tell her to go for what she wanted. Now there was no one who would truly appreciate what this meant to her.

Except Chase. He would. But she certainly couldn't tell him. And maybe she was wrong; maybe he wouldn't care. Maybe he never really had. She didn't know anymore. She only knew that she missed him. Odd silences, up-and-down moods and all, she missed him. Despite whatever that fiasco had been the night of the picnic.

Throughout the next week she received call after call of congratulations from colleagues and competitors, some sincere, some dripping with envy. She had been touched by her father's warm "Atta girl!" while her mother's lukewarm "That's nice, dear," had been no more than she had expected. She had tried calling Sean, but he had mulishly refused her calls; the nurse told her that he had refused to talk to anyone for two days now. She sighed, seeing her brother's last chance for any kind of life slipping away.

"You can't live his life for him." Chase's words echoed in her mind. She knew he was right, but it was so hard. "Sometimes the best thing you can do is nothing at all. And that's the hardest thing of all to do.'' Oh, Chase, what happened? I never meant to ask for more than you could give.

Or was it that? Was anything, any closeness, even friendship, more than he could give? She wondered if she would ever know, would ever understand.

The office insisted on throwing a party for her that Friday at the local restaurant that was everyone's favorite hangout. She appreciated their good wishes, and she tried to relax and have a good time, but by the time midnight rolled around, she was more than ready to go home. She thanked everyone profusely, then made her excuses and left, thankful that she had managed to nurse a glass of seltzer water for hours and could safely drive home.

She pulled into the carport at twelve-thirty, noting with a calm she was almost proud of that Chase's motorcycle was there. She'd finally reached the only conclusion that made any sense about that night that had marked her body and scarred her soul: he'd intended to do that to her. For whatever reason, he'd wanted to go back to his shadowed, haunted existence, and he'd had to get rid of her to do it. Beyond that, she didn't understand and had tried diligently not to think about it.

She thought she heard someone calling her as she walked to her door, and she turned to see Mrs. Trimble hurrying her way. What on earth was she doing up so late? Stevie wondered, and why did she look so upset? Apprehension sprang to life in hot-cold ripples as she went to meet the older woman.

Chapter 6

From his place in the shadows of his own patio, Chase watched her. He'd been sitting there since he'd gotten home well after dark and found her parking space empty. It had been three hours of torture, wondering where she was. Was she working late?

Face it, he'd told himself harshly. It's Friday night. She probably has a date. He acknowledged the churning that thought brought to the pit of his stomach even as he coldly told himself that he had absolutely no right to feel that way. He would just wait here until he was sure she was home safe, he told himself. What he would do if she didn't come home at all, he didn't know.

His fingers had clamped on the arms of the patio chair convulsively. To think of her with some other man, one of those "three-piece-suits" she'd always laughed about, had been bad enough. To think of her spending the night with him, wrapped in his arms, in his bed...

He made a low, choking sound. It's what you wanted, isn't it? he asked himself. She's out of your life. You gave her no choice. That he had had no choice himself did nothing to ease his pain.

It wasn't until he'd heard her car that another, horribly worse thought occurred to him. What if she brought someone here? What if he had to spend the night knowing she was with another man on the other side of that wall that suddenly seemed all too thin? In her bed, that big, beautiful brass bed he'd seen, covered with the bright, colorful quilt that so suited her? A vision of her long, silken legs, locked in a passionate, naked embrace with some junior executive...

He'd nearly run then, certain he didn't have the nerve to even look at her if she wasn't alone. Then he'd seen Mrs. Trimble hurrying across the courtyard, looking worried even in the limited light, and he had stopped dead.

He saw Stevie, lovely in a deep blue dress with a full skirt, a wide black belt that emphasized her slim waist and black heels that gave a sexy curve to her luscious legs, and tried to ignore the fist closing around his heart at the sight of her.

He watched as she turned to see the older woman approaching, then crossed to meet her with a lithe, leggy stride emphasized by the sheer black stockings she wore. He watched as the shorter, heavier figure reached out with a hand to touch her arm; he could only hear an occasional word.

"...all night...to find you...call right away..."

He got to his feet as he saw Stevie go rigid, tension radiating from her. She listened for another moment, nodded shortly, then turned and ran for her door. Chase watched her fumble with her keys as she tried to balance her purse and something else in her hands, and the light beside her door showed too clearly that she was trembling.

He hesitated after she'd gone inside. He knew she wouldn't welcome his intrusion, but... The light that remained on at Mrs. Trimble's decided him. He sprinted across the courtyard toward the light, tapping on the door before he could change his mind.

The kindly older woman looked startled, staring up at him. "Are you all right? You look ghastly."

He looked, Chase thought dryly, like some forgotten corner of hell. He had a mirror; he knew about the dark circles sleepless nights had left beneath his eyes, and the hollows in his cheeks, courtesy of his nonexistent appetite.

Mrs. Trimble looked as if she didn't quite believe his assurances that he was fine, although she answered his hurried question readily enough.

"Why, some people have been trying to find her all night. From some hospital, about her brother. It must be very serious. There was even a policeman here looking for her."

He barely remembered to thank her as he caught movement out of the corner of his eye: Stevie, heading for her car at a pace that belied the high heels she wore. He was after her in a second.

He caught up with her just as she was reaching for the door handle. Looking at her drawn face was like looking in his own merciless mirror.

"Stevie."

If she was surprised to see him, it didn't show, or perhaps there was just no room for anything but the pain that had turned her clear blue eyes shadowed and dark. She pulled the door open without saying a word, tossing her small black purse onto the seat.

"What is it?" The question burst from him.

"I have to go," she said dully. "Excuse me, please."

He told himself that her cool, formal politeness was no more than he deserved, but he couldn't just let her go, not looking like this.

"No. What's wrong?"

She tried to get into the car; he stopped her by blocking the opening with a muscled arm.

"Stevie, please."

She recoiled at the new softness of his voice. "Don't."

He understood. With an effort, he stiffened himself. "Tell me," he said sharply. It was an order.

"My brother," she said, biting off each word with icy precision, "tried to kill himself this afternoon."

Chase paled. "Oh, God, Stevie...."

She shivered, as if every ounce of strength she had was going into keeping her voice even, into not cringing at the pleading note in his voice, leaving nothing to control the quaking of her body.

"Now, if you'll excuse me, I have to go to him."

She wasn't going to give an inch, he thought. And he couldn't blame her; he'd done this to her himself. Any sign of softness, of caring, from him was going to drive her away, possibly over the edge he knew she was teetering on. But he'd be damned if he was going to let her go alone, not when her whole world was on the verge of coming apart.

"Get in," he commanded. "I'll drive."

She stared at him.

"You're in no condition to drive. Move over."

"No."

He read her look, knew that she didn't think she could take his presence on top of everything else. He hesitated, but the little tremors that were visible up and down her slender frame decided him. He reached for her arm.

"More tough-guy stuff, Mr. Sullivan?" she spat out.

Only then did he fully realize just how much he'd hurt her. His expression stayed even, giving no hint of the turmoil it was masking.

"If that's what it takes," he said coolly. "Get in."

She capitulated suddenly; he guessed it was more because she didn't want to waste any more time than because of any decision to do as he asked. She answered him when he asked where they had to go, and gave him directions in flat, mechanical tones.

It was a long, silent ride. It seemed hours before he saw the sign marking the small hospital. He found a parking place, then had to hurry to keep up with Stevie as she headed for the entrance marked Emergency.

Chase would have given anything to be able to comfort her as they waited for the doctor, but she made it quite clear that she wanted nothing to do with him. She paced the shining linoleum floor, her heels clicking, giving the impression that if she didn't expend her tension that way, she would fly apart. She was breaking his heart; he couldn't watch her.

The clicking stopped, and he looked up to see a man in a white coat approaching. The look on Stevie's face was worse than fear, worse than worry; it was a dull, numbed acceptance, as if she'd already heard the worst. He felt the stinging of moisture in his eyes and prayed to a God he wasn't sure he believed in anymore that Sean was all right.

He was, the doctor said. He had used a piece of broken mirror on his wrists, but the cuts had not been severe, and the paramedics had been able to stop the bleeding before he'd gotten here from the rehab camp. He was resting comfortably, albeit unhappily.

"We tried to locate your parents, but his file didn't have their number or address, only yours." The young man betrayed nothing but professional interest. "He didn't want us to call even you, but of course we had no choice in this case."

Stevie nodded, her shoulders slumping. She looked unutterably weary as the tension that had kept her going drained away.

"If you wish to call them, there's a phone over there."

"I . . . You're sure he'll be all right?"

"He will be fine, physically. There is a standard seventy-two hour commitment for observation, however. His mental state is questionable."

"May I see him?"

"Yes, but I'm afraid you'll have to wait. I have another patient, and our policy in these cases is not to leave the patient alone with just one person, even a family member." He looked at her apologetically. "Not that we expect violence, but it's for your own protection, as well as the patient's."

Chase moved then. "What about me?"

Stevie made a little sound of protest, but the doctor looked at him consideringly, taking in his height and the breadth of his shoulders.

"Well, it's not exactly procedure, but we are short-handed tonight. I suppose it would be all right."

Chase froze the moment he was through the hospital room door. He'd thought he could handle it; he hadn't expected the wave of remembered terror that flooded him. He battled it, wrestling it down, and at last was able to look around.

If Stevie took after her father, it was obvious that this boy took after their dark-haired, brown-eyed mother. He was pale and thin, and the empty space beneath the sheet next to his right leg was painfully obvious. He was propped up in the hospital bed, looking at Stevie with eyes that—incredibly, Chase thought—held anger.

"I told them not to call you." The boy's voice matched his eyes, and Chase straightened suddenly.

"Sean," Stevie began.

"Just go the hell away, will you? Haven't you done enough?"

"What do you mean?" she asked faintly.

"Did you think I wouldn't find out?" he snapped. "I wish they hadn't found me in time."

"Sean!"

"What the hell did you expect?" He struggled to sit up. "Was I supposed to just go on and on, letting you work yourself ragged to pay for me? I'm not worth it, Sis, so just get the hell out. Forget you've got a brother. Or half of one."

"How did you—"

"Did you think I was blind along with crippled? I saw the chart, saw who they were sending the bills to. And don't give me that insurance crap. Our parents might buy it, but I know better. No more, Stevie. I'm not going to let you waste your life taking care of a useless—"

"Sean, please," Stevie said, reaching out to touch his hand.

"Don't touch me!" the boy exclaimed, jerking away. Stevie tried to move closer, and he raised the hand as if to strike a blow.

Chase uncoiled with the speed of a striking snake. Sean gave a startled yelp as his arm was caught in an iron grip before the blow could fall.

"Let go of me, you..." Sean's words trailed off; he had gotten a glimpse of deadly cold green eyes.

"Chase," Stevie whispered, "let him go."

"I will," he said coldly. "When he quits acting like a spoiled brat."

Disbelief filled the boy's eyes. "What? Who the hell are you, anyway?"

"Who I am doesn't matter. Apologize to your sister."

"Chase—"

"Don't defend him, Stevie. You've done more than enough for him. More than he deserves."

"You don't even know me," Sean protested, more than a little wary of this ominous stranger who had a grip on his arm that was frightening in its strength, yet strangely careful about avoiding the bandages at his wrists.

"I know you're a little boy who's pouting because life isn't going exactly as he expected. A child who's sulking because somebody took away his pretty dream. An immature, whining kid who doesn't even have the grace to appreciate that he has a sister who loves him enough to put his welfare above her own."

Sean gaped at him; Stevie was stunned into silence. "I do!" Sean finally sputtered. "Why do you think I tried—"

"You've got a rotten way of showing it," Chase cut him off sharply. "You put her through hell in the first place, wondering if you were ever going to grow up enough to handle this. But you didn't have the guts, so you put her through more hell with this stunt."

"Stunt? I—"

"It takes a hell of a lot more guts to live than it does to take the easy way out."

"What do you know about it?" Sean burst out angrily. "You've got both legs!"

Chase dropped the boy's arm as if touching him was suddenly distasteful. He started to turn away, his inner battle clear on his face. When he turned back, his eyes were a bright, blazing green.

"You think you're the only one who's ever been in pain?" he snapped. "You think you're the only one who's lain in a hospital, afraid you were going to die, and then, when it got real bad, afraid you weren't? The only one who's hung on from painkiller to painkiller, wondering if you'd ever be able to live without it?"

His voice had become a harsh, bitter thing. "You've got your parents. You've got—" He stopped for a gulping breath. "You've got a sister you don't deserve, and you can walk down the street without looking over your shoulder, if you'd just get off your butt and do it. You think you've got the corner on suffering?"

Chase bit back the urge to yell, and his voice went low and rough with the effort. "You don't know how lucky you are. I'd give you this damn leg—if it would get me what you've got."

He whirled, then, striding across the room to stare out the small window. He stood rubbing his arms against the chill that had come over him. He couldn't help it any more than he could help the shaking; why did these places all smell alike?

After minutes of shocked silence, he heard the soft murmur of their hushed voices. He stared into the night. At last he heard the click of her heels, and without another word or a glance at the boy in the bed, he turned and followed her out of the room.

She stopped at the desk to sign some papers; for the commitment, he guessed, or maybe just once more making herself responsible for his bills. She hadn't said a word to him; he wasn't surprised, after the way he'd blown up at her precious brother. Made a fool of yourself again, he thought bitterly. But he stayed close, sensing that she was rapidly coming to the end of nerves already stretched to the limit.

"Are you going to call your parents?" he asked when she had finished with the papers.

"No. It would only worry them."

"And heaven forbid anyone should worry except you!" He couldn't help his frustrated exclamation, but, to his surprise, she didn't get angry. She just folded her copy of whatever she'd signed and tucked it into her purse as she headed for the door.

"If he wants to tell them when he gets out, that's up to him," she said briefly, sounding strangely calm.

"Fine," he grated. She protected her brother, her parents, everybody except herself. And she needed it the most. "I suppose you apologized to him for me, too," he bit out as they stepped outside.

"No." Her voice still held that odd note of preoccupation. "Everything you said was true."

He stopped dead. "It was?"

She turned to look at him, her face shadowed in the dim light of the parking lot. "You were right. I can't do it for him. I tried. All I did was make it easier for him to feel sorry for himself."

"Stevie—"

"Thank you for making me see that. I would like to go home now."

It got through to him then, her strange, distant tone of voice, her rigid, wooden calm. As clearly as if he could see the spreading fissures, he knew she was on the edge of shattering.

"Stevie," he said, his voice catching as he reached for her.

She twisted away, her breath suddenly coming in deep, wrenching gulps. She was visibly shaking. "What do you want from me?"

Her voice was the cry of a wounded animal. What did he want? He wanted to hold her, to soothe her battered spirit; he wanted tonight, and all the rest of her nights, and her days, and everything he knew he couldn't have.

She was swaying now, as if a wind had come up that was more than her frail strength could stand. He broke then, moving suddenly, pulling her into his arms. She made one feeble effort to resist, then collapsed against him. He held her close, stroking her hair with a hand that was infinitely gentle, crooning softly.

"It will be all right, Stevie. Everything will be all right. Relax now, you've done all you can do. God, you've done more than anyone should have to. It's all right, love, just let go now...."

He felt a shudder go through her, heard her voice, muffled as her face was pressed against his chest. "I...I don't understand you."

He chuckled wryly, harshly. "Oh, Stevie, neither do I. I'm sixteen kinds of a fool, but I can't stay away from you. I tried. I swear I tried."

She lifted her head, peering at him, at the green eyes barely illuminated by the distant lights. "You...wanted me to hate you," she breathed, and it wasn't a question.

He should have known she would figure it out. "I had to make you hate me," he said, unable to hold back the words. "Don't you see? I couldn't do it on my own. I couldn't fight myself and you, too."

"That night—"

"Lord, Stevie, I've hated myself since that night. I've relived it a thousand times. I've barely stopped myself from coming crawling back, from begging you to forgive me. That's why I didn't dare be around you, because I knew I'd weaken."

He drew in a long, shaky breath and expelled it in a short, rueful laugh. "But I'm running out of places to go on Sundays. I've burned I don't know how many tanks of gas, I've seen every inch of coastline between L.A. and the border, and some woman in La Jolla called the cops on me because I kept sitting in front of her house all day."

Stevie stared at him, wide-eyed and wondering.

"I thought it would only take time to get you out of my head. So where do I end up last Sunday? San Diego State. I walked over every foot of that school, thinking about you, what it must have been like for you, how you must have looked then...."

"I didn't think you—"

"Cared? God knows, I tried not to. I almost had myself convinced, too. Until tonight. Sitting there wondering where you were, thinking you were with some guy, afraid you were going to bring him home."

"You... tried not to care?"

"Harder than I've ever tried at anything in my life. For your sake."

"Why... my sake?"

He gripped her shoulders, backing up a step, yet still supporting her. "That's the clincher," he said tightly. "I can't tell you why."

"Can't? Or won't?"

"Both. Don't try to soften it, Stevie. It's rotten. It stinks. But I can't change it, and you've got every right to tell me to go to hell."

"You're . . . in trouble, aren't you?"

He laughed grimly. "Not the way you mean. Not with the police or an ex-wife or anything like that. I only wish it were that simple."

"What you said in there . . . your family . . ."

"Stevie, don't ask. I can't tell you, and I can't stand to keep shutting you out."

She caught her breath. "You don't want to shut me out?"

He stared at her, then closed his eyes in pain as he pulled her close once more. "I've never wanted to shut you out. But I don't have a choice."

She stood, her cheek pressed against his chest for a long moment before she spoke. "What do you want me to do?"

"What you *should* do is say, 'Good riddance, get the hell out of my life.' "

"That's not what I asked."

He shuddered despite himself, and her arms slipped around him. "Stevie, I can't—"

"What do you want?" she repeated insistently.

"I want . . ." He swallowed heavily. "God help me, Stevie, I want you. I can't. I don't dare. But I do."

"That's all I wanted to know. Can we go home now?"

He stared at her. That was all she wanted to know? What the hell did that mean? It couldn't mean what it sounded like. "Stevie—"

"Please? I don't think I can stand up much longer."

He remembered then that moment when she had swayed as if buffeted by a nonexistent wind, and a qualm struck him. She'd been through an emotional wringer tonight. She needed rest, not to be standing here in the dark trying to deal with the complicated chaos of his life.

Keeping his arm around her for support, he headed for the car. She wobbled as they stepped off the curb, and he felt her slender body stiffen as she tried to steady herself. In a smooth motion so swift she didn't have time to protest, he turned her sideways and swept her up, one arm carefully supporting her shoulders, the other her knees.

"Chase—"

"Hush."

She obeyed meekly, telling him worlds about her weariness. He'd never felt this fierce, protective urge before, even when he'd made the hardest decision of his life. He wanted to build her a fortress somewhere, where she would be safe and secure, where the ugly side of life she'd seen too much of lately couldn't reach her.

But he knew she wouldn't want it like that. She was one of those people who faced life head-on, handling what fate dealt them. I should take lessons, he thought bitterly.

He reined in the sour feeling that rose in him, realizing that his frustration was coloring his view of everything. His life was out of his control and had been for nearly three years, ever since, God help him, he had "done the right thing."

He had to remember that. He had to ignore how good, how right, she felt in his arms. Had to ignore the piercing shaft of desire that shot through him, making his body knot in response. He had thought, had hoped, that these weeks away from her would ease this raging need, or at least give him the strength to control it; the hot, thrusting ache that settled in his groin told him he had been vastly wrong on both counts.

He managed the lock, then set her with infinite care in the passenger seat before fastening the seat belt around her securely. He walked around the car and slid behind the wheel; she hadn't moved.

The ride back seemed even longer than the trip out. Again it was a silent journey, but this time it was a silence full of a sense of a conversation unfinished, words unspoken. He wished it wasn't so far back to the apartments.

Somewhere along the way he glanced over to find Stevie dozing. Her face looked thin and drawn in the unsteady light, and the primitive instinct to protect rose in him again, so strong it stopped his breath for a moment. For the first time in years he wanted to rail at the unfairness of life having let him find a woman who roused this incredible feeling in him now, when he knew that the only way he could truly protect her was to get out of her life.

It was after 3:00 a.m. when he at last turned into the parking area and carefully slid the car into her space. Only the ingrained habit of months had made him pause in the driveway to look around; all appeared safe, no skulking, shadow figures, no out-of-place cars.

She stirred slightly, then murmured something as he got out and came around to her side. This time when he lifted her up, she instinctively, sleepily, slipped her arms around his neck. She turned to rest her head against his chest, and he swallowed heavily as he shut the car door and headed for the building.

He managed to open her door without setting her down, but she roused a little at the click of the lock. By the time he gently lowered her to her feet next to the big brass bed, her eyes were open and fastened on him intently. And her arms were still around his neck.

"Are you all right?" he asked softly. She nodded, but made no move to release him. "You'd better get some rest." His voice was a little uneven. Still she held on. He didn't dare move; if she came an inch closer she was going to know exactly what she was doing to him. "Stevie?"

"Don't go," she whispered.

Molten liquid poured through him as his body reacted to that breathless plea; his eyes searched her face, certain he was wrong about her meaning, certain that she just didn't want to be alone. But he was a poor choice for company, he thought acidly, visions of the last night he had been here flashing painfully through his head.

"No, Stevie. You don't want me here. Not after what I did."

A emotion he couldn't name flared in her eyes, and with a sudden burst of strength she straightened, her arms at last sliding from his shoulders.

"Stop it," she said softly, her voice harsh but strong. "That was a stranger. It wasn't the man I know, and it sure as hell wasn't the man I saw tonight, the man who ripped himself open to try to get through to a kid he'd never even met."

He winced. He'd never meant to let all that out; it had just seemed to burst from some buried place deep inside him when he'd seen that hand raised against Stevie.

"So I'm forgiven? Just like that?"

She drew a long breath. "I know you wanted to...drive me away. I don't know why, but I know you must have had a reason. And—" she cut him off as he started to speak "—I know you won't tell me that reason. I also know I've never been more miserable in my life than I have been since you walked away."

"Stevie," he whispered harshly, "don't do this."

"Don't do what? What I want, for once?" She bit back a tight little laugh. "I've spent my whole life trying to please everyone else. First my mother, who wanted the perfect, angelic little girl in frilly dresses with bows in her hair. I tried, but I always wound up in jeans, climbing a tree or playing baseball with the boys. Then my father, who paid my way through college when he couldn't really afford it, and even though he never said a word, I knew I owed him everything. I had to be a success, not for me, but for him."

Her mouth twisted bitterly. "Then it was Curt. Whatever he wanted, I did. We were going to be married, weren't we? He had a right to expect it, didn't he? And then—" her voice broke "—then Sean. I had to be strong for him, because if I broke down, if I let the panic show, he would give up...."

Chase couldn't have spoken even if he'd had the words; his throat was too tight. He stared at her as she took a shuddering gulp of air.

"So for once I'm going to think about me. I'm going to be selfish. Even if it means making a fool of myself."

"A fool?" he asked, his voice a mere rasp of sound. She raised her eyes to his, the trepidation there outdone by her determination. He knew in that moment just how difficult this was for her, how hard she'd had to push herself to speak.

She made herself look at him, fighting the urge to lower her eyes, conscious of the flaming color in her cheeks. "Yes. Over you. Because you're what I want. For me. For once, just for me."

He groaned deep in his throat as her words sent a sheet of white-hot fire through him, a fire fueled by furious need and long-suppressed passion, a fire he'd never expected to have to battle because he'd never expected to be wanted in return.

"Stevie, please, don't do this to me," he begged.

"You said . . . you wanted me. Did you mean it?"

"Oh, God," he groaned, reaching for her. In the last quivering second before he touched her, before the living flame of her flesh beneath his fingers put the torch to the last remnants of his will, he stopped. His hands clenched convulsively into fists, and he dropped them to his sides.

"I meant it," he choked out. "More than I've ever meant anything. But I can't . . ." He swore softly, viciously. "That trouble you asked about... It exists, I can't change that. You don't know what you'd be getting into, and I can't tell you. It could spread to you."

She stared at him for a moment. "That's why? You were afraid for me?"

He knew she meant the night of the picnic. His fists tightened even more, his nails digging into his palms.

"I can't let you risk it."

"You can't protect me from the world, Chase. Any more than I can protect Sean. It's my risk."

"Damn it, you don't even know what the risk is!"

"No, but I can guess at how serious it is. I know what it would take to make you act the way you did. But I don't care. And if you can't tell me, I won't ask."

Chase stood there, stunned. It was crazy. She couldn't possibly want him that much. To accept this insanity, to take chances she knew nothing about, unquestioningly. Not Stevie, with her bright, crackling intelligence, her lively mind and sometimes soaring imagination....

"Stevie, no," he said desperately. "You're not thinking straight. You're tired, you're worried about Sean—"

"I am," she cut in bluntly, "for the first time in my life, worried about me." She lifted her chin, and he saw a spark of her old fire and sassiness. "Besides, it's not your decision to make," she said softly. "All you have to decide is if you meant what you said. That you...want me. This is new to me, and I'm trying to be as honest as I can. I don't want any promises. I'm not asking you to dress it up and make it pretty for me. I just...want you." She took a ragged breath. "I know that I'm not very...experienced, but I can learn."

"Stevie," he grated, his already raw emotions gouged by her hesitant, embarrassed words.

"That's all that was wrong before, really." She faltered, then went on. "I just didn't know."

"Before?"

"With Curt. He said...virgins weren't worth the trouble. That I was..." Her brave front crumbled then, and her color rose even higher; she lowered her eyes. "He said if I'd been better in bed, he wouldn't have had to...go elsewhere."

"And you believed him?"

Chase had thought he couldn't feel any worse; he'd been wrong. Again. Anger at the unknown man who had so wounded her feminine esteem battled with the grim knowledge that he had done some wounding of his own.

"At first," she whispered. "It took me awhile to realize that since he'd lied about everything else, he'd probably lied about that, too."

She made a little movement as if to shrug it off, to say it didn't matter; the anguish in her face told him the truth. That tormented look was his undoing; he pulled her into his arms.

"The son of a— Stevie, I am so sorry."

"Why should you be sorry about Curt?"

"I'm sorry there are bastards like that in the world. I'm sorry you ever met him. Most of all I'm sorry he was your... first."

She made an odd little sound. "He was my... only." She pulled back then, and he felt her square her shoulders as she once more raised her head. "Until now."

Pain, longing and fear gripped him. Fear that he wouldn't have the will to resist her. And fear that he would. He went pale with the strain.

"Why?" he groaned. "Why are you trying to give this to me?"

"Because you're the only one who's ever made me want to give it."

Sweet, sizzling desire swept over him in a blazing wave so intense it left all other emotions in cinders and seared his control to ashes. He wanted to take her right here, right now, to kiss her breathless, to caress her until she unraveled beneath his hands. He wanted to slide his rigid, pulsing flesh into her, watching her eyes go smoky blue as he thrust again and again. He wanted to go up in flames with her, and he didn't care if there was anything left afterward as long as he could ease this wild, turbulent need.

He couldn't help it. He had to have her, just this once. Suddenly it was a need as elemental as his next breath, and, at the moment, a great deal more important. He didn't realize how his face changed, how the mask he'd worn for so long slipped, baring to her gaze the gnawing hunger he'd hidden for so long.

"Stevie," he whispered, "you're sure?" He couldn't quite believe it, that this incredible, strong, gallant woman truly wanted him, in spite of everything. "You've got to be sure, because I... I don't think I could stop."

For answer she backed out of his arms, her eyes fastened on his as she kicked off her shoes and her hands went to the wide belt at her waist.

Chase closed his eyes for a moment, sucking in a strangled breath as that white-hot flame ripped through him again. A sudden qualm overtook him. He was no stranger to control; it was a skill he'd learned the hard way, and well, over the last three years. Knowing the essential need for obscurity, he'd learned to keep himself rigidly in check no matter what the provocation.

But that control was in splinters now, shattered by the whispered words of a blue-eyed gamine. She wanted him. He couldn't doubt it, not when he opened his eyes to find her staring at him, those eyes hot with a look that made him shudder.

What if he couldn't hold back? He was nearly out of control now. But he had to, had to find some way to slow down. Not for anything, not even the blessed release his body had been demanding since the first time he'd laid eyes on her, would he add to the damage done to her by that son of a bitch she'd been engaged to. The bastard hadn't had the brains to treasure the incredible gift he'd been given. How could anyone, given a chance with her, not cherish the exceptional person she was?

He would find the strength. Somehow he would find it. He'd given her enough pain already. She deserved so much better. And if it killed him, he would see that she got it.

Stevie's fingers were trembling as she fumbled with the buckle of the belt. With hands that were none too steady themselves, Chase reached out to help her. The belt fell away, the heavy buckle thumping on the floor. His hands slid up her arms to her shoulders and gently pulled her closer.

One hand went to her cheek, cupping it gently, while his thumb brushed her full lower lip in the lightest of caresses. His fingers slid to the back of her head, threading through the silk of her hair as he tilted her face upward. The memory of the painful, brutal kiss he'd inflicted on her glimmered with haunting clarity in his mind as he lowered his head with agonizing slowness, giving her every chance to turn away.

She didn't. She tilted her head back farther, her lips parted in anticipation, and he could feel her breath soft and warm against his face. A shiver went through him, along with a last flickering doubt at his ability to carry out his resolution. He smothered it; he would do it. He would find the restraint.

Her mouth went warm and pliant beneath his gentle pressure, but still he pulled away after a brief, fleeting touch. She made a small sound of protest and reached up for him, making him clamp down another notch on his reeling senses as he kissed her again. Slow, he ordered himself, denying the incredible need to taste her, to plunder the honeyed warmth of her mouth.

She returned his kiss with delicate sweetness, sighing softly, sending such a piercing stab of pleasure through him that he nearly groaned aloud. He'd never known that a simple kiss could be so incredibly arousing, so exquisitely perfect.

Slow, he repeated to himself, drawing back a bare fraction. His lips traced her face, the fragile yet defiant line of her jaw and chin, the lovely arch of her brow, the soft curve of her cheek. She made a little sound he wasn't sure he'd heard, so loudly was the blood pounding in his ears, and lowered her eyes. He pressed the soft kisses on her eyelids, feeling the tickle of the thick lashes against lips that had never been so sensitive before. Slow. He hated the word.

He'd neglected to tell Stevie about his plan to move slowly. She slid her hands to the back of his neck, tangling her slender fingers in the thick, dark hair at his nape. She pulled him relentlessly closer, increasing the pressure of her mouth on his. A low, hungry growl rumbled in his throat as her tongue met his, seeking, tasting. Every sign, every movement, that proved the truth of her wanting him sent a rippling shudder through him.

She made no move to stop him when his hands went to the zipper of the blue dress, although he gave her every chance. She read his eyes and knew that, despite his words, he would stop even now, if she asked it of him. She gave him her answer; she turned her back to make the task easier for him.

Chase held his breath as the dress settled in a deep blue puddle at her feet, then let out a groaning exhalation as she turned back to face him. She was clad only in the sheer black stockings that had so tantalized him, and a silk and lace teddy that was the same color as the dress. The shimmering fabric clung to her lush, trim curves and outlined the taut, aroused tips of her breasts.

A sudden image of that ripe, tempting fullness, bared to his anguished gaze the night he'd hurt her so badly, sent his heated blood surging through him in hot, heavy waves and at the same time gave him back some of the control he'd thought vanquished by her onslaught on his senses. He lowered his head to kiss her yet again, cupping her face in hands that he ordered fiercely to stay there, to ignore the need to move down to that soft, warm flesh.

He managed it, for a moment. Then his hands were sliding down to her shoulders, fingers splayed to stroke the incredible smoothness of her skin. Then farther, feeling the heat of her easily through the thin, lustrous fabric. He grasped the slender indentation of her waist, his spread fingers reaching to the swell of her hips. He tried to stop there, but as if on their own volition his hands moved down to cup the trim, tight curve of her buttocks.

Convulsively, he pulled her against him, pressed her softness close, groaning as his swollen flesh strained against her. He tore his mouth from hers, gasping for breath, caught unaware by the savage sweetness of it.

The feel of that rigid hardness seemed to stun Stevie; she made a small, moaning sound as she swayed against him. Afraid he had moved too fast, had frightened her, he lifted her chin with one finger. Her eyes were huge, full of the urgency, need and heat that he knew must be reflected in his own. And in the blue depths was an echo of the astonishment he was feeling.

"I . . . didn't know . . ." she whispered.

"Oh, Stevie," he breathed. "Neither did I."

The tip of her tongue crept out to her lips, as if she were savoring the lingering taste of him. It was as shattering as if she had run that tongue over his skin, and his body clenched fiercely. Unsure of how long his legs would hold him, he lifted her up and lowered her to the bed with exquisite tenderness.

Quickly he slid off his worn boots, socks, then his shirt, not daring to look at the slender figure on the colorful quilt, waiting for him. For him. Disbelief flooded him, and he turned to drop quickly down beside her, as if only the feel of her, warm and alive beneath his hands, could convince him that this was real. Yet when he reached to touch her, reached for the silken straps of the teddy, he hesitated.

Stevie moaned. She wanted him to hurry, even though she wasn't sure toward what; at the same time, she wanted this spun-gold heaven to last forever. But when she met his gaze, she understood. She'd told him to forget that night, but even then, she'd known he wouldn't. It would take more than her forgiveness to erase the hell she'd seen in his eyes.

So she gave him what he needed. She reluctantly pulled her arms from around him and twisted them free of the straps of the teddy. With a sudden spurt of abandon that startled her, she tugged them down farther, then wriggled free of the interfering swath of cloth. She slid the stockings down the long, curved length of her legs, then cast them aside.

"Oh, Stevie...."

As she lay back, his eyes were on her, glittering green and bright, as bright as they had been the night a fever of a different kind had been burning inside him. Ever so slowly he moved, his hands going to cup and lift the tender flesh of her breasts, and she saw his eyes close as if the intensity of touch alone was all he could bear. A tiny moan of anticipation escaped her.

He opened his eyes, no longer able to deny himself the pleasure of looking at her. He saw her nipples tighten and rise under his gaze, heard her smothered gasp of pleasure. Her astonishment that just a look from him could do this to her was plain on her face; his own response to that knowledge was cataclysmic. His body cramped with need, and every muscle tensed with the effort to slow down. It took a tightly clenched jaw and a fist closed in a killing grip around one of the bars of the brass bed to keep himself in hand.

Slow. He'd repeated the damn word until it was engraved on his brain as if by acid. Slow. So it was with agonizing slowness that he traced her full curves with his mouth, feeling them growing taut and firm as he did. At last, unable to resist any longer, he moved toward that delicious puckered crest, deep coral now, and so very tempting. His lips closed over her, sucking, pulling, tasting, the rhythm of his mouth matching the pounding of his heart, until she was so sweetly hard in his mouth that he groaned with pleasure.

She arched her back, thrusting herself up to him, never guessing what the instinctive movement did to him. All she knew was that the path he had blazed was widening as his mouth was relentlessly sending those flaming sensations racing along it.

Stevie whimpered, tiny little cries of delight that fired Chase. He was sure now, sure of her response, and with that certainty came the renewed determination that he would make her forget that making love could be any other way than this, could be anything but this fierce, hot, searing sweetness.

"God, Stevie," he said hoarsely, "you are so beautiful."

She was kissing him, light, sweet little butterfly kisses across his jaw and down the taut, straining cords of his neck. Her hands, slender fingers leaving a fiery trail, moved over his chest, and he jumped in startled surprise when they reached and caressed his flat, brown nipples and a spurt of stunning pleasure shot through him. It would seem he had some things to learn himself. . . .

He couldn't believe the smoothness of her, the feel of skin so soft and smooth it made the fine silk that had covered it feel like coarse burlap. His hands slid down from her shoulders, his fingers tracing the straight indentation of her spine. Then he was at the sweet, tight curve of her buttocks, and he cupped that taut flesh eagerly, his body straining once more for the feel of her pressed close.

The world that had been threatening to spin away slowed with the realization that the fluttering sensation he'd been feeling at his belly was the touch of her fingers, reaching for the snap of his jeans. He stiffened suddenly.

She had so filled his senses, his mind, he had been so fully intent on her needs, her pleasure, that for a few heated moments, he had actually forgotten. Forgotten he had an ordeal yet to face, one that could change everything, that could wipe that hot glitter of desire from the deep blue eyes and turn them cold with disgust. Or, worse, flat with pity.

"Chase?" A world of doubt was suddenly in her voice. "Did I . . . do something wrong?"

With a violent shudder he rolled away, sitting up beside her. "No," he said tensely, shutting his eyes as he turned his head from her. He strained to pull himself together, to put out of his mind the vision of her fading rapidly beyond his reach. At last he turned back to her.

Her eyes were wide with confusion, need and a trace of hurt that tore at him. She drew her knees up, hiding her body from him, an agony of shyness in her face.

"Stevie, I—"

"You . . . changed your mind?" Her voice was brittle, tight and brought an unbearable pressure to his chest.

"No! God, no." He took a long, tortured breath and swallowed heavily before he said dully, "But you might change yours."

Chapter 7

Stevie stared at him, bewildered. A long, strained moment stretched out before he went on.

"I ... had an accident." He gave a small, muffled laugh. "I guess you figured that out, from that scene in the hospital." With a tremendous effort, he lifted his head to meet her gaze. "I'm ... pretty marked up." That small laugh, harsh this time, came again. "No, 'pretty' isn't the word for it."

He couldn't understand the look in her eyes. It was disbelief. She didn't believe what he was telling her? Well, she would soon; there was no denying the evidence. But then he was even more confused, because the disbelief changed, became a growing spark of anger in her clear blue eyes.

"Chase Sullivan, I ought to ... to punch you! I've never been so insulted in my life!"

He gaped at her.

"I don't believe you! How can you have the nerve to sit there and ... and ..." Words failed her for a moment, but her eyes did not; they were flashing fire. She sat up, shyness forgotten, her bare breasts heaving with the force of her anger. "How dare you insinuate that it would matter to me?"

NO COST! NO OBLIGATION TO BUY!
NO PURCHASE NECESSARY!

PLAY "LUCKY 7"
AND GET AS MANY AS SIX FREE GIFTS...

HOW TO PLAY:

1. With a coin, carefully scratch off the silver box at the right. This makes you eligible to receive one or more free books, and possibly other gifts, depending on what is revealed beneath the scratch-off area.

2. You'll receive brand-new Silhouette Intimate Moments® novels. When you return this card, we'll send you the books and gifts you qualify for *absolutely free!*

3. If we don't hear from you, every month we'll send you 4 additional novels to read and enjoy. You can return them and owe nothing but if you decide to keep them, you'll pay only $2.92* per book, a saving of 33¢ each off the cover price. There is **no** extra charge for postage and handling. There are **no** hidden extras.

4. When you join the Silhouette Reader Service™, you'll get our subscribers'-only newsletter, as well as additional free gifts from time to time, just for being a subscriber.

5. You must be completely satisfied. You may cancel at any time simply by sending us a note or a shipping statement marked ''cancel'' or by returning any shipment to us at our cost.

This lovely Victorian pewter-finish miniature is perfect for displaying a treasured photograph—and it's yours absolutely free—when you accept our no-risk offer.

PLAY "LUCKY 7"

Just scratch off the silver box with a coin.
Then check below to see which gifts you get.

YES! I have scratched off the silver box. Please send me all the gifts for which I qualify. I understand I am under no obligation to purchase any books, as explained on the opposite page.

240 CIS ADET
(U-SIL-IM-10/91)

NAME

ADDRESS   APT.

CITY   STATE   ZIP

7	7	7	WORTH FOUR FREE BOOKS, FREE VICTORIAN PICTURE FRAME AND MYSTERY BONUS
🍒	🍒	🍒	WORTH FOUR FREE BOOKS AND MYSTERY BONUS
●	●	●	WORTH FOUR FREE BOOKS
🔔	🔔	🍒	WORTH TWO FREE BOOKS

DETACH AND MAIL CARD TODAY

"Stevie, I—" he began, then stopped. God, she was beautiful! And she was right, he admitted ruefully. He should have known better than to think that she, like the few others he'd been with, would be either repelled or morbidly fascinated at the sight of him.

"Is that really what you think of me? That a few scars would make a difference?"

"One," he said mildly.

"What?" His tone had taken the wind out of her sails.

"One. Scar." He gave her a sideways look. "But it's a beaut."

Her anger drained away. "Oh, Chase," she said softly. "I'm sorry."

"So am I. I should have known."

"We all have scars," she whispered. "It's just that some don't show."

He looked at her for a long moment, a moment of silent communication that was somehow more intimate, more intense, than all that had gone before. Then, with the quick, sure movements that spoke of a decision irrevocably made, he reached for the zipper of his jeans.

He kicked free of the snug denim, leaving himself covered only by the briefs that strained to contain him. He lay back, knowing he at least would not see horror in her eyes, but unsure of what he *would* see. Saying that it didn't matter was easy when you hadn't seen it.

For a moment Stevie couldn't seem to tear her eyes from the surging swell of his hardened flesh, which more than tested the limits of his cotton briefs. But then she saw a flicker of light across puckered, unnaturally shiny skin, and she shifted her eyes.

He hadn't exaggerated. It was a wide, jagged, brutal mark. It began just above the band of elastic at his hip, inside the left hipbone. Below the fabric it reappeared, twisting outward over the top of his thigh to curve with vicious suddenness down the side of that muscled leg, stopping abruptly six inches below the joint of hip and thigh. This was not the neat, sutured incision of surgery; this was the uneven rip of trauma, of torn flesh too ragged to be mended neatly.

Chase saw the tears that were tracing their way down her cheeks, and he turned cold inside. He didn't want her pity; he couldn't stand her pity. Then she lifted her eyes to his, and the chill evaporated. There was pain in her eyes, and warm, sweet sympathy, but not pity. Then she reached out, tracing the ridge of white, drawn flesh with gentle, healing fingers, showing no repugnance, only the wish that she could ease that long-ago pain.

"Oh, Chase," Stevie whispered, "you must have gone through such hell. And what strength it must have taken."

He reached for the hand that was making that puckered flesh burn as if the wound were fresh, pulling it up to his mouth and kissing the slender fingers. Then she was up in his arms again, raining hot, sweet kisses over him, heedless of where her lips touched, just needing the feel of his body beneath her mouth.

His hand slid down her body as his mouth returned to her breasts. He groaned aloud when his fingers found their goal; she was hot and slick and ready. For him. This undeniable evidence that her need, her desire, matched his own made him shudder in response. His body surged, thick and hard with desperate wanting. His raging flesh knew what that wet heat meant, that with one quick move he could be sheathed in the caressing satin core of her, and it didn't care to listen to any ideas his mind had to the contrary.

After one shocked still second when his fingers first entered her, he again began to move, to stroke, and a small, rippling sound of surprise and pleasure broke from her. It was her surprise that allowed him to once more rein in his senses, to slow the rapidly spiraling heat that seemed greater than any fever.

Instinctively she moved, rocking against his hand in a steady rhythm. A tiny, breathless sound came from the back of her throat as she felt the probing thrust of his searching fingers, teasing, stretching her, making her ache for more.

Stevie felt as if she were floating, mindless, her body suspended, held only by the burning points of fire that were her nipples and that throbbing center of aching need beneath his hand. Her blood was pounding in her veins, the world was spinning away, and in her head was a triumphant cry: this is how it's supposed to be!

A low, rippling cry that sounded like his name escaped her, hot and sweet against his ears. She quivered, the searing pool of heat deep in the core of her growing, fed by three points of fire that were bursting into conflagration beneath his hands and mouth. Then the fire began to spiral outward, building heat and light and pressure until she thought she would die from it.

She was beyond hearing her own broken cries, beyond knowing she was arching toward him with utter abandon. She only knew she was flying, soaring, straining to reach that unseen, unknown goal, and then she was there, shattering into a million glowing, floating sparks, drifting weightless on a soft, warm cloud, then settling with infinite slowness and peace into the haven that was Chase's arms.

It seemed impossible that her body had come to rest in one piece, in its old shape and form. From that sheltered, warm place, she became aware of the tension rippling through the lean, strong body beside her. She opened her eyes, knowing they must be wide with the wonder she was feeling.

Chase was wrestling with his own feeling of wonder. Never in his life had anything like this happened to him. Never had giving someone pleasure been so important or given him so much in return. And never, ever, had it had such an effect on him. Just watching her, seeing her respond to his touch, hearing her cry of shocked, rapt pleasure as she went to pieces in his arms, had nearly sent him over the brink. Not even as a teenager, with hormones at full throttle, had he come so close to losing control so prematurely.

He held her close, only aware she had opened her eyes by the soft tickle of her lashes against his neck. He lifted his head to look at her. Her lips were swollen from his kisses, her cheeks flushed, and she looked wonderfully sated and languorous. Her eyes were filled with the wonder of discovery, and he knew he had succeeded; she wouldn't be looking at him like that if there was anything left of the grim memory of the night of the picnic.

Stevie looked up at him, soaking in the tenderness that glowed in his vivid green eyes. She saw the sweat that beaded his brow and heard the deep, harsh breaths he was taking. Slowly she realized that he was holding himself carefully, rigidly, and that small tremors seemed to ripple through him. She lifted a hand to his arm and felt the rock hardness of muscles strained to the breaking point.

Concern penetrated the pleasant fog she was floating in, and she lifted herself on one elbow to look at him. As she moved, she shifted her hips, and one silken thigh brushed his hot, engorged manhood. He sucked in a swift breath, and his eyes closed suddenly, an expression on his chiseled features that bordered on pain.

She felt a little foolish and a lot naive, but most of all she was filled with a spreading, glowing tenderness for this tormented, haunted man who had given to her so completely, with no thought of himself. The look on his face, the tautness of his body, told her eloquently what her flight had cost him. She smiled as she reached out to him.

Chase's eyes flew open at the feel of her arms sliding around him. He caught a glimpse of a smile so warm, so soft, so loving, that it took his breath away before she buried her face against his chest. Then she was kissing him, sweet, warm little kisses pressed on the heated skin beneath her lips.

Her hands slid downward, moving over the taut ridges of his rib cage, coming to rest on his hip, half on the heated skin, half on the fabric that kept him from her touch. She found it disturbingly unsatisfying; she wanted hot, living skin beneath her fingers. She wanted Chase under her hands. She paused, but before she could decide what to do he had moved, tugging with his free hand at the interfering cloth, lifting himself to remove the barrier.

His rigid, pulsing flesh sprang free, burning like a brand against the smooth skin of her belly. She could feel the tickling caress of the dark curls at its base, and her fingers flexed again convulsively. Yet, frozen by her shy uncertainty, she couldn't move.

Even through his blinding need he read her. His hand stole to hers, covered it, then moved it with exquisite gentleness. He stopped just as the tips of her fingers reached that thicket of dark hair and pressed her hand to his lower belly. She felt rather than heard him swallow thickly.

"Touch me," he said hoarsely. "Please."

Tears stung Stevie's eyes as his hand left hers, making no effort to move it that last, critical inch. He had let her know what he wanted, yet clearly shown he wouldn't force her. Then her hunger overcame her, and she slid her palm across his skin, her fingers curling instinctively around him.

She heard his gasp, a short, sharp intake of breath that condensed into a low groan. She felt the quick, involuntary movement of his hips as he pressed himself against her hand. But it all came through a haze, a fog of shock and heat and shuddering pleasure at the size and feel of him.

Slowly, tentatively, she caressed the hard length of him, marveling at the taut smoothness, loving the satin weight of him against her palm. A moment of doubt assailed her; would she really be able to take him? Was it possible?

The thought sent a rippling wave of sensation through her, a wave that seemed to hit the limits of her body and then careen back, until her entire being was a churning storm of heat and pressure and aching need. Her doubt disappeared, replaced by a frantic need to do just that—to take him inside her, to have that hard, hungry flesh stroking her, piercing her. . . .

Through the mists of his pleasure at her hands on him, Chase felt her shudder. The thought that touching him had such an effect on her would have startled him had he not discovered that just touching her, just feeling her response to him, was the most overwhelming sensation he'd ever known.

While he'd always tried to give as much pleasure as he'd gotten, never had he known he could derive so much from just the giving itself. He never would have imagined it was possible. But with Stevie, all things seemed possible. Her every move, her every little sound as she responded to him, gave him as much—if not more—pleasure than the long-awaited touch of her hands on his body.

That touch was more confident now, and he couldn't stop his hips from moving, pressing forward in time with her stroking caresses. She cupped his aching flesh, traced his throbbing length until his breath was coming in ragged, choking gasps.

He was dying. That had to be it. He was spinning off into some misty netherworld, only the feel of her hands telling him that he still clung to life. He'd never been so rigid, so hot, so achingly full; he was hard to the point of agony, and still she kept on.

"Stevie...stop. You've...got to...stop," he said, panting.

She made a small sound of protest, her hands continuing to move, to stroke.

"Please... It's been too long. I want you too much.... I can't *take* this!"

She moved then, to whisper in his ear, her breath hot and searing, "Then take me."

The flesh he'd sworn could grow no more, could get no harder, quivered and expanded at her shy but impassioned words. He had no choice; he couldn't leash the wild demands of his body any longer. He moaned, a low, husky murmuring of her name as he moved between her thighs. She opened for him willingly, eagerly, and his pulse hammered in his ears at the sight of her waiting there for the first touch of the hot, hard flesh that had ached for her for so long.

He wanted to go slow, to savor every sweet second as he sank into her, to watch her face as she took him in, but the first slick caress of her eager softness destroyed the last remnant of his will. Her body yielded to him, parted for him, then closed around him with searing, clasping heat.

He groaned. "You're so tight, so hot...."

Then she moved beneath him, arching her hips upward, demanding more of him, her hands sliding down his back to clasp his lean hips hungrily. He surrendered without a thought, driving forward to bury himself in her hot, satin depths again and again and again.

It all boiled up inside him, the months of longing, the years of loneliness, the enforced restraint of these last weeks when she had been so near and yet so distant. Simmering, seething heat uncoiled within him with unstoppable force. Her sweet, welcoming body freed it, and it ripped away any lingering thoughts of control.

"Stevie!" Her name ripped from him, and his fingers tightened convulsively on her shoulders as his hips drove against her again. "I'm...sorry.... I can't wait!"

His body went rigid, his head thrown back as a cry of agonized pleasure burst from him, and he erupted into the hot, dancing depths of her. Wave after pulsing wave swept him, then returned, ever widening, until astonishment tore awed words from him.

"Stevie...hold me...can't stop!"

Her hands went around him, keeping him close, savoring the tremors that shook his powerful body as she had savored the feel of him pulsing deep and hard inside her, as she had savored the savage heat of him as he gave himself to her.

At last the tremors eased, and the slamming of his heart eased to a mere pounding as his surroundings began to intrude on the edges of his whirling vision. Slowly he became aware that his whole weight was pressing her down, but when he tried to lift himself, she made a small sound of protest and tightened her arms around him. Just that small resistance was enough, and he dropped back weakly.

After a moment he tried again, but again she resisted. "I'm too heavy," he protested huskily.

"No," she said, shaking her head. "It feels...wonderful. Don't move."

He lifted his head. "Stevie," he began, but she lifted a finger to his lips, hushing him, as if she knew instinctively what he was going to say. "But I was too quick. I—"

"Stop," she said firmly. He did, but his eyes were troubled. She searched for the right words. "What did you feel, a few minutes ago, when..." She blushed, but made herself go on. "When it was only me?"

His brow furrowed as he remembered the intensity of his emotions when she had been writhing in his intimate embrace. "I ... loved it. Watching you, feeling you respond ..." His eyes widened. She nodded.

"Why should it be any different for me?" Better in fact, she thought. He'd had so much farther to go, to let down those towering walls that had held him apart for so long.

To his amazement, he felt himself flush. To be watched like that, by those wise blue eyes, when he was so out of control ... Yet hadn't she given the same to him? She had trusted him that much, with the ultimate vulnerability, how could he not return that trust?

"You," he said, pressing a soft kiss on her forehead, "are—" Words suddenly failed him; how could he name all the things she had become to him? "I don't know what to say to you," he whispered, overwhelmed.

"Just the one thing I want to hear," she said softly. He lifted his head to meet her gaze, seeing a sudden intensity in her eyes, still smoky with sated desire as she looked at him. "That you're not sorry."

"Sorry?"

"I couldn't stand it if you were. If you went back into the dark again."

He stared at her, amazed both that she had guessed so much and that he was surprised at all. She had confronted something that probably would have crashed in on him in the full light of day, that he had broken all his rules, that he had put her in danger of being sucked into the very darkness whose existence she had guessed at.

"Promise me?" she asked, suddenly fierce. "No regrets?"

Regrets? No, no regrets. Worries, but never regrets. "I promise," he said softly.

The change in him that night was nothing less than miraculous. The dark, shadowy man she had known nearly disappeared, and the relaxed, open one she'd had only glimpses of took over. The cautious, wary looks were rare;

the lethal, flashing grin was frequent and never failed to send her insides into a tumbling free-fall.

Nobody was more amazed than the other tenants of the building, as Stevie well knew; they chose her to vent their astonishment.

"Why, I just heard a noise and looked out, and there he was, fixing that ugly crack in the wall I've been telling Mr. Henry about," Sheila told her.

"He did it right there, just sat down and sketched out the perfect solution. It will be so much cheaper than a complete remodeling job, but it will do everything I need." This from an astounded but grateful Mr. Rubin.

"I never would have pictured him liking animals at all, he's so... rough-looking. Or at least, he used to be. But he got Cissy out of that tree and never even laughed at me," Mrs. Trimble marveled, crooning over her rescued Siamese.

Stevie was more than a little amazed herself. They had spent the rest of that first miraculous weekend cocooned in her apartment, never setting foot outside, seeing and talking to no one, except for a brief phone call to check on Sean. They had talked endlessly, and she had immediately noticed that he was much more open about himself, although in very general terms.

"I can't, Stevie," he had told her sadly when she'd asked about the sister he'd once mentioned. "I'm sorry."

It hurt, but she nodded in understanding. "I said I wouldn't ask, but I may slip now and then. I'll try to remember."

The pain in his eyes was greater than hers, and she went to him immediately, pressing sweet, soft kisses on any part of him she could reach. His distress was washed away by the rising tide of their mutual need. They hadn't even bothered to leave her sofa that time; they were much too frantic.

To her surprise, he told her about the scar. She had steeled herself not to ask that question, sure somehow that it was connected to all the other things he wouldn't talk about. But on that lazy Sunday afternoon, when she had awakened to the smell of coffee, bacon and eggs, and had opened her eyes to the whimsical, endearing sight of Chase, naked, with a tray full of breakfast in his hands, he had told her.

The breakfast had gotten slightly cold as, touched by the sweetness of his gesture, she had pulled him down to her with the inevitable results. In the warm aftermath she had pressed a line of loving kisses along the ridge of puckered flesh. He had wryly told her that if she didn't stop, even the steaming coffee would be cold by the time she got to it, and she had sat up with a grin.

"It's killing you not to ask, isn't it?" he said gently as he scooped up a forkful of eggs.

She stopped with a piece of bacon dangling ungracefully from her fingers, startled. "I . . . Yes," she admitted. "But I promised I wouldn't."

He sighed. "I got hit by a car."

She set the bacon down, staring.

"It was pretty bad, at first. It tore up some things inside, and they had to do a lot of patchwork." His words were awkward, choppy, and she wondered if he'd ever told anyone.

"As it turned out, I was pretty lucky. The hip healed up straight, and there was no one place that took all the impact." His lips quirked upward, twisting in a smile that was not all cheerful. "The laceration went every which way. Made it uglier but did a lot less damage."

"It is not ugly," she said fiercely. "Any more than life is ugly because there are parts of it that aren't perfect. It just means you've gone through hell and survived. It's a sign of your strength. It's not ugly," she repeated emphatically.

"Well, it sure isn't pretty," he drawled, his kidding tone not very successful.

"Only because it's all you see. When you get up, it's the first think you check, as if you wish it had disappeared while you slept. It's the first think you look at in a mirror. You see that scar, and nothing else. You don't see what I see."

She was right, he realized with a little shock. It was the first thing his eyes went to if he was in front of a mirror. "What . . . do you see?" he asked her softly.

She eyed him carefully, her gaze sliding hotly up and down his naked body. "I'll tell you later," she said huskily. "After breakfast."

And she had. In intimate, sensuous detail, she had told him, making him color with her extravagant praise for every inch of him. With special attention to several inches that particularly fascinated her. Then, being, as he told her solemnly, fair-minded, he returned the favor. It had been a long, luxurious day, and they had only left the big brass bed when hunger of another kind had driven them to the kitchen.

The time had seemed to sail by since that weekend that had started so horribly and wound up being the most beautiful of her life. They spent every spare moment together. Chase took to keeping normal hours, telling her with a sheepish grin that Charlie had immediately guessed why. He even began to take whole weekends off, and they filled every hour of them.

The went to the zoo, to more baseball games, to the movies and a play or two. They went to the scenic town of La Jolla, with its shops and art galleries, and he ruefully showed her the spot where he'd parked that had resulted in him explaining his presence to a rather gruff police officer.

"He asked me what my problem was," he told her with a wry grin. "I told him it was a five-foot-six strawberry blonde. He just laughed and left me alone."

Stevie had blushed and managed to put out of her mind the fact that he was still more vigilantly aware of his surroundings than anyone she'd ever known. She also tried to forget the night of the latest picnic.

It had been a warm summer night, another perfect evening in that idyllic time, with no warning about the sour note to come. By tacit agreement, the first picnic they had attended together was not mentioned beyond Stevie's blithe "ancient history."

She intended to enjoy this one, having missed the last because she was in no mood to be cheerful when all she could do was think about Chase and ponder the horrors of that night. And she did enjoy it. She enjoyed being with the people she had become so close to; she enjoyed seeing Mr. Henry again and didn't even mind Sheila's complaining that Dan had a last-minute emergency and would be late.

But most of all she enjoyed watching Chase. And watching the rest of the group respond to the change in him. He teased Mrs. Trimble to a fine blush, making her giggle like a schoolgirl. He had Mr. Rubin roaring with laughter over his outrageous suggestions for additions to his deli's menu. He had Mr. Henry beaming over the minor repair work he'd done mostly while waiting for Stevie on the nights she'd had to work late, nights she kept to the bare minimum these days.

He even got Sheila to laugh with a story of a well-known politician who had ordered his house built with huge mirrors on the ceiling and walls of one large room. All the sordid speculations of the people working on the house had been blown to smithereens with the discovery that the man's wife was a former ballerina, and the room was her dance studio. If Sheila noticed his story was carefully devoid of names or places, she was tactful enough not to mention it.

It had been shortly after that that he and Stevie had made a run to the grocery store for more chips and soda for the monthly gathering. They had unloaded all the bags from her car and were going back to rejoin the group when, just as they crossed the driveway, there was a squeal of tires and brakes and the sound of a racing motor.

Stevie guessed it was probably Dan; she was familiar with his somewhat reckless driving. It was Chase's reaction she didn't understand. Dropping the bags, he grabbed her, shoved her against the wall of the building and pressed himself tight against her, as if trying to smother her.

"Chase?" she said, bewildered.

"Hi, kids!" Dan called cheerily, having parked his battered car haphazardly. "Don't let me interrupt your necking session!" He waltzed by with a laugh, totally unaware of the havoc he had caused. Stevie knew, because she could hear the hammering of Chase's heart, could feel the tremors that shook his tall body, but she had no idea why it had happened.

She could see why he would be jumpy about speeding cars; he certainly had reason enough, along with a daily reminder in the scar he carried. But why he'd reacted as he had, pushing her back and screening her with his own body, even though they were well out of the path of the car, was beyond her.

After a long, tense moment, he moved away from her, leaning back against the wall beside her. She could see the rapid rise and fall of his chest, and even in the poor light, she could tell that he was deathly pale.

"My God, Chase," she breathed. "Are you all right? Was it the car? Why—"

"I'm fine." His voice was brittle. "Forget it."

"But—"

"Please. Just forget it."

She stared at him, the silence drawing out. For the first time her confidence in her ability to accept the silences, the things he would not tell her, was shaken. And it was shaken because, for the first time since the night they had become lovers, she could see in his eyes the haunted look she'd hoped had been banished forever.

She tried desperately in the days that followed to do as he asked, to just forget it, but she found herself watching him even more intently, dreading the moment when that look would reappear, though she tried to hide her concern.

They went shopping in Tijuana, where he mysteriously disappeared, then reappeared with a bag he wouldn't show her. It wasn't until the next day, when he told her he would take her for the ride on his motorcycle that she'd been pestering him about, that she found out what he'd bought.

Her jaw dropped when he brought out the leather jacket. "It's not just for looks, you know. The leather protects you, and it's smooth, so if you do go down, you slide. It's when your clothes grab and you start to tumble that you get hurt."

"How comforting," she said dryly, but she put it on. He made her wear the helmet, grinning when she accused him of just wanting to go without it himself and using her as an excuse.

She soon understood the fascination the two-wheeled vehicles had for people; the sounds, the feel, even the smells, of the world around you were so much clearer, so much closer. Not to mention the sheer pleasure of clinging to Chase's broad back, her arms tightly around his waist, his taut buttocks close between her thighs.

When she climbed off the bike back at the apartments, she felt exhilarated and laughed gaily as she pulled off the helmet and ran slender fingers through her tangled hair. She was three feet away from the parked cycle before she realized he was still astride it, sitting motionlessly.

"Are you just going to sit there?"

"Maybe."

"Why?" She came back curiously.

"I'm waiting until I can walk," he grated.

"Until . . . ?" She stared at him blankly.

"Did you have to sit so damn close?"

"Well, where else . . . ?" She trailed off as his meaning got through to her. Her eyes flickered downward, to the unmistakable bulge behind the zipper of his snug, black jeans. "Oh, dear," she teased, "you do have a . . . sizable problem there, don't you?"

"You should know."

"Oh, I do." Her eyes were sparkling, alight with laughter.

"I'm glad you find it so amusing," he said, fixing her with a stern glare that wasn't quite convincing.

"I was only making an observation." She giggled. "But what *are* you going to do about it?"

"You did it. You do something."

"Now whatever could *I* do?" she asked innocently.

"That," he said, his own eyes now alight with an answering sparkle, "is for you to figure out."

He swung off the bike, and as he stood there, looking much as he had the first time she'd ever seen him, a sudden, overwhelming tenderness filled her. She'd been awed, almost intimidated, by him then, and never would she have guessed at the man hidden behind the daunting exterior.

He watched the softening of her expression, the sudden warmth in her eyes. "And you can do it right after you tell my why you're looking at me like that," he said huskily.

"Like what?"

"Like you're . . ." Words failed him; he'd never had anyone look at him like that before, as if he was their world.

"I am," she said softly, putting everything he'd seen in her face into her voice.

"We'd better get inside in a hurry," he said, his own voice hoarse.

They had barely closed the door before she began to show him what she meant. His heavy leather jacket hit the floor with a thud, and she had his shirt half off before their lips parted for the first time. The need that had been simmering all day suddenly boiled over, and they were frantic as they tore at each other's clothes.

They left a trail of discarded garments to the bedroom before, naked, they fell back crosswise on the big brass bed, stroking, petting, caressing, until they were wild with need. Stevie tried to pull him down atop her, but he rolled away. He lay back, a hot, teasing glitter lighting his piercing green eyes.

"You did it," he repeated. "You do something about it."

Her cheeks flamed, but it was a measure of how far she'd come, how secure she was with him now, that she never hesitated. She leaned over him and began to trail hot kisses over his body in a blazing path.

Chase sucked in his breath at the sensations that rippled through him, wondering what he'd let himself in for. Her mouth caressed his shoulder, ran along the line of his collarbone, lingered in the hollow of his throat. Then she moved downward, smiling as the scattering of hair in the center of his chest tickled her tongue.

He was quivering under her tender ministrations by the time she slid down over his belly; by the time she traced the now-familiar path of the wicked, twisting scar, he was shuddering. She had even managed that, he thought with an awed sense of wonder. When he looked at that mark now, it was no longer the ugly slash that marred his body, it was a favorite path for Stevie's mouth, and looking at it sent waves of desire through him instead of bitter distaste.

"Oh, Stevie!" It broke from him as she nibbled gently at the scar where it angled past the point of his hip. She drew back, and with eyes hot and smoky blue reached for him.

Chase groaned as her fingers found him and began to move in the ways she had learned so well. He levered himself up on his elbows, and her hands stopped as she looked at him.

"Please," he panted. "I want to...watch you touch me."

She smiled a soft, sensuous smile that did nearly as much to him as the touch of her hands. She returned to her slow, teasing caresses until he was arching into her grasp, his breath coming in harsh pants.

When at last she lowered her body to his with voluptuous delight, he felt himself unravel with a speed that shocked him, and left him drained and spent. Stevie met his ecstatic release with her own, then collapsed on his chest, a slight, welcome weight he cherished.

Days later they were soundly asleep, tightly entwined in the middle of her brass bed, when a dull thud made them stir. Rather, it had made her stir; Chase came instantly, alertly awake and rolled out of bed with a swiftness that startled her into a full awakening.

She stared at him as he crouched there in the darkness, listening, looking like some wild creature scenting the breeze for danger. His nakedness did nothing to detract from the image; in fact, it only emphasized the coiled tension of his body. What faint light there was in the room seemed drawn to that expanse of golden skin, and she caught a brief flash of white where it skittered across the scar, the scar that, in her suddenly vivid imagination, could just as easily have been the mark left after some fierce battle with a wild, primitive beast in some ancient time.

She sat up as he reached for and tugged on his jeans, but stopped when he whispered harshly, "Stay here."

"Chase—"

"Stay," he snapped. Then he was gone, more silently than seemed possible for a man his size.

Stevie scrambled out of bed, grabbing and yanking on her own clothes. She didn't understand this. Were it not for his reaction, she would have assumed the noise had been an animal, or one of the countless sounds engendered in any building where several people lived in close quarters.

She was sliding her feet into her tennis shoes when she came to a halt, her breath catching in her throat as she realized what Chase must have known all along: the sound had come from next door, from Chase's apartment. Chase's empty apartment. She slammed her feet forward and began to move, running awkwardly to avoid tripping over the laces she hadn't taken time to tie.

His door was open. She paused, her heart hammering. She smothered a tiny cry as a shadow moved, silhouetted against the faint light from the bedroom. Then something about the way it moved, about the tightly controlled grace, told her it was Chase.

She ran across the room, pausing only when something in the kitchen caught her eye. An open drawer. The gun, she thought, her heart beginning its racing beat once more. She bit her lip and started toward the bedroom door.

She saw the shadow near the window whirl. Saw the glint of metal in his hand.

"Chase!"

She heard a short hiss of breath as the hand came down. "Damn it, Stevie, I told you to stay there!"

There was something cold and hard and frightening in his voice, and Stevie shivered involuntarily. Then he flipped on a light, and she saw his face. It was full of fear. Fear for her. A fear barely kept tamped down by the iron control that had made his voice sound like the cutting tip of a whip. The chill faded.

She ran to him then, and he hugged her tightly.

"I'm sorry, Stevie. I didn't mean to scare you."

"It's all right. What happened?"

He hesitated, but she saw his gaze flick to the back window. She looked, and in the dim light she saw the marks where someone had tried to pry it open. And she only now noticed the bolts he had put through the window frame that had stopped whoever it had been. Another measure to guard his fortress, she thought a little wildly.

She tried to calm herself, saying evenly enough that they should call the police. Chase brushed off the idea.

"No. He didn't get in."

"But . . ." Her eyes searched his face, all the things she didn't know about him and the trouble he was in tumbling around in her mind.

"Please, drop it, Stevie. It's all right."

She didn't believe him. And she knew he didn't even believe himself. But she said nothing as they went back to her apartment. They lay in her bed for several long, silent moments, until finally she reached out to touch him. She felt the rigid tension in him, and when she rose up to look at him, those bleak, haunted eyes looked back at her.

She attacked him fiercely then, nipping, clawing, demanding his full attention, as if in that way she could drive out the demon who possessed him. She was an irresistible spitfire, and the thought that swirled in her mind was an unspoken cry, directed at that hovering, unknown darkness: he's mine! You can't have him back!

After his first moments of surprise, he responded in kind, as if her fury had called up some answering turbulence in his own soul. It was a wild, violent coupling, two creatures slaking a savage need, and when it was over they lay gasping, panting, aware that, for a time, the demon had been driven back.

Chase stood in front of the mirror the next morning, ruefully aware that his first glance today was not at the scar on his hip but at the red welts on his back and shoulders from her nails. What a wildcat she'd been last night, he thought, a little echo of the heat of that encounter rippling down his spine to settle tauntingly between his thighs.

And I, he said to himself wryly, will be wearing a shirt all day, in the middle of the summer, naturally on the day we're starting the outside roof work. He wasn't about to give the crew anything more to speculate on; they'd had quite enough fun with him already.

He reached for the razor that had taken up residence in her medicine cabinet, as had several other things, since about the only thing he went to his place for anymore was to change clothes.

And to chase burglars.

His hand stopped in midstroke, as if the accumulation of shaving cream behind the razor had suddenly become too heavy to move. All the images he'd buried since last night rose up to haunt him, and he tried desperately to push them back into their dark, shuttered hiding place.

It was just a burglary, he told himself. Happens all the time. Just a plain, ordinary burglary, and merely a fluke that, of all the apartments, the crook had chosen his. He realized even as he was doing it that he was burying misgivings that shouldn't be buried, but the alternative was too horrible to face. Especially after the night he'd just spent with Stevie.

Yes, she had been a wildcat, he thought as he once more slid the razor over his jaw. She had also been magnificent, wonderful—and absolutely beautiful. Her fiery spirit had taken over, virtually ordering him to put everything else out of his mind.

And I'd better put this out of my mind, he thought, or I'm going to be late. Again. Even Charlie would run out of patience someday, although the affable man had told him that he could be late for months and still not make up for all the extra time he'd put in.

Wiping away the last of the shaving cream, a reflective smile curving his mouth as he remembered the day Stevie had shaved him, he dressed quickly, except for his boots. He carried them as he quietly padded back to the bedroom where Stevie was still deep in sleep, her hair spread wildly on the pillow, and a mark or two of his own doing on her tender flesh. He knew she wouldn't care—she had revelled in their wildness as much as he had—but he wished he didn't have to leave without acknowledging the specialness of what had happened.

He compromised by leaving her a note, then pressing a gentle kiss on her bare shoulder, over a dark mark left by his clutching fingers. He smiled as he left, thinking of her blush when she read his short "Thanks, Wildcat—C."

He left, refusing to think about the hovering darkness she had single-handedly beaten back.

Chapter 8

For Stevie, that night was firmly etched in her mind as a treasured memory. Along with that first precious night, it joined several other things that seemed to glow with sweet brilliance in her head, pushing away the shadows.

There was the evening they'd spent with Dan and Sheila, the first they'd shared with anyone other than themselves, the first time they'd joined others as a couple. She had been afraid it would prove awkward, that the Bartletts, especially Sheila, might press for answers that Chase wouldn't give. But Dan, with his professional sensitivity, had kept the conversation rolling on a multitude of topics, keeping it off anything personal.

She had wondered about it at first, but then a sudden image from when Chase had been so ill, a memory of a look of understanding exchanged between the two men and words that at the time had seemed too pointed, came into her mind, and she realized that Dan had seen that cruel scar. And he was perceptive enough to recognize Chase's reluctance to talk.

So it had been a memorable evening complete with pleasant company and a delicious meal, and Stevie had allowed

herself the luxury of thinking it could last forever. She had
giggled in an unusual rush of feminine delight when Sheila
had cornered her in the kitchen to say enviously, "My Lord,
girl, I had no idea that behind that gruff exterior there was
such an absolutely gorgeous man! I mean, really, those killer
green eyes. And those eyelashes! Not to mention a bod to
die for."

Just as special to her, however, was the night she had sat
in her apartment, rushing to finish a layout for an account
that had abruptly been dropped in her lap when Beth
Walker's child had decided it was time to join the world. She
had been wrestling with the rough draft that was all she had
to work with, trying to understand why, no matter what she
did, no matter how she tried to rearrange the elements, the
ad still lacked punch. She had almost wished she was at
work; the computer would at least have made the futile ex-
perimenting quicker.

Her sigh of disgust had drawn Chase's attention from the
book he'd been quietly reading, and he had set it down to
come and peer over her shoulder. He'd opened his mouth to
say something, then snapped it shut.

"What?" she asked.

"Nothing."

"C'mon, now, you saw something. What? I need help
here," she teased.

"What do I know? I'm just a working stiff."

She had eyed him coolly. "Uh-huh. Who just happens to
have one of the best design eyes I've ever come across. So
give."

Something odd came and went in his eyes; then he
shrugged. "Dump the landscaping."

She looked startled, then glanced at the layout once more.
It was for a large home development company, the first ad
for their latest project, on a bluff slightly inland from the
ocean in the booming Oceanside area.

"It's too much," Chase said succinctly. "It detracts from
their main selling point, which is the ocean view. Looking
at that—" he nodded at the layout "—all you see are those
damn bushes."

Stevie studied the sketch on her drawing table carefully. She picked up her gum eraser and carefully began to remove the abstract blobs representing bushes, along with the tree that had taken up the top of the drawing. She hadn't been comfortable with the tree in the first place, but she had been hesitant to change Beth's work, even though it was only a rough draft.

"It's not a bad house," Chase said. "Just let it stand alone."

Finished, she set down the eraser and took a step back. The house now leapt out from the page. It rose from the bluff as if it belonged and led the eye from its modern lines to the expanse of water, leaving no doubt in the buyer's mind that the view would be well worth the price.

She looked up at Chase, a speculative look in her eyes.

He just shrugged. "You've been looking at it too long."

She smothered a rising question, knowing he wouldn't answer it, but she couldn't help wondering why he'd never done anything with his obvious talent. She remembered the sketch he'd done for Leo, outlining the remodeling of his store. Even on the back of a menu, done with nothing more than a pencil stub, it had been a marvel of quick, sure lines, meshing into an efficient and economical design. It seemed such a horrible waste. The night remained vividly in her memory.

As did the questions. A construction worker with a true artist's eye. Who read anything and everything. Who knew the work of Kahlil Gibran. Who seemed as comfortable with a book as with a hammer. She smothered them all and added the image to her treasury of memories.

That night was followed by the night he'd found the certificate she'd been given announcing her nomination for the Ad Council award. It had slid behind the entry table unnoticed, the night she'd gotten the word about Sean. She'd wondered idly where it had gotten to, but she'd been so wrapped up in other things—Chase, to be exact—that she had eventually forgotten about it.

When she came into the living room to find him holding it, she abruptly remembered the day she'd gotten it. The day she'd been so achingly aware that there was no one to share it with, no one who would appreciate it. She had thought of Chase then, but he had seemed so far out of reach....

He proved her instincts right. He showed her clearly that night that he knew exactly what an achievement it was. He told her in no uncertain terms how proud he was of her. His words brought tears to her eyes, tears she didn't even bother to try to hide. He carted her off there and then, tucking her into the passenger seat of her car like a princess and driving to her favorite restaurant in La Jolla.

There, in the redwood-and-glass building clinging to the side of the cliff overlooking lovely La Jolla Bay, he had ordered her favorite meal of rare prime rib, and a bottle of ridiculously extravagant champagne. Then, when she was feeling deliciously mellow, he had taken her home and made long, languorous love to her well into the night.

"And when you win," he'd told her, "we're really going to celebrate!"

The final presentation wasn't for weeks yet, and she had felt the sting of tears once more at this promise of a shared future. But she kept silent, not wanting to risk destroying the mood.

She remembered the morning after that incredible night, when she had awakened before him and spent a long time just watching him sleep. He lay sprawled facedown, one arm thrown over her ribs, his hand gently cupping her breast. His other arm was under the pillow his head was burrowed into, leaving only the dark tangle of his hair, his beard-shadowed jaw and one dark-fringed eye visible to her loving gaze.

The covers were in a tangle from their lovemaking. Only the sheet remained over him, and that only from midthigh down. She'd had to resist the urge to reach out and cup the tight, tempting curve of his buttocks, and the thought of how that swell of muscle felt beneath her hands when he was driving into her body had made her flush with heat.

The most surprising thing she had tucked away in her mental storehouse of memories was the day they'd gone to get Sean. Stevie had called the hospital on the morning when he was to be released, only to find that he had already left, that the bus from the rehabilitation camp had picked him up. She'd been puzzled, but grateful that he had decided to go back.

She'd been disappointed when she called the camp and was told Sean wasn't receiving any calls, but she'd accepted it philosophically enough.

"You really mean it, don't you?" Chase had asked when she had hung up. "You're not going to let him tear you up anymore?"

"You were right," she'd said, slipping between the arms he held out to her. He'd pulled her onto his lap, holding her close. "I can't do it for him, and I can't make him do it. All I can do is love him enough to let him find his own way."

"You've come a long way," he said softly.

"I had a lot of help." She met his gaze with a warm, tender look.

After that, it had been a surprise when Sean had called a few weeks later and asked her to come get him.

"There's isn't anything more these guys can do for me," he'd said, his voice sounding oddly tense.

Stevie had sighed, supposing that if he hadn't made any progress in three months, he wasn't going to make any, and she had agreed to get him on the following Saturday, determined that she wasn't going to fall back into the old trap of trying to make her brother do anything.

She hadn't thought Chase would want to go, not after the painful scene at the hospital. She'd thought a lot about that night, regretting that she had let him be subjected to that, especially now that she knew what horrible memories hospitals held for him. He'd spent three months in one after he'd been hit, he'd told her, and another three in a clinic learning how to walk again using battered and weakened muscles. But when she told him of Sean's request, he had merely nodded and asked what time she wanted to leave.

She had been pacing the floor of the tiny lobby at the camp's office, nervous despite her promises to herself. If Sean made another scene, if he said one angry word to Chase about what had happened, she—

"Hi, Sis."

She wheeled around, her eyes automatically lowered to the level from which the voice had come. The wheelchair was being pushed by a pug-nosed little blonde with a bouncy ponytail, who, for some reason, was grinning from ear to ear, while Sean was looking the way he had looked ever since the accident: angry and bitter.

There was a lightweight blanket covering his leg and foot, and she thought with a sigh that he was still hiding from the world. He looked healthier, with a touch of color in his face, as if he'd been out in the sun, and looked even a bit heavier, as if he'd been eating better, but that sour look was still on his face.

She saw his eyes go past her to where Chase was leaning against the wall, arms crossed casually, his air of insouciance marred by the intense gaze of his vivid green eyes as he watched the young man in the chair.

"Brought your bodyguard, I see," Sean said, that same odd note in his voice that she had heard on the phone. "Did you think you'd need him?"

"I wasn't sure," Stevie said shortly, suddenly out of patience with this stubborn brother of hers. "But if you say one nasty thing, little brother, one smart-aleck word to him, I'll knock you on your butt so fast it'll make your head spin, wheelchair or not!"

Sean stared at her, while Chase smothered a stunned smile at her words. Then the most unexpected thing in the world happened; Sean threw back his head and laughed. Great, roaring gales of laughter, until he was holding his ribs.

"Damn, Stevie, if you only knew how long I've been waiting to see that temper of yours again!" he finally gasped.

It was her turn to stare.

"I was so sick of everybody treating me like an invalid. You, Mom and Dad... I decided if that was what you thought, then that was what I'd be."

His eyes went past Stevie's stunned face to rest on Chase once more. "But then your friend there got me to thinking. About a lot of things. For a lot of long, late nights. And I decided I'd had enough of people feeling sorry for me."

"Oh, Sean, I—"

"Quiet," her brother said, a gleam coming into his brown eyes. "I'm not through with you yet."

Startled, she backed up a step. That brought her practically up against Chase, who had straightened away from the wall. She went silent with shock as her angry, bitter brother tossed away the pale blue blanket and, incredibly, amazingly, stood up. On two legs. On two feet.

"Oh, God."

She swayed, and Chase's hand shot out to steady her. He felt her tremble as Sean took the two short steps between them and put his arms around his suddenly weeping sister.

"I'm sorry, Stevie," he murmured into her hair. "I'm sorry I've been such a prize bastard."

"Sean—"

"I know I've got a long way to go. I'm still angry that it happened to me. And I can't quite face myself in a mirror. But I'm going to try. And if I ever put you through hell like that again, you have my permission to—" he smiled sheepishly "—knock me on my butt, plastic leg and all."

She was smiling through the tears brimming in her eyes, and she hugged her brother fiercely. She kept an arm around him when he turned to look at Chase.

"I owe you an apology."

Chase shook his head. "What you just did," he said, looking at Stevie's joyous face, "made up for everything."

Sean studied the tall, lean man opposite him for a moment, searching his face, his eyes, until he apparently found what he was looking for. He nodded, an odd little jerk of his head, and Chase returned it: message received and understood.

"In that case, thank you," Sean said. "What you said—"

"Was nothing you hadn't heard before."

"I know. But only from doctors, nurses and shrinks. It didn't mean a damn thing. But you . . . you've been there. I could tell. It made it different somehow."

"Welcome back." Chase spoke with a heartfelt sincerity that only one who had been to the dark side and made it back would understand. Sean didn't miss it, and as he hugged Stevie once more, he nodded in silent acceptance.

"So, sister mine, are you going to introduce me to this killer bodyguard of yours now?"

She laughed at the realization that this intensely personal conversation had been carried on by two men who hadn't really ever met. And, she thought as she made the formal introduction, it was indeed two men; her little brother had gone a long way toward growing up.

To Stevie's surprise, in the following weeks Sean and Chase became close friends. When Sean was down, when he found himself slipping back into that old, dark well of self-pity, it was Chase he wanted to talk to. When he called her apartment, he made no comment about the fact that Chase was always there when he asked for him, just casually accepted his presence. He assumed that where Stevie was, Chase would be.

"You don't have to come," Stevie said when Chase told her that Sean had assumed he would be joining her for dinner at their parents. He had hushed her objections with relative cheer.

"I know. I want to." He gave her a sideways look. "But if your mother starts on you again, I make no promises about keeping my mouth shut."

Stevie knew her father guessed immediately at the change in their relationship by the way he kept looking at Chase. The older man's alert blue eyes followed the tall, dark-haired figure as he carefully yet inconspicuously stayed at Stevie's elbow.

Maggie Holt was wrapped up in Sean and blissfully ignored everyone else. "It's so good to have you here," Maggie cooed, as Sean, looking a little more comfortable with the new leg, moved to his seat at the table.

"Thank Chase," Sean said simply. "If he hadn't given me a swift kick in the pants I wouldn't be—" he glanced down pointedly "—standing here now."

"Here, here," Stevie said softly. Her father nodded as if in sudden understanding, and her mother stared as if she'd never seen Chase before.

It was over dessert that it began again, the comments Maggie always seemed to make, so habitual they seemed unconscious. Little digs about Stevie's apartment, her clothes, her car. Each time Chase abruptly and obviously changed the subject, and Sean willingly jumped in to carry the new topic. Yet still Maggie persisted.

When at last she openly criticized her daughter for not having the gumption to go out and get a better job, since the one she had obviously didn't pay enough to support her spendthrift habits, Chase lost his battle to control his temper.

"Mrs. Holt," he said icily, "with all due respect, shut up!"

"Well, I never!" the older woman exclaimed, outraged. "And in my own house! Steven, do something!"

"I think not," Steven Holt said mildly, his eyes fastened on Chase with intense interest.

"Good for you, Dad," Sean chimed in, and his mother turned to him in shock. "It's about time she faced the truth."

"The truth?" Maggie was staring at her son, slack-jawed.

"Yes. Like I had to."

"Sean . . ." Stevie was pale, her eyes wide and worried.

"You shut up too, Blue Eyes," Chase said, the tone of his voice making what had been an insult to her mother a caress for her. Sean cast Chase a glance of thanks before going on. "It's time you learned just how Stevie spends her money."

And it all came out. Stevie had the pleasure of seeing her critical mother for once at a complete loss for words. But her father wasn't surprised, and she realized with a little shock that he had known. Chase realized it, too, and fixed angry eyes on the older man.

"This should have been said long ago," he said. "How could you let it go on?"

Steven Holt seemed to find the answer to all his questions in the fierce, protective demeanor of the man at his daughter's side. "I only just realized. I'm afraid it took me awhile to put two and two together," he explained, seeming pleased, rather than offended by Chase's tone.

They left shortly after that, with Stevie feeling so emotionally exhausted that she couldn't stop the little shivers wracking her. When they got home, Chase carried her inside, undressed her with tender, strangely sensuous care and put her beneath the covers. He shed his own clothes and slide in beside her, pulling her gently into his arms, into the curve of his body.

She felt the hard pressure of his arousal against her bottom, but when she had tried to turn to him, he held her still. "Not now," he'd whispered. "Go to sleep, love." And she had, with the dampness of tears on her cheeks, tears for the tenderness she'd found in the man who held her.

It had been the first night they'd spent together without making love, and the fact seemed somehow significant to Stevie, important because it proved to her that there was more than just incredible, fiery passion between them. She had added the memory of that night to all the others she was collecting, all of them precious and made more so by the realization that she had come so close to not having them at all. And by that nagging fear that the shadows were still there, just out of sight, waiting.

Chase paced Stevie's living room ceaselessly. She was late. And Stevie was never late. If she said she would be somewhere at a particular time, she was, on the dot. One of her pet peeves was people who thought that no one's time but their own was important and kept people waiting indiscriminately.

He glanced at his watch again, swearing under his breath when it uncaringly told him that it really was nine o'clock. He'd called the office and been told that she'd left shortly after seven. Even if she'd stopped somewhere, which she hadn't been planning on, she should have been here by now.

It was that damn car, he thought. It had finally given out on her. If she wouldn't do it herself, *he* would buy her a new one. Except that she'd never take it, he thought grimly. Stevie had definite views about where the lines were drawn on that kind of thing. Maybe he'd buy one himself, then get her to drive it. He could tell her that he'd rather ride the bike most of the time.

He dropped down on the sofa, staring unseeingly across the room that had become so familiar. It felt so comfortable to him, so much like a home....

The old, aching longing rose up in him, and he tried wearily to beat it down. It was getting harder and harder each time. He wanted more than anything in the world to know that Stevie would always be there, to tie her to him forever. He wanted everything he'd had to put off-limits so long ago—a home, a family....

Pain twisted inside him at the thought of Stevie, pregnant with his child. At the thought of a tiny scamp of a girl, a miniature of her mother, with the same bright blue eyes and silvery laugh. They had taken precautions after that first night, but he half wished they hadn't. He slammed a fist into his palm, cursing himself, the world and anything else he could think of.

These last months of peace, of safety, had lulled him. That and Stevie's sweet, precious love. He'd begun, on some subconscious level, to think perhaps it was possible. That maybe it was over. Because of that he'd ignored the signs, the hints. The prowler, the sensation of being watched again that he hadn't been able to shake, the—

The shrill ringing of the phone shattered his thoughts. Damn, he thought as he went for it. The car had broken down.

"Is this Mr. Sullivan?"

The detached female voice was unfamiliar, but then, he didn't make a habit of answering Stevie's phone unless he thought it was her. But the woman had asked for him by name. He said yes.

"This is the sheriff's office. Please don't worry. It's not an emergency, but do you know a Stevie Holt?"

He tried to hang on to what she'd said. Not an emergency. "Yes," he said tightly. "What's wrong?"

"She's been involved in an accident. She's not injured, just shaken up," the woman hastened to assure him, "but her car is undrivable. She gave us your name. Could you come and pick her up?"

She'd given them his name. She had to be all right, then, didn't she? He swallowed, trying to get a grip on his fear. "Of course. Where is she?"

He wrote down the directions, hung up and headed for the door. And stopped as soon as he had it open. Just because she wasn't hurt didn't mean she was up to a trip on the back of his motorcycle. He thought for a minute. The Bartletts were out, and Mrs. Trimble didn't have a car, but Leo did. And his lights were still on.

In a matter of minutes he was climbing into the relatively new sedan, Leo Rubin's keys in his hand and the man's concern for Stevie still echoing in his ears. The incredible thing, he thought as the motor turned over, was that she didn't even realize the effect she had on people.

He felt a moment of panic when he found the location the dispatcher had given and there was no sign of her. Had she been hurt after all, something that hadn't shown up right away? Then another thought hit him; had it been a phony call? A setup? To get to him? Or was that just on his mind after his gloomy thoughts earlier?

Then he saw a marked sheriff's unit in the parking lot of a small coffee shop that appeared to be open. He parked next to it and went inside. He found her immediately, huddled in a booth, seeming somehow smaller and more delicate than ever before.

She was sitting across from a uniformed sheriff's deputy who was altogether too California blond and handsome for Chase's comfort. Yet Stevie's glad cry, and the speed with which she threw her arms around him when he sat down beside her, soothed any pangs of jealousy he was feeling.

The deputy nodded to Chase, an expression not far from envy on his face. Intensely aware that Stevie was holding on to him fiercely, Chase nodded back. "What happened?" he asked.

"Hit-and-run. Guy came out of nowhere. Must have been doing eighty." His eyes shifted to rest on Stevie's bent head. "She's lucky. If it had happened a few seconds later, or if she hadn't had her seat belt on . . ." He shook his head, and Chase closed his eyes at the horrors the man's words invoked. Horrors he knew all too well.

"Any description on the car?" he asked after a moment.

"Big. Dark. Black, or maybe dark blue. One witness thought it had out-of-state plates. Not much to go on."

Somewhere in the dark recesses of Chase's mind, a small, bright light began to glow.

"We'll do the best we can, but don't count on anything," the deputy said, then got to his feet. "Good luck, Stevie." He held out a business card. "Call that number next week if you need a copy of the report. Or me, if I can help."

Stevie lifted her head from where it was buried against Chase's arm, then took the card.

"Thank you, Dave." Her fingers might be shaking, but her voice was fairly steady. "It was nice of you to wait with me, especially since you're off duty now."

"No problem."

Dave looked at Chase, the envy more obvious now. But he smiled good-naturedly, resigned; Stevie had made it clear how she felt.

"Take care of her," the deputy said.

Chase nodded. Great. Hanging around with her when he should be going home. Talk about above and beyond the call. But how could he blame the guy? And she would probably be better with a guy like this. At least Dave could offer her all the things he himself couldn't. He laughed bitterly to himself. Fine thing, when you have to admit she'd be better off with a cop. At least he would only take a chance on getting himself killed, not her.

He felt a little quiver go through the slender body in his arms, and he tightened his grasp. Knock off feeling sorry for yourself, he ordered, and take care of her like the man said. "Are you sure you're all right?"

"I'm fine," she insisted. "The paramedics looked at me and put on a Band-Aid or two. I banged my knee on the dash, but I'm fine. My car, on the other hand, is history."

He tweaked her sassy little nose. "I hate to break it to you, but it was nearly that anyway."

"It wasn't that bad!"

"Look at it this way," he said, glad to see her flash of spirit, "at least it went out in a blaze of glory."

"Yeah," she said glumly, then shuddered. "It was scary, Chase. He came out of nowhere. He must have had it floored. It was like he was heading right for me. I mean, I wasn't even moving, I was just parked—"

"Parked?"

She nodded. "It was making a weird noise. I was going to stop and look, so I pulled over." She gestured out the window, and he could see the remnants of flares and some shards of glass still lying in the street. "I was just about to get out. . . ." She shuddered again, violently this time.

"Stevie?" With a growing dread he held her shoulders and stared at her. The light in his mind grew brighter.

"I had the door open. I had even started to get out, but then I saw the grocery bag had fallen on the floor." She looked up at him sheepishly. "I stopped to get you some of that ice cream you're so crazy about, from that little store over on Garnet."

He closed his eyes for a moment, his own fingers shaking now, his stomach knotting. He should have known it was something like that.

"What happened, Stevie?" The light was glaringly bright now.

"I reached over to pick it up. Then he hit me." Her eyes were wide with remembered shock. "If I had gone ahead... God, I already had my foot out, on the ground, but I had to move it to reach the bag. I had my hand on the seat belt, to unfasten it, when it happened." She was shaking steadily now. "He took out the whole car door. If I'd gotten out..."

She would be dead. He didn't need a picture painted. That glaring light exploded inside his head. A three-piece-suit mouthing the same words he'd just heard from the deputy. A big car. Dark colored. Out-of-state plates. Waiting until the victim stood beside the car, open, vulnerable.

Hit-and-run. Untraceable car. And sheer, unforeseeable luck, the only thing preventing a gruesome, bloody death. Twice. The brilliant light dimmed, then faded, leaving a blackness that was impenetrable by comparison.

"Chase?" Her voice sounded distant, far away. "God, Chase, I'm sorry. I shouldn't have told you. I didn't think. I was just so shaken, I..."

He felt her hand on his cheek and summoned up every last ounce of control he had. He shoved the dark, grim memories back into that vault where they'd stayed silently for all these weeks, waiting only for this moment. Later, he told himself coldly. Stevie comes first. Take care of her, then do what has to be done. He felt as if he'd been encased in ice.

He reacted normally, on the surface. He answered her questions; he explained about Leo's car. He tucked away the young deputy's card for her when her fingers were shaking too badly to manage it. He said he would get Dan to check her over again if he was home when they arrived.

Dan was, and although he agreed with the paramedics' assessment, he offered her a mild sedative to help her sleep. She refused, but Chase took it from Dan as he walked him to the door.

"Good idea," Dan said. "She may be glad of it later. She's kind of numb now, but that will wear off."

"I know."

Dan looked at him. "Yes, I suppose you do." He turned to go, but looked back. "I'm glad you were here for her."

"Yeah," Chase said flatly. But inside he couldn't stop thinking, If I hadn't been here, it would never have happened. If I'd gone when I should have, when I started feeling like someone was watching me again, this wouldn't have happened.

I should have gone after the attempted break-in, he thought, the acid of guilt searing deep into his battered soul.

But no, I worked so damn hard at convincing myself it was just an ordinary burglary, because I knew if I didn't, I'd have to leave. Leave Stevie. And, coward that I am, I couldn't face that.

Later, his mind ordered. Handle those thoughts later. The icy control clamped down again as he went to get a glass of water for the pill she didn't yet know she was going to take.

The icy control melted to molten lava when he went back into the bedroom to find her waiting for him, wearing a filmy blue nightgown that drove him crazy.

He remembered the first time she'd worn it, on an evening when they'd curled up in front of the television to watch a movie. He hadn't seen much of the film; all he'd been able to think of was the way that gown had clung to her, how its sheerness was just enough to hint, which hadn't mattered, because his mind supplied the details. They'd wound up on the floor, the flickering light of the forgotten television dancing over their naked, straining bodies.

That gown had become a symbol since then, worn when she had one thing in mind above all else. Just knowing she had it on was enough to fire his blood. He was amazed the flimsy garment hadn't been torn to shreds before now.

Now. Then. Such small words to have such power. By tomorrow, what was now would be then. Stevie would be then. Past tense. No longer in the present. And deep inside him, all that was bright and beautiful, all the sunlight she had brought into his life, went down to a dark, dusty death.

When he went to her, peeling his clothes off on the way, it was with the sense of a final chapter about to be read; his mind knew the book would soon be over, but his heart and body were determined to hang on as long as possible. When he touched her, it was paying homage to a dream, a sweet, ethereal dream that he had held for a while, time stolen that must now be returned.

With quietly whispered commands he ordered her to lie still and proceeded to stroke, kiss and taste every silken curve and hollow. He tasted her lips, traced her brow, teased the delicate shell of her ear with the tip of his tongue. She began to shiver, and still he continued his onslaught. He nibbled gently down the column of her neck, pausing at the hollow of her throat to savor the quickened, pulsing beat. Alive. She was alive. And he would make her know it as she never had before. It was the last gift he could give her.

She reached for him, but he pressed her back to the bed. "Please," he whispered. "Let me."

Her arms fell back, spread in an attitude of surrender, of giving her body up to his will, to do with as he pleased. He smothered a groan and once more called up the control he hadn't had to use for so long. She mustn't know, mustn't guess. . . .

He bent to her again, his hands going to the firm curves of her breasts, circling, caressing. At last she moaned, arching her back, thrusting upward nipples aching for his touch. He took them, pressing them with a rotating motion that tore her breath from her in a gasp, then rolling them between thumb and forefinger until she was moaning his name.

He lowered his head, kissing the firm, rounded flesh, tracing it with his tongue with agonizing slowness, always circling but never quite touching the erect crests. He waited until he heard her whispered plea, then took first one, then the other, fiercely into his mouth, nipping just hard enough, tugging with just enough strength, to make her cry out in pleasure.

He continued until she was writhing, her legs parting involuntarily as the heat grew so intense she couldn't bear it. He trailed his mouth over her, tracing the much loved paths over her slender rib cage, across her flat stomach, over the point of her hip.

As he kissed and tasted her skin, his hand slipped down to find that sweet, pulsing spot, to stroke it, massage it gently. She was hot and wet and ready, opening for his touch as she opened for his body, and he savaged his lip with his teeth in an effort to maintain his frozen control.

"Chase," she gasped. "Please! Now. I need you now."

"Soon," he promised, pressing his lips to the indentation of her navel. He laved it thoroughly, then moved to kneel between her legs. She gave a small sigh of relief and anticipation, which broke off into a ragged cry as he bent his head to let his tongue take the place of the hand that had been tormenting the throbbing place between her thighs.

Her body stiffened in shocked surprise, then went soft and supple beneath his mouth. Her breath came in gasping pants in time with the stroking of his tongue. Her hands clenched, nails digging into the cloth beneath her. Chase slipped his hands beneath her hips and lifted her to him, increasing the pressure and tempo of his probing tongue.

Soon she was moving, arching, lifting herself to him with utter abandon. Her hands moved to his head, her slender fingers tangling in his hair, her moans running together now as her body surged toward completion.

She went rigid, and with a sharp cry of his name, shudder after shudder swept her. He moved swiftly then, fitting himself to that pulsating sheath and thrusting forward, hard and deep. She gave a second, gasping cry, and her hands went to his lean hips, fingers digging into his flesh as she forced him even deeper.

For long, exquisite seconds, his every muscle tensed to tearing tightness with the strain, he stayed motionless, feeling the convulsions, letting her rippling flesh stroke him, caress him, until he was so swollen he wondered that she could still hold him.

Then, as the waves of her pleasure ebbed, he began to move, not allowing her to reach that lazy plateau of aftermath but instead, driving her upward once more with every powerful thrust of his body into hers.

He knew, as she arched up to him, opening her legs wider so that the only place they were touching was that hot, swirling core of her body, that she was climbing with him; he knew her body so well now. . . .

And he knew, when her hands went to his shoulders, what she wanted, knew that he wanted it, too, and the rest of the world slipped away as he gave it to her. He moved faster, driving harder and deeper with every slamming thrust of his hips, pounding into her body until she was calling his name at every echo of hungry flesh against hungry flesh.

At last, at the very moment when he knew one more thrust would finish him, she clenched around him, a harsh, moaning sound ripping from deep inside her. Her back arched, and her legs locked with supple fierceness around his waist, holding him deep within her. He erupted in a spurt of searing, pouring pleasure, giving himself to her over and over and over, until, as it had been the first time, he thought it would never stop. The pulsing waves went on, until his very vision began to fade and he thought he might as well die right now, in this moment of supreme ecstasy, rather than facing the living death to come.

Stevie drifted down from that wondrous, high place, thinking, as much as she was capable of thinking in this state, that there was something different about this night. She always felt treasured when Chase made love to her, felt cherished and special, but never before had she felt this overwhelming, shining, shimmering warmth, as if she were being cradled in the softness of his tender care.

Perhaps it was just reaction, she thought, but she didn't really believe it. And when at last she stirred, opening her eyes to meet his vivid green gaze, she knew she was right; there was something she'd never seen there before, something her pleasure-numbed mind couldn't put a name to.

"I love you," he whispered.

Stevie's eyes widened. That she loved him, had for a long time, she had long ago accepted. But she'd never said the words, afraid to damage the fragile balance of their relationship. And she had never expected to hear them from him. Her heart soared. "I lo—"

"Shh," he said, forestalling the vow returned. "Not now. Tell me later. In the morning. You need to rest now." He sat up, reaching for the glass of water he'd set down.

Stevie made a face when she saw the pill he held out, but when he softly pleaded with her, she finally accepted it. Not being used to such things, it hit her quickly, and she felt herself drifting away. She heard him repeating those sweet, longed-for words, over and over. And just before the darkness enclosed her, she felt him lift her hands to his lips, and she thought what an odd effect this drug was having on her, because she could have sworn he was crying.

Stevie awoke with a dry mouth and the odd, aching feeling brought on by being in one position too long. She wondered if she had moved at all during the long, drugged night. Even through closed eyelids the room seemed too bright; either it was very late, or that was another by-product of whatever had been in that damn pill. She swore she would never take one again, no matter how Chase pleaded.

Chase. A soft smile curved her lips as she remembered last night. He had given and given to her last night, made her feel enclosed in shining warmth and love as never before. She reached for him, longing to return the favor in the morning—or was it afternoon?—light, but found the bed empty.

Of course, she thought. He wouldn't still be asleep. She pried one eye open to peer at the bedside clock, noting with chagrin that it was indeed afternoon.

"Stevie?"

She rolled over, startled at the sound of that unexpected voice. "Sean?" She gaped in surprise when she saw him sitting in a chair pulled up to the side of the bed. He looked as if he had been there for a while.

"How do you feel?"

She sat up, rubbing bleary eyes. She plucked at the silken gown that had twisted around her, then stopped to stare at it in confusion. How had she gotten back into it? she wondered. Sean saw her look and something strangely sad came into his warm brown eyes.

"I'm fine," she said, ignoring the various aches that were making themselves known. She looked at her brother, puzzled. "What are you doing here?"

"Chase called me." His voice sounded flat, his words clipped.

Stevie's brow furrowed. "Why? I'm fine, you didn't have to—where is he?"

"Gone."

"But it's Saturday. He doesn't have to work. Where did he go?" And why had he—and she knew it could only have been him—dressed her in the blue gown again, as if he'd known she would awake to someone else?

"He didn't tell me."

The tightness of Sean's voice could no longer be denied, and a sense of nagging unease began to grow in Stevie's chest. "Sean, what's wrong?"

When he finally answered, it was in flat, measured tones that held as much pain as she'd ever heard from him, even in the bitterest days after his accident.

"He called me early this morning. Told me to get over here. No questions, just get here." He held up a hand as Stevie opened her mouth to speak. "Let me finish. When I got here, he told me about the accident. He said he'd rented you a car for a couple of weeks because yours was totaled. It's out back. He said he'd called Mom and Dad, and told them you were all right. He called your insurance company and left a message. They should call you on Monday."

As he mechanically listed, in that dull, flat voice, all the things Chase had done while she slept, dread was expanding inside her. Why wasn't Chase here, telling her this? Sean took a deep, rasping breath, and she knew with instinctive fear that she was about to find out.

"Then he told me to stay here. To take care of you. Because he couldn't."

"Where is he?" Stevie asked again in a tiny voice.

"He told me to tell you the dark had caught up with him. He said it was because of him. The accident, I mean. That he should never have let you take the risk."

Sean repeated the words that had meant nothing to him; his sister's pale face told him they meant everything to her. "He's gone, Stevie. There's no easier way to put it."

A low, harsh sound came from her, and Sean moved quickly, if awkwardly, from the chair to the bed, gathering his trembling sister into his arms.

"It was only an accident," she moaned.

"I don't understand, Stevie. I told him that this didn't make any sense. I was shouting at him, and every word...it was like I was hitting him. He just stood there. Even when I told him he was crazy, that even if he didn't know it, he loved you.''

Stevie jerked in his arms, a low whimper tearing from her as she remembered those sweet, sweet words whispered in the dark.

''I'll never forget his voice. He just said, 'I know it,' but it was like I'd tortured it out of him. Then I told him that if he knew that, then he had to know you loved him, too. At least, I tried to tell him. He cut me off.''

Just as he cut me off last night, Stevie thought numbly.

''He said the weirdest thing . . . in that terrible voice, like he was begging. He said, 'Please, don't give me that to carry, too.' Stevie, I've never seen anyone look like that before. His eyes . . . I can't describe them.''

He didn't have to. Stevie knew exactly what he meant. That haunted, tortured look was a permanent part of her memory. And in that moment she knew that it hadn't been the sedative that had made her think Chase had been crying.

''He's really gone?'' she asked brokenly, knowing the answer.

Sean tightened his arms around her. ''He's gone, Stevie. He must have stayed up all night to do it, but everything's gone.''

''He . . . didn't h-have much,'' she stammered, unable to stop the shaking that had overtaken her. *That's why he was so determined I take that damn pill. So I wouldn't know what he was doing.*

''He left me the key, for your landlord. Said the rent's paid up until the end of the month.'' He was quiet for a moment, pondering, then decided it was best to get it all over at once. ''He left something, though. For you.''

She lifted her head then, hope dawning in her devastated eyes. But when Sean handed her the framed drawing of the house, that lovely, magical house that had been the only personal thing he owned, the crushing, utter finality of her loss came sliding down on her with the force of an avalanche.

She wanted to cry, but no tears would come. Some vital part of her had been torn out, leaving a yawning, empty cavern where her heart, her emotions, the ability to feel, her very soul, had been. With them had gone her capacity for the healing release of tears, leaving behind agony compounded by the knowledge that she had always known this could happen. And now she would never know why.

Never. The word echoed in her mind with the aching pain of a funeral bell. Never. Never again to see him, never again to talk to him, to hear that rare and precious laugh, never again to see that overwhelming grin, and never again to see his eyes light with that ceaseless hunger when he looked at her.

Never to touch him again. Never to feel that smooth, sleek skin, stretched taut over lean muscle, never to rest her head on the muscled expanse of his chest, never to let her fingers tangle in the thick, dark silk of his hair. Never to hear him gasp with pleasure as she slid her hands over him, never to see that strong, powerful man let himself be turned to putty beneath her touch.

"Please go, Sean," she said woodenly. "Thank you for... being here, but please go now."

"I can't. I promised him I'd stay."

She bit back a bitter retort. "You don't have to."

"I do. I promised him," Sean repeated.

She lifted her head then, looking up at him with eyes that were a frightening duplicate of the green ones he'd seen this morning; mortally wounded, full of a pain beyond words.

"Stevie," he said earnestly, "I don't know what this is all about, what his reasons are, but I know one thing. He loves you, and leaving was tearing him apart."

Her hands tightened on the frame of the drawing. She had a sudden feeling that she had been living on borrowed time since the night the prowler had tried to break into his apartment. Somehow it was all tied together—his reaction that night, and the night Dan's car had come screeching around the corner, his own accident, and then hers. And hers, that terrifying near miss, that hair-breadth escape from death, had been the crowning blow.

He had convinced himself that what had happened last night was somehow his fault. She didn't understand why, but it told her why he'd done what he did. "It could spread to you...." He'd said that the first night they'd made love, and she hadn't listened. She had hoped in the gloriously happy weeks they'd had since that he had forgotten it. But he hadn't. And now he was gone. Gone and alone, back in that horrible darkness she'd thought she'd rescued him from forever. And the tears she couldn't cry for herself, she found she could cry for him.

"She means well, Stevie."

Sean handed her a glass that was wet with condensation. Even this close to the beach, the dog days of September were taking their toll. She had just hung up from talking to their mother, a stressful experience at best.

"Well, somewhere between the meaning and the putting into practice, she loses something," Stevie said sardonically, taking a deep sip of the fruit-flavored rum drink Sean had fixed.

He had stayed with her for two weeks after Chase had gone. He had called her office to say she wouldn't be in, that she was suffering aftereffects of her accident—not quite a lie. He had slept on her couch, fixed food when she thought she could force it down, been there to listen when the pain overwhelmed her, and kept his own thoughts tactfully to himself.

She tried now and then to ask him how his rehabilitation program was going, but he merely hushed her with a short, "It's going." He said nothing more about the promise to stay Chase had extracted from him, not while the wound was so raw. He just quietly, gently fulfilled that promise.

He had even helped her in her futile efforts to discover where Chase had gone. But Chase had left no word with anyone. Even Charlie Starr knew nothing, only looked at her sadly and said, "I knew something was doggin' that boy."

She tried mailing a card, but it came back from the post office as undeliverable, no forwarding address. And Charlie had told her that the motorcycle had been registered to Starr Construction; Chase had asked him if it was all right when he first started, and Charlie had seen no reason to say no. Since changing the registration would be a certain trail, she was grimly sure he wouldn't do it.

In unspoken agreement, neither she nor Sean ever mentioned going to the police for help, even in looking for the motorcycle. Stevie believed what Chase had told her, that it wasn't that kind of trouble, but she wasn't taking any chances. And Sean pointed out that they probably wouldn't be able to do much to find someone who had obviously disappeared of his own free will.

She had surrendered then, sliding into a nearly unbroken silence that tore at Sean's heart. He would distract her with a game of cards, or even the Monopoly they had loved as children, when that seemed to be what she needed, and he left her alone when that seemed to be what she wanted.

He had, Stevie thought now, as he lowered himself into a chair with only a trace of awkwardness, gained a maturity in the last six months that sat well on shoulders broadened by months of powering a wheelchair.

Where before he had been merely an attractive, carefree boy, he was now, at twenty-two, a young man with the kind of character and strength that glowed quietly from within. And it had shown in the way he had taken care of her in those first horrible days. He had put aside his own problems, had buried the countless difficulties he faced, the daily reminders that his life would never be the same, to take care of her. Her little brother had indeed grown up.

"That's a rather odd look, sister mine. What's up?"

"I was just thinking that some girl is going to be very, very lucky someday."

Sean blushed; in that way, he was still the boy she remembered. "I don't know about that. Most of 'em prefer all the original equipment."

"But not all. There'll be a special one out there."

Sean looked at her, then spoke tentatively. "Chase said something like that to me once."

"Oh?" she said, proud of the evenness of her tone; she knew Sean was gauging her reaction.

"Yeah. He said you meet people who pretend to forget about it all the time. And some who really do forget about it—that's rare. But when you meet one who can make *you* forget about it, that's the one to hang on to."

Stevie closed her eyes. He'd told her that she'd made him forget, that she'd completely changed the way he looked at the jagged scar that marked him. "But he didn't hang on," she whispered.

"Because he couldn't, Stevie," Sean said softly. She had told him, in those first long, sleepless nights, what little she knew. "He was afraid for you. And he loved you. I know he did."

"I know. He told me."

Sean sat forward suddenly. She hadn't said this before. "He told you he loved you?"

"That night. Before he made me take that damn pill." She opened her eyes. "And he wouldn't let me say it back."

Sean's eyes widened. "'Please, don't give me that to carry, too,'" he quoted, and Stevie nodded. "What he was doing to himself was all he could stand," Sean said slowly, understanding now. "He couldn't take thinking of how he would be hurting you, if you loved him back."

"But he wanted me to know . . ."

"Stevie?" Sean was beside her suddenly, removing her glass and taking her hands between his. "You don't . . . hate him, do you?"

"Hate Chase?" She shook her head sadly. "I love him. I'll always love him. No matter where he is. Or what he's done."

Sean hugged her. "Don't think that, Sis. He would never do anything . . . like that. It's what's been done to him. I know him too well to think otherwise."

Stevie clung to him, marveling at the turnabout, at her baby brother being the one to comfort her, and more, that he had the ability and sensitivity to do it, despite the long road that he still faced himself. She loved him dearly, and she was so very, very proud of him. Whatever else Chase had done, he had helped bring this about, and for that alone, she would love him forever.

Chapter 9

Chase shivered in the chill desert air, despite the heavy sweater under his leather jacket. He knew that his action had nothing to do with the temperature; he'd been cold long before he'd left the warmth of the California coast. He'd been cold since he'd left the warmth of Stevie's home. His home.

The fluorescent light of the gas-station canopy formed an odd, geometric shape, glowing eerily in the middle of the stark blackness of the night. The farther he got from it, as he walked across the scrub-covered sand, the more surreal it looked, like some oddly square spacecraft hovering over the concrete apron.

His mouth twisted grimly at his own thoughts; he recognized the efforts of a mind desperately trying to avoid the one thing that was eating away at it like acid. It hadn't worked before, and it didn't work now. Nothing could ever erase the corrosive memory of that moment when he had had to turn his back and walk away from her.

Oh, God, Stevie....

He whirled, turning his back on the eerie white glow. The stars were so clear here, the darkness so complete away from that oddly box-shaped light. The New Mexico landscape appeared to stretch on unbroken forever, with this tiny outpost, this last fragment of civilization, seemingly dropped out of the sky amid mile after mile of emptiness.

Emptiness. He closed his eyes against it, thinking that in this dark, barren, desolate nightscape he had found the very essence of what he had become, what was left of him.

How easy it would be, he thought, to just keep walking. To let the emptiness swallow him up and put an end to this hell once and for all. It was so much worse this time. So much worse, knowing the pain he'd left behind. At least there had been a finality to it before, an end for those left behind. But not this time. Stevie would never know. She would know only that he'd left her, and she would hate him for it.

And he would deserve it. His hands clenched into hard, futile fists. He'd had no right to get involved with her. Self-contempt welled up inside him, so strong it made him tremble under its force. Because he hadn't been strong enough, hadn't been able to resist the sweet temptation, she would suffer, she would pay the price.

He opened his eyes, and the black emptiness rushed at him, seeming to cast him into some fearful, diabolic, bottomless pit, sending him spinning into nothingness with a force that made him dizzy. He sank to his knees, holding his head between his hands, trying to stop the whirling.

He'd never, not even in the darkest days he remembered from after the accident, felt so desolate. The darkness around him filled up the emptiness inside him until there was no room for anything else.

After a while, the spinning stopped. The darkness stayed. He sat there, shivering with a cold beyond the physical, wondering if Stevie would know, would sense it somehow, if he took that long, one-way walk.

"Why should she care, after what you did?"

He hadn't meant to speak out loud, and the surprising way the quiet words broke the stillness startled him. But the truth of what he'd said seemed to hang there in the air long after the words had died away.

She wouldn't care. She would get over him. Someday she would find someone else. He tried not to think about it, tried to banish the thought he'd planted in his own mind. Yet he knew it would happen; he could hardly expect her to moon around over him for the rest of her life. She was too young, too attractive, too alive, to stay alone for long.

She would find someone. One of those three-piece-suits, someone safe, someone who would give her all she deserved. Someone who would slip into her life without a ripple, bringing no shadows, no ghosts. He would be the one who would wave to Mrs. Trimble in the mornings, the one to eat Leo's chicken soup. . . .

He shook his head at the sudden, unexpected sense of longing that filled him. Who would have thought that he would miss something as simple as the gentle companionship of those people, the people who had made room for a withdrawn loner in their lives?

Because of Stevie. She had brought him into their fold; they had accepted him for her sake long before they had accepted him for his own. It all came back to Stevie. Everything came back to Stevie. He shuddered. No matter who he was, that future phantom, he would never love her as much as he did. No one would. No one could.

But whether she cared or not, even if she hated him, he knew she would be with him forever. Her image was in his mind as firmly, as permanently, as was the memory of the golden days she had given him. Maybe the time would even come when he could look back on those precious days without this searing, driving pain.

The thought of how long that would take, of how long he would have been without her by then, made the empty reaches of the desert look even more inviting. Maybe he could find a nice, obliging rattlesnake. . . .

"Hey, mister, you okay?"

His slumped body jerked at the words of the young gas-station attendant. No, his battered mind screamed. Yes, he said. Or tried to. His voice caught, and he had to try again.

"Yeah. Fine."

"Well, I finished gassin' your bike. She's ready to go."

Chase didn't move, just nodded, then turned to stare back out at the bleak yet oddly enticing landscape.

The boy hunkered down beside him. "Gotta be careful out here at night. It's easy to get lost if you go too far in the dark."

Chase grimaced. "I was . . . just thinking that."

"Most people don't have sense enough to realize it. Desert's nothing to fool with. My grandpa lived here for twenty years, but he walked out one day and never came back."

"Maybe that's what he wanted."

The boy looked at him quizzically. "I've told a lot of folks that, but you're the only one ever guessed why. He did it the day after Grandma's funeral."

Chase closed his eyes. "I know just how he feels."

"Somebody die on you?"

Yeah. Me. "No. I just had to . . . leave somebody."

"Well, at least they're alive, then. That's somethin'."

"Yeah."

And she'll stay that way, as long as I stay away. I'm what put her in danger. She'll be fine now. Safe. They won't go after her.

A sudden chill, deeper, stronger even than before, swept him. They *would* leave her alone, wouldn't they?

He scrambled to his feet. What if they went after her again, before he got clear, before he was able to surface somewhere else and draw their attention? What if . . . ?

"Damn you," he swore under his breath.

He whirled and headed back to the eerie square of light. He swore again, fiercely, sharply, as he grabbed the helmet and strapped it on. You should have thought of that, he berated himself. If you hadn't let your heart run your head, you would have. But no, you were too busy feeling sorry for yourself, too busy thinking of how much you were hurting. You were too busy running to save yourself to worry about what might happen to her if you did. You already broke her heart. Now you've risked her life. Again. And left her alone to face a situation she couldn't even begin to imagine.

He straddled the bike, tugging a wrinkled twenty-dollar bill out of his pocket and tossing it at the young attendant in the white shirt.

"I'll get your change," the boy said, looking a little bewildered by the bizarre actions of his customer.

"Keep it," Chase shouted over the roar of the engine as he fired up the bike.

The boy stood there, gaping at what had turned out to be a twelve-dollar tip, then lifted his head as the big motorcycle and its black-clad rider with the odd, haunted green eyes raced back in the direction they had come from.

"They were right. You look ghastly."

Stevie looked up at the words, a smile crossing her face as she saw Beth Walker in her doorway.

"You're back!" she said unnecessarily, taking in the woman's businesslike suit. "And back in shape, at that," she added; that suit hadn't seen the light of day since the fourth month of Beth's pregnancy.

"I'm not here to talk about *my* shape, Stevie."

Stevie got up and walked around her desk to give her friend and mentor a hug, hoping to forestall what she feared was coming.

"So, how's the new addition? Did you bring pictures? Is Sam popping his buttons about having a son?"

Beth eyed her dryly. "He's three months old, gaining weight like a pig, and Sam is beside himself. All of which you know. The grapevine around here is still intact. Now," she said in her best executive tones, "what is with you? I've heard nothing since I've been back except that the Stevie Holt that was here when I left doesn't exist anymore."

Stevie backed up to lean against her drawing table. "Has there been a problem with my work?" she asked carefully.

"You know better than that. It's been flawless, as usual. Thank you, by the way, for bailing me out on the Banes Development account. I don't know what possessed me to clutter it up with all that jungle life."

Stevie didn't think her expression changed; Lord knew she'd had enough practice by now at keeping it even. But

Beth knew her rather well. The older woman stepped forward and took her hands.

"What is it, Stevie? Your brother still?"

"No. He's fine. Really making progress." She raised her eyes to Beth's concerned brown ones. "I'd rather not talk about it. Please."

Beth hesitated. "All right," she finally said. "As long as you know that if you change your mind, I'm here." She let go of Stevie's hands. "Perhaps this will cheer you up. Call it an early Christmas present."

"Very early," Stevie said with a laugh that didn't sound as cheerful as it should have. "It's not even December!" She reached for the letter Beth was holding out to her.

"It has to be early," Beth said airily. "You'll need time to go buy a fabulous dress."

"A dress? What for? I don't—" She stopped, her jaw sagging as she scanned the sheet of paper she held. She raised stunned eyes to Beth, who was grinning widely. "I...I won?"

"I made them wait, so I could give it to you. I wanted to see your face." Beth laughed. "It was worth it. I know you've never known just how good you are. Now you do." She turned to go, then looked back over her shoulder. "Make it an outrageous dress, Stevie. You can afford it now. Even old tightwad Dunn agrees this is worth a darn good raise."

Stevie tried hard to maintain a cheerful front when she arrived home to find Sean waiting for her. He was in a sour mood, grumbling something about having had lunch with some of his former teammates, none of whom knew quite how to act around him. And, he admitted gruffly, he had felt very left out of their football talk.

"I'm trying," he muttered, "but damn it, it hurts!"

When she told him her news, he buried his peevish disposition with an effort and congratulated her. Stevie smiled; he might have a distance to go before he completely accepted his fate, but the Sean of a few months ago would never have been able to do what he had just done. The Sean who hadn't yet run into Chase Sullivan. She smothered a sigh.

Sean studied her for a moment. "It's Chase, isn't it?"

"Oh, Sean," she said, "I'm beginning to think I'm a nut case or something. Why can't I get him out of my head?"

"You love him," Sean said simply. "And knowing that he loved you, too, that he didn't want to go, makes it worse."

"But it's been so long—"

"You don't put a timetable on things like that, Sis."

Stevie shook her head, looking at the letter she'd shown him. "All I can think of is the day I found out about the nomination. I felt so alone, because you were so far away, and so was Chase. Then he came back, and he took me out to celebrate. He said when I won we'd really paint the town. I was so happy. I remember thinking I'd won something much more important than that nomination. He wasn't afraid anymore...."

"And now you've won the prize, and he's gone again," Sean said softly, hugging her again. "I'm sorry, Stevie. For both of you. I know he'd do anything to be with you. Except put you at risk."

"But I'm not!"

"He thinks you are. And maybe he knows."

She broke down crying then, although she'd sworn she was through with tears. Sean held her, and when at last she regained control, he lifted her chin with a gentle finger.

"I know I'm only your little brother, but I'd be honored if you'd let me take you out tonight. Please?"

Stevie found it hard to resist when she knew what an effort Sean was making to set aside his own troubles for her sake. She smiled through the last of her tears and nodded.

"Scoot, then, and take a shower. You'll feel better."

When she came out, wrapped in her thick velour robe, Sean was standing in her bedroom, staring at the wall across from the bed. She had hung the picture of the house there, in the same spot it had occupied in Chase's apartment.

"Don't think I'm...masochistic or anything," she said softly. "It just helps to have it there."

"I wasn't thinking that," Sean said. "I was just wondering something." He glanced at her. "This was so special to him..." He smiled when she raised an eyebrow. "It had to be. He left it for you. But what I was wondering...it looks like an original, an architect's rendering. They usually have the name of the firm on the bottom, don't they?"

Stevie nodded, not sure what he was getting at.

"If this does, they might know something. I mean, if it was done for him, they must have some record of the work."

Stevie stared at him. "I never thought of that."

"It might not help you find him now, but maybe... I know you've never stopped wondering why..."

Without a word, she reached for the drawing. Sean caught her wrist. "Are you sure? It might be a dead end, and even if it's not, do you want to dig it all up again?"

"It's never been buried," she said briefly, then lifted the frame from the wall.

Sean had been right. Folded out of sight beneath the frame, wrinkled but still readable, were the names of the firm and the architect. "Forsythe and Ralston—Seattle," it said. "John Cameron, Architect." The firm's name was printed on the paper much like a letterhead; the architect's name was hand lettered in the clean, elegant sweep of calligraphy. But the line labeled Designed For was blank.

"Not much," Sean said.

"But more than I had," Stevie said. She replaced the drawing in the frame with tender care, then walked to the phone. Sean hung the drawing back up, then followed her. She was standing with her hand still on the receiver, a piece of paper with a number written on it in her hand.

"They're still there. Information still has a number, anyway," she amended.

"Stevie..." Sean began, starting to wish he'd never brought up the subject.

"I have to, Sean. I have to try. So I can understand. If I can understand, maybe I can...go on."

It was all Stevie could do to wait until the next morning. She was at her office at seven, pacing, staring at the design on her glowing computer screen without really seeing it. She made herself wait until eight, then dialed the number.

She hadn't expected a dead end quite so soon; the polite voice on the other end told her that Mr. Cameron was no longer there. Could someone else help her?

"I don't know," Stevie said tiredly. "I . . . came across a piece of his work that I was very interested in. I wanted to talk to him about it."

"A piece of his work?" The woman sounded puzzled.

"Yes. A house."

"It must not be very recent, then."

"I don't know. It's—why do you say that?"

The woman coughed, then said awkwardly, "I'm sorry. It's just that . . . Mr. Cameron was killed almost two years ago. And he did only commercial work for quite some time before that."

"Oh." Stevie didn't know what to say. Her last hope had just gone up in smoke.

"It's such a shame. I never knew him, but everyone here says he was brilliant."

"He was," Stevie said quietly, an image of that soaring, beautiful house in her mind. She took a breath. "Is there any way of finding out who he might have done this work for?"

"Perhaps. Is there a project number on the rendering?"

"No. There was just his name, and the name of the firm."

"No client name?"

"No. But it might—" she had to pause for a second before she could say it "—it might have been Chase Sullivan."

"Let me check. Hold on a moment."

Stevie heard the click of the line being put on hold, then a spurt of cheerful music that only irritated her.

After a few moments the woman came back. "No, I'm afraid there's nothing under that name. However, Mr. Forsythe did say that Mr. Cameron often did private work, for friends. Perhaps that's the answer."

"I . . . Maybe."

Stevie puzzled over the problem for a while, and at lunchtime headed for the library. The reference librarian pointed her toward the shelf of phone books, and she quickly found the one for Seattle.

It was a long list, especially when she included the Camerons in the outlying areas of the big city. Back in the office, uncomfortably aware that she was using Walker and Dunn's time and phones, she began to make her calls. She would square it with Beth later, she told herself.

She'd found three John Camerons, none the right one. And a Charles and a David who had sons named John, again, not the right one. She sighed. She was frustrated already, and she was only up to George. By the time I get to William, she thought glumly, I'll be a basket case.

She never got to William. On the second George, she hit pay dirt. At the first mention of John Cameron's name, the woman on the other end went cold and distant.

"My son is dead. I do not discuss him with anyone, Miss Holt, so you can tell your editor to forget it."

The abrupt disconnect sound came before Stevie could even get a word of explanation in. Editor? What did the woman mean?

She carried around the idea that came then for a few hours before she went in to see Beth.

"I need a couple of days off. Tomorrow. And Friday."

Beth raised an eyebrow at her tone, but nodded. "All right." She glanced at her watch. "It's nearly four. Why don't you go now?"

"Thank you." She turned to go.

"Stevie?" She looked back. "Is this going to...help?"

"One way or another."

Stevie tried to ignore the chill of November in Seattle as she walked up the long driveway. The house was big and formal looking, standing out starkly white against the deep greenery surrounding it. There was no sign of life save for the curl of smoke issuing from one of the three chimneys that were visible. Taking a long, deep breath to steady herself, she knocked on the door.

The petite woman with the kindly face didn't look like someone with the potential for the kind of anger she'd heard on the phone. "Mrs. Cameron?" Stevie asked doubtfully.

"Yes. May I help you?"

It was the same voice. Not daring to take the chance of mentioning John Cameron and getting the same reaction, including, no doubt, the door slammed in her face in place of the phone receiver, Stevie spoke hastily.

"I wanted to talk to you about Chase Sullivan." She watched the woman carefully for any reaction. There was none.

"I'm sorry, I'm afraid I don't know the name."

"I thought...I hoped he was a friend of your son John."

Pain, still fresh, appeared in the woman's eyes. But no anger, at least not yet. "My son is dead."

"I know," Stevie said gently, "and I'm so terribly sorry. I've...seen one of his designs. He was very, very good."

"He was the best." The woman suddenly looked at her sharply. "You sound— Why, you're that Holt woman who called from California, aren't you?"

"Yes. But I don't work for a newspaper or anything like that. This is strictly...personal. And only about your son indirectly. Please, may I speak to you?"

"I told you on the phone. I don't talk about my son. I don't talk about either of my sons. They were mine, and they're dead." The pain was there again, stronger, harsher. "And I don't know the person you mentioned. Good day."

The echo of the slamming door seemed even louder in the cold air. Stevie stood there, fighting her roiling emotions. What now? She shivered again. They didn't know Chase. No one knew Chase. He didn't exist anymore. End of search. She had to get that through her head.

Feeling battered, she turned to walk back to her car. She was about to get in when a sound made her lift her head.

"Miss Holt?"

She whirled to see a tall, leggy figure wrapped in a red parka, the fur-trimmed hood pulled so tightly around the face that it was impossible to see any features. The figure made a gesture for her to follow, and without really thinking, she did so, back around the garage to a small grove of trees.

The red-jacketed figure headed straight for a small building which, as they got closer, Stevie realized was a child's playhouse. More like a fort, actually, with a rough wood exterior and what appeared to be a lookout tower. She ducked inside in the wake of her mysterious guide.

"There's a light, but if I turn it on, Mom'll be out here like a shot. This place is like a shrine to her."

"A shrine?"

"Yeah. It was the first thing Johnny ever designed. He was twelve, and he knew exactly what he wanted. Drove Dad crazy." It was a young feminine voice, but it was so dark in the tiny, shuttered room that Stevie couldn't see anything other than a vague outline.

"You're ... ?"

"Cassie Cameron. Johnny was my brother." The same pain as in her mother's voice, but more acceptance. "I heard you, from on the stairs. Are you really from California?"

"Yes. San Diego."

"I'd love to go there. I've got to get away before I smother. I want to be a model, but I'll never make it here."

Stevie tried to keep a grip on her nerves, wondering what all this was about. "I ... There must be agencies here."

"Yeah. But my folks won't even talk about it. They want me to stay right here and go to school."

"I suppose most parents would feel that way. Modeling is very ... chancy."

She could almost feel the girl staring at her. "Are you a model? You're pretty enough."

"No." Stevie laughed, a little faintly. "But I work with them a lot. And don't kid yourself, it's work. Hard work."

"I know that. I've tried to tell Mom, but she just won't listen. They want me here." The "under their thumb" rang as clearly in the little room as if she'd said the words.

"Well, if you ever do get to California, I know a couple of people. Maybe I could get you an interview, at least." Now why did you say that, Holt? You haven't even seen this girl.

"Would you?" Cassie exclaimed.

"I can't promise anything. And nothing might come of it, anyway," she warned.

"I don't care. I have to try. Even if I don't make it, I have to try," the girl said vehemently.

"Is that what you wanted to talk to me about, Cassie?"

"Partly." She paused. "You came all this way just to talk to my mother. I'm sorry she was rude. She's..."

"She's lost two sons," Stevie said, remembering what the woman had said. "She has the right."

"Yeah, I guess so. But we all miss him. Johnny, I mean. I don't remember Jason at all. He was killed when I was only a year old. But Johnny... Johnny was special." Stevie heard a small sigh. "It's been tough."

"Especially on you?" Stevie guessed.

"Yeah. How'd you know that?"

"You're all they have left. It's only natural that they want to cling to you. And with that on top of your own grief, it must have been tough," Stevie said sympathetically.

"You understand," Cassie said, astonished. "Why?"

"My brother was badly hurt a couple of years ago. My parents went a little nuts, too." Stevie wasn't quite sure why she was saying this, only that something about this girl drew her.

As if she'd come abruptly to a decision, Cassie went on. "Why did you think this guy was a friend of my brother's?"

"He... had one of his drawings. Of a house."

"One of John's?" She sounded surprised. "He hadn't done houses for a while."

"So I've heard. But this one is... special. On a cliff, overlooking the ocean—"

"My God! You've got it?"

Startled, Stevie strained to see her. "Yes, I—"

"We've been wondering forever where it went to. It was the only thing they didn't send us after he was murdered."

Stevie's throat went dry. "Murdered?"

She could tell the girl was staring at her.

"You really don't know, do you?"

Stevie shook her head before she realized that the girl couldn't see any better than she could. "No wonder your mother is bitter," she said, shaken. The man who created that beautiful house, murdered? It seemed too horrid to contemplate.

"Yeah," said the girl. "She'll never forgive anyone. My dad for not talking him out of it, the district attorney for talking him into it and most of all, the government for not protecting him like they said."

Stevie struggled to make sense of it. "What happened?"

She heard a soft little sigh. "He was working on a house for some bigwig from San Francisco. Johnny always liked to oversee things personally. Anyway, it turned out the guy was like a racketeer or something, and the FBI and IRS had been after him for a long time. Then some investigator they'd had on him turned up missing." There was a long, silent moment. "Johnny saw them bury him. At the house."

Stevie sucked in her breath. "And he testified?"

She heard a bitter laugh. "Yes. They promised him protection, especially after Granger's men tried for him twice before the trial. Afterward, when the papers were blasting all over that it was Johnny's testimony that won the case, they heard Granger had a contract out on him. So they put him in that 'protected witness' program."

Stevie heard a harsh, short sound and didn't have to ask what had happened. "Cassie—"

"That Frazier guy, from the FBI here, he promised Johnny would be all right. But within six months he was dead. They sent us his ashes. We didn't even get to say goodbye."

"Cassie, I'm sorry." She heard the rustle of nylon and guessed the girl had shrugged.

"It's over now. Only Mom won't let it be." Her voice changed, the sound of suspicion biting deep. "But how did you get that drawing? It was the house he wanted to build for himself someday. He'd been working on it, on and off, ever since he decided he wanted to be an architect."

"A... friend gave it to me. It was very special to him, too."

"But I know Johnny would never have given that to anyone. He wouldn't even let Mom hang it in the house. Said it was too private, too personal."

"I don't know how he got it—"

"This Chase guy? Damn it, I can't see you. I can't tell if you're lying if I can't see you!"

There was a sudden movement, then a flare of light. Stevie shut her eyes instinctively.

"There. Now, tell me about this guy. I want to know how he got that drawing."

Stevie opened her mouth to answer, and at the same time she opened her eyes. The words she meant to say vanished, replaced by a stunned gasp. She swayed on her feet, and her face went starkly white as she moaned.

"My God."

It was like looking at Chase. They were softened by youth and femininity, but the thick, dark hair, the vivid green eyes, the determined jaw, were all there.

"Oh, God," she moaned again.

"Are you gonna faint or something? You look awfully pale."

Desperately, Stevie tried to slow the hammering of her heart, the spinning of the world around her. "Cassie... how was your... brother killed?"

The girl backed up a step, eying her warily.

"Please, Cassie!"

"He was hit by a car. Hit-and-run. He never had a chance. It was Granger, or his thugs, but we couldn't prove it. They found the car later. It had been stolen in Oregon."

"Out-of-state. Big. Old. Dark." Stevie parroted the long-ago heard words without even realizing she spoke them aloud.

"Yeah. How did you know?"

"Do you... look like your brother?"

"Well, yeah, I guess. Everybody says so, but—"

Stevie backed toward the door. She had to get out of here, out of this room, away from this eerie reminder. She had to sort this out....

She whirled and left the small building at a run, the cold making her ankles ache as she went. She was aware of Cassie staring after her, but she didn't dare look at the girl again; seeing this feminine version of Chase had shaken her to the core.

She felt as if her mind had short-circuited. As if it had been overloaded by such a surge of shock that it had shut down under the strain. She drove with intense concentration, consciously making the decisions that were normally automatic. Brake, turn signal, look both ways... each formed in her brain with careful intent, desperately, as if by filling her mind with these routine commands she could stave off the chaos that threatened to overwhelm it.

She came back to herself with a little start, looking around with a touch of dread. She had no idea where she was, only that she had left the outskirts of the city and was much closer to downtown. She checked the next two street signs she passed, then pulled over and stopped. With hands that were trembling slightly, she reached for the map the car rental agency had given her.

Boeing Field, she thought. I passed that, didn't I? And the Kingdome. And I know I saw a sign for Pioneer Square somewhere.... She found it then, pinpointing her location. She looked up, glancing around until she spotted a phone booth. It took her only a moment to find what she was looking for in the directory.

She found the Federal Building easily, barely sparing a glance for the incredibly blue water of Puget Sound to the west, and took the elevator to the seventh floor. She was prepared for battle; she didn't know the protocol for getting in to see an FBI agent, but she wasn't about to let anything stop her now. But the mention of the name ''Cameron'' seemed to smooth the way miraculously, and she was quickly ushered down a long hallway.

Charles Frazier was younger than she had expected. With his golden blond hair, ears that protruded slightly and soft, brown eyes, he reminded her of a cocker spaniel that had belonged to one of her childhood friends. She took the chair he indicated.

"When they said a Stevie Holt was here about the Cameron case, you weren't what I expected."

"May we skip the niceties, please?" Stevie said tightly. "I'd like a simple explanation of what's going on."

"Going on?" Frazier asked blandly. "Why, nothing. It's over and done with. It's a very old case, Miss Holt."

Stevie sighed. "Will you please just tell me?"

"Why?"

Stevie floundered, searching for words to make him understand, to make him tell her what she had to know. "I . . . I've lost someone very important to me. He's . . . connected somehow to this. If it's an old case, it can't matter now, can it?"

After a moment in which Stevie felt she had been thoroughly inspected and sized up, he seemed to come to a decision. "We'd been trying for years to put Granger away. But somehow the maggot always slipped through the net. Witnesses disappeared, or he got off on technicalities. It would have been the same all over again, except for John Cameron."

He picked up a pencil and toyed with it, but his eyes never left her. "My partner was trying to find evidence to make something stick. Granger murdered him. John saw them bury him. Luckily he had the brains to realize what he'd stumbled onto, and he got out of there before they found him."

He dropped the pencil. "He stuck it out, even after they tried to get to him twice before the trial even started." He grimaced. "They called Granger 'The Spider' in the newspaper stories. It fit him. His web stretched everywhere."

Frazier drew a long breath. "John knew it wouldn't stop, but he wouldn't quit. I will never forgive myself for letting them get to him, letting them mow him down in the street."

A flashing image of a harsh, twisting scar on a lean, hard body went through her mind. Stevie's hands clenched.

"Mr. Frazier—"

"It's over, Miss Holt." Something gentle shone in the brown eyes for a moment. "Believe me, the best thing you can do is let it rest. John is dead. And now Granger is, too. There's nothing—''

"What?" The blood had drained from Stevie's face.

"I said there's nothing to be gained. Even Granger's wife is dead. And his son left the state a few months ago."

"Granger," Stevie whispered, stunned. "He's dead?"

The brown eyes narrowed again. "Yes. Colon cancer, fittingly enough. It's what he was. But he's dead, and his organization with him. They're all in jail, or dead themselves."

She stared at him. "You mean," she said slowly, speaking as if each word was a blow delivered to her heart, "that there's no danger anymore?"

Frazier sat back in his chair, staring at her intently. "Danger, Miss Holt? To whom?"

Another image shimmered in her memory, an image of a pair of tortured green eyes, and suddenly Stevie's tenuous hold on her emotions gave way and her temper flared.

"Please drop the facade, Mr. Frazier."

"What?" He looked startled.

"Why have you let this go on, knowing Granger was dead?"

"I . . . don't understand."

"Correct me if I'm wrong, Mr. Frazier, but in your so-called *protected*—" she put heavy, sardonic emphasis on the word "—witness program, you do have ways of contacting the people you are supposedly protecting?"

"Of course—"

"Then I repeat," Stevie cut in, "why have you let this go on?"

"Ms. Holt, I'm afraid I don't understand."

"Stop it!" Stevie leapt to her feet, nerves already strung taut finally snapping. "Drop this silly game! It may be what you're used to, all this secrecy nonsense, but it's about time you stopped and thought about what you've done!"

Frazier stared at her. Admiration flared briefly in his eyes, followed by a moment of frank, male appreciation. His gaze rested for a moment on the bright red-gold of her hair, then flicked to the door, as if he were worried about someone overhearing her angry outburst.

"Uh, Ms. Holt—"

"And don't patronize me! I want a simple answer! You've let him go through hell all this time—for no reason!"

"Him? Who?"

Stevie fixed him with a seething glare. "You know exactly who I mean. Perhaps you *are* as stupid as you seem, but if not, I would appreciate it if you would not insult *my* intelligence by pretending to be."

"Ms. Holt," Frazier said evenly, "if you are referring to John Cameron, as I told you, he died two years ago."

The cocker spaniel had disappeared. The soft brown eyes had hardened; the relaxed body had tightened with tense awareness. This was what she had expected—the alert, intent agent, the trained professional. For some reason that fanned her anger; it meant the man had simply failed at his job.

"Mr. Frazier," she said icily, "as *you* must know, I would hardly have come here if I didn't know better."

Frazier leaned back in his chair, studying her, and another oddly canine image rose in Stevie's mind. Only this time it was of a hunting dog on an intriguing scent.

"I think you'd better explain exactly what you mean."

The sudden note of command in his voice was unmistakable, but Stevie's blood was up, and she refused to be intimidated.

"The only person who has any explaining to do is you. And I'm getting very tired of this game."

Admiration flickered in his eyes once more. "All right. Let me tell you a story. A hypothetical one, of course."

"Of course," Stevie said sourly.

"Suppose there was a man who had gotten on the wrong side of a very ugly, very powerful person. A man who could put that ugly, powerful person in a very nasty place for a very long time. And suppose, at great risk to himself, he used the power he held over that evil man for the good of a great many people. Knowing what might happen."

"But depending on the people he was helping to help him?" she asked bitterly.

"Yes." The word was flat, with no attempt at denial; Stevie had to give him credit for that. "And suppose, despite all the right procedures to insure this brave man's safety, a fluke, a one-in-a-million chance, makes it all for nothing. The ugly man finds him and turns loose his jackals."

"A fluke?"

"Yes. One wrong person in the wrong place, one person who recognized him and was willing to sell him to that ugly man, who even in prison had the power to strike."

"And nearly succeeded."

"Very nearly. For several days, we thought he had. It was touch and go. But instead, another innocent soul paid the price for our mistake."

"Another?"

"A fifteen-year-old boy. He never even made it to the hospital. And you can imagine what something like that would do to someone like our hypothetical hero." There wasn't a trace of mockery in his tone; he used the somewhat melodramatic title of hero with flat seriousness.

Stevie warmed toward him slightly. "Yes," she said quietly, "I can."

"I will never forget having to tell him about that boy." For now, at least, Frazier dropped the pretense of speaking hypothetically. "I think he made the decision right then. He was in horrible shape, weak, but he wouldn't budge."

He caught himself and went back to that brisk tone. "Now, under those circumstances, this hero might reach the conclusion that it would be better, especially for his family, a family that could be used as leverage, if he died."

She winced. "So, for all intents and purposes, he did."

"Theoretically," Frazier said smoothly. "And a certain federal agent, feeling, perhaps, tremendously guilty about what had happened, might make arrangements to help him with that plan. Such as releasing the news that the attempt on his life had been, regrettably, successful."

Stevie's eyes never left the man's face, and he shifted in his chair as he went on.

"And, after watching him go through three months of hell in a hospital, that agent might arrange for a private clinic and the necessary therapy to get him back on his feet." He met her gaze. "All in an effort to make up for his own failure, of course, so that he could sleep at night."

The warmth Stevie had felt evaporated suddenly. "I might be touched by that," she said fiercely, "if I wasn't wondering how that agent could sleep at night now, knowing that the man he professes to be so concerned about is still living in hell—for no reason."

"Ms. Holt—"

Fury rose in her again, and she made no effort to hide it. "Why haven't you told him? My God, he's been safe for months, and he doesn't know! How can you let him go on thinking he's in danger, that it could happen again at any second?"

"It's simple, Stevie," he said softly, using her first name intentionally. "I don't know where he is."

"You . . . what?" She gasped.

"I don't know where he is," he repeated, then leaned forward to gaze at her intently. "But you obviously do."

Stunned, Stevie shook her head. "No. I don't. Not anymore."

"But you did. When?"

"I . . . Three months ago." Her anger faded into confusion. "I don't understand. Didn't you stay in communication . . . ?"

"Normally, yes, we do. And I saw no reason to expect anything different this time. What I didn't count on was that . . . our hypothetical hero had different ideas. And he was stubborn enough, smart enough and tough enough to pull them off."

He smiled ruefully. "He disappeared. He set us all up like clay pigeons and walked away. We never had a clue. I tried every channel, and I've got access to more than a few. Nothing. It was as if he really had died."

"You sound . . . impressed."

"I was," he admitted. "And embarrassed, when I realized that he'd done a better job of it than I had. That was when I gave up trying to find him. I tried again when Granger died, but nothing. I even ran ads in every paper in the Northwest, trying to at least let him know...."

Stevie met his eyes levelly. "I'm sorry. I said some uncalled for things."

"You didn't know. From your standpoint, you were right." His eyes narrowed. "Now, if you don't mind, just what is your standpoint?"

He'd earned it, she supposed. So she told him. She didn't tell him of the intimacy of their relationship, but she had a feeling he guessed. When she had finished, he was looking at her with a warmth that surprised her.

"He was...engaged when all this happened. She was excited at first, with all the attention, the publicity, but she dropped him like a hot rock when she realized the trouble was real." He nodded reflectively as he looked at her. "He was long overdue for some luck, but I'd say he got about even when you came along."

"Thank you," she acknowledged. "But it doesn't help much now, does it?"

He sighed. "I could try calling the San Diego office."

"But you don't think it would do any good."

"No. He's gotten too damn good at this."

"He thought he had to." She got to her feet. "Thank you. I'm sorry I was rude."

He rose, too. "Forget it. I hope..." He let out a breath, realizing the unlikelihood of what he'd been about to say. "If you *do* find him again, would you let me know? We...became friends. I'd like to know he's all right."

"Hypothetically, of course," she said, not at all sarcastically.

He winced, then caught her tone and smiled. "Of course."

She took his extended hand. "Thank you for...what you tried to do."

It all made sense now. Horrible, agonizing sense, she thought as she lay sleepless in the hotel bed that night. A hundred little things came whirling back, beating at her weary brain like tiny, flapping wings. His words to Sean that night in the hospital, about looking over your shoulder. Not having a phone, and therefore no listing of a name anywhere. And the realization that came to her only now that at no time had she ever seen him buy anything except with cash. Groceries, dinner at a restaurant, even gasoline, all paid for in cash. Even the rent, she thought, remembering that Mr. Henry had said he had paid the rent in cash, as usual. Then she had just thought it a personal oddity, an unusual habit perhaps, in this day of credit cards and checkbooks, but nothing more.

All those symbols of his withdrawal from the world, from people, from anyone who might get too close, might discover his secret. That haunted look, the result of too many terrible memories, the look of a man who had done what he felt he had to, but at horrible cost. To himself and to his family, who had already suffered the loss of one son. The Jason Chase had loved, and Cassie barely remembered, dead in some Asian jungle... and on the twelfth panel of names on the Vietnam memorial.

That day came back to her with painful clarity. "We both did what we thought was right," he'd said. "It got him killed, and me—" She shuddered. She knew now what it had done to him.

Her heart ached for him, twisting inside her like some mortally wounded creature. She ached for his pain, the agonizing physical pain of his battered body, clinging to life after being mowed down by two tons of speeding metal. She ached for the emotional pain of leaving the family he had loved, and who had so clearly loved him, a leaving made all the harder because it had been his own decision, the ultimate self-sacrifice made for their safety.

But the final, finishing blow that destroyed her fragile control was the harrowing knowledge that he was hopelessly adrift in a fiendish hell that wasn't of his own making, and she had no way to rescue him, no way to tell him that it was over, he was safe, that he could come out of the dark forever. And as dark as this night was for her, she knew it was nothing compared to the shadows that engulfed him.

For the first time in her life, Stevie understood why more suicides were reported in the days before Christmas. Enduring the holiday cheer of others when your own life was a grim struggle to get from one day to the next was a torture she had never imagined possible.

Her efforts to find Chase—she couldn't think of him as John Cameron—had yielded the result she'd expected: nothing. Just a dark, yawning cavern of nothingness into which he had disappeared. Thinking of the ads Chuck had run, announcing the death of "The Spider," she placed similar ads in every paper she could think of, including a construction workers' newsletter. The staff there had been very sympathetic, even making room for the ad in the issue that had been about to go to press, but it had been as fruitless as the rest. Still, she kept the ads running, hoping against hope that somewhere, somehow, he might see them.

She had even dug out the card given to her by Dave Barton, the sheriff's deputy who had helped her the night of the accident. He'd listened to her story, with particular interest in the similarity between her own accident and the one that had nearly killed Chase.

"What a mess," he said and gave a low whistle.

"Yes. I know this isn't your job—"

"No problem. What can I do?"

"I was hoping you could give me some advice. Or tell me what, if anything, the police can do."

"Well, we could put out his description, countrywide—hell, even statewide. Maybe somebody might come across him. I mean, he's got to go out, even if it's only to get food, so there's always a chance."

Stevie knew he was trying to sound optimistic; she'd heard that tone from Sean enough lately. "I realize the odds against it are very high, but I have to try."

After that Stevie had slipped back into a plodding lethargy, into a vicious cycle of weariness and sleeplessness that seemed never ending. She threw whatever small amount of energy she had into her work, leaving nothing for her life outside the office; if she'd been asked, she would have said she had no life outside the office.

On the Saturday night of the awards ceremony, Stevie studied her reflection in the mirror, dreading the evening to come. She was already irritated by having had to once more drive all the way around the block to get into the carports because of the black coupe that was half blocking the entrance as usual; the thought of the evening before her did nothing to ease that irritation.

Beth had had to literally drag her out of the office to go shopping for the "fabulous dress" she had insisted Stevie needed, and eventually, in the face of Stevie's lack of enthusiasm, she had picked it out for her.

It was a strapless wrap dress in a bold black-and-white print, bordered with a wide black band that emphasized the graceful curves of the overlapping hemline and the matching curves of the bustier bodice. It was short enough to bare an amount of leg, and the big, matching fabric bow at her left hip emphasized her slender waist. It made her hair gleam warmly and her golden skin glow.

It was a sexy, sassy dress, and Stevie hoped it would at least give the impression that she was happy to be there. She had had to get it in a size smaller than usual. Misery was a great diet aid, she thought grimly, but she wouldn't recommend it to anyone.

Beth had also selected the pair of long, delicate, filigree silver earrings, and Stevie had agreed they were all the jewelry that was necessary. She would wear simple black heels, she decided, and leave it at that. The dress was striking enough; anything more would detract from it. Not that it mattered, she thought bitterly. Without Chase, she found it hard to care.

Although she knew Sean, looking elegant in his tux, was waiting for her in her living room, she took a moment to sit on her bed and look at the picture that had led to her discovery of Chase's story.

She wished with all her heart that he could keep the promise he'd made to her that night in La Jolla. She wondered if the pain would ever ease, if her battered heart would ever heal, or if she would spend the rest of her life searching, haunted by the knowledge of the nightmare he was living.

''I love you,'' she whispered to the picture, swept by a longing so strong it made her ache. And then by a horrid bleakness that what they'd had was now reduced to a half-formed hope that, wherever he was, he knew that she loved him.

She tried to pay attention to the ceremony, but she had a feeling she remembered more about her junior high graduation than she would remember about this. She was one of five winners, all of whom sat at the front tables reserved for their respective companies; her parents and Sean were one row back. Even her mother had seemed impressed with the glittering ceremony, if not by her daughter's accomplishment.

Stevie didn't remember what she'd said when they handed her the award, but since no one seemed to be laughing or staring at her, it must have made some kind of sense. She walked across the podium and joined the other winners. She looked across the hotel's big banquet room, full of her colleagues and family, and empty of the one person she really wanted to see. She tore her mind out of that old familiar rut.

It was a lovely award, she thought. Set on a broad, golden base, a large piece of heavy crystal, a free-form, flowing sculpture caught the light and sent it skittering in all directions. She stared at the award idly, wondering what on earth she was going to do with herself next week when the office was closed for the holidays. She had always been grateful for Beth's policy of closing for an entire week, but this year she was dreading it.

She looked up and shook hands with the last of the winners as he joined them, and her eyes automatically followed him as he walked to the end of the row of recipients. Then her gaze kept going, and as the final round of applause echoed throughout the big room, she froze, her heart suddenly racing in her chest.

She had to be mistaken, she told herself desperately; it was wishful thinking. Yet didn't she know that profile better than she knew her own face? But she had only gotten a quick glimpse and in the shadowed light of the backstage area at that. It couldn't be. Then the nearly hidden figure moved with the hard-won ease and grace she remembered so well, and she knew that it could be.

Chapter 10

She nearly knocked over the little man who had won the last award as she rushed toward the steps. She saw Sean, with her parents a few feet behind. She jumped the last two steps despite her high heels and grabbed her brother's arm.

"He's here! Backstage!"

Sean, bless him, didn't doubt her for a second. "You go that way—" he jerked his head toward the stage door "—I'll go around to the hallway door. He'll probably try for a side exit." He turned and started off, the slight roll in his gait as he hurried barely noticeable.

She knew her parents were staring at her in puzzlement, but she didn't dare take time for even the briefest word. She darted through the milling people and pulled open the door that led to a small supply and lighting control room behind the raised podium.

The outer door was closing as she came in, plunging the room into blackness. She fumbled next to the door for a light switch, having seen the chaos of equipment scattered around the floor. Precious seconds tripped by as her frantic fingers searched; then at last the room was flooded with light. She dodged the clutter as she ran to the door, praying that Sean would be able to head him off in time.

The minute she was in the hallway, she knew she'd been right. He'd kept his promise; she would recognize that tall, lean, graceful body anywhere. She also knew she didn't have a chance of catching up with his retreating figure. She couldn't call out to him; he obviously wouldn't come back. Not to her, not thinking what he thought. Desperately she looked for Sean, but he was nowhere to be seen.

In her search, her eyes fell on a pay phone flanked by a white house phone, and an idea flashed through her mind. With one eye on the figure that was much too rapidly nearing the side exit that would take him out of her life forever, she picked up the white receiver.

They were as quick as she had asked them to be. The page for John Cameron to call the hotel operator echoed through the hall, and Stevie saw the dark-clad figure that was now at the door go rigid. He half turned, his head cocked toward the ceiling speaker in shock. And in that moment Stevie saw the beautiful sight of Sean slipping through the door from the outside. He stood silently just inside the door, a bare three feet behind Chase, with his eyes on his sister.

Chase, too, saw Stevie now, striding down the hall in that extraordinary dress like some mythic huntress, the piece of crystal glittering in her hand like a mysterious, magic weapon. She saw him shudder, saw the incredible strain in his face, saw him grow paler with her every step. When she was only ten feet away he finally broke, backing up with violent haste, as if confronted by a dream that had haunted him forever.

"You could probably knock me down and walk over me," Sean said, his soft, intent words carrying to Stevie easily, "but I promise you, that's what you'll have to do."

Chase whirled, his face going from pale to chalk white when he saw his way blocked and realized that Sean meant exactly what he'd said. His shoulders slumped in sudden, total defeat, as if he'd fought to the limit of his endurance and beyond. With a slow, weary movement, he turned back to look at Stevie.

She wanted to touch him, to hug him, to bring him so close that he could never leave her again, but she made herself stop a foot away. She knew she should tell him now, but her throat was so tight at the sight of him that she doubted if she could have spoken if her life depended on it. No, she *knew* it, because her life *did* depend on it, and she couldn't say a word.

He looked ghastly. He'd gone from muscular leanness to gauntness; his cheeks were hollow, his eyes shadowed and exhausted. His hair was a little shorter, although it still brushed the back of his neck, and it looked shaggier, as if he'd cut it himself. Little tremors rippled through him, and his arm trembled when, after a tense, silent moment, he lifted it to touch the piece of crystal in her hand.

"I... had to... see you get it," he whispered brokenly.

She found her voice then, although it was hoarse and tight with emotion. "I think I hoped you would."

He glanced at Sean, then back at her. "Stevie, please... I have to get out of here."

"No, you—"

"You don't understand," he said desperately, backing up, but coming up against Sean once more.

"But I do." Her voice was stronger now. "All of it. It's over, Chase."

He shook his head, and Stevie thought that men on the rack had probably looked less tortured. She had to make him understand.

"Stevie," Sean said warningly, nodding his head toward an approaching group of people. Chase saw them, too, and began edging away.

"Chase, stop," she said quickly. "Granger's dead. The Spider's dead."

His normally tan complexion faded from the white of shock to the gray of trauma. She saw his eyes, glowing green embers in his drawn face, flick upward to the speaker in the ceiling, and she knew that he had only now realized that she had been behind that page, that calm announcement of a name he hadn't heard for so long.

"You shouldn't have paged me, shouldn't have used that name. It's too dangerous."

"Chase, it's all right. You're out of danger. *We're* out of danger. He's dead."

"You . . . know?" His voice was a hoarse, low whisper of sound.

"It's over," she repeated, her voice husky with the love she'd kept bottled up for so long.

Chase swayed on his feet, as if he had absorbed one blow too many. Sean steadied him with a hand on his shoulder. Then the cheerful, chattering group was upon them, several of them insisting on waving and calling congratulations to Stevie.

"Let's get out of here," Sean said, steering them both away from the milling groups lingering outside the banquet room. Numbly, Chase let him do it. Stevie recognized that look; she'd seen it on her own face in a hotel mirror in Seattle and knew it meant a brain too shocked to function.

They obeyed when Sean told them to just wait by the elevators that went to the upper floors of the hotel's main tower. Stevie was silent, knowing that Chase was in no shape to hear her. He was leaning against the wall, eyes closed, his skin still possessed of that frightening gray tinge.

She was startled when Sean reappeared, thrust a room key into one of her hands and took the crystal sculpture from the other.

"Fifth floor. Get off and go right." She gaped at him as he punched the elevator button. "You need to talk. Alone and uninterrupted. I'll explain to the parents and Beth and anyone else. Go."

Stevie's heart swelled with love for this amazing person who was her brother, and it lit her face. He was going to make it, she thought. He'd hit bottom, but he was coming back. She opened her mouth but stopped when he grinned and shook his head.

"I know," he said. "I'll make it yet." He nudged her and Chase into the now-open elevator.

Stevie found the room quickly, and the first thing she did was pour a large dollop into a glass from one of the bottles she found in the small bar in the sitting area. She pushed the glass into Chase's hands. "Drink," she ordered. "And sit down."

He did so silently, still with that look in his eyes that reminded her frighteningly of the bright flare of a light before it burned out. She sat down on the chair opposite the sofa he had literally collapsed onto, clinging to only one thought: she had to get that look out of his eyes.

She gave a little start at a knock on the door; Chase never even blinked. Thinking it was Sean, she opened the door and was surprised when she found a hotel employee there with two boxes in the hotel's colors, cheerfully labeled Care Packages For Stranded Travelers. She took them, realizing they must contain all the necessities for an unplanned overnight stay, and blessed her brother once more.

She set the package on another chair, then sat down again. Chase had taken a gulp of the liquor—brandy, she thought—at her first order, but now he sat in silence, staring down at the small, half-empty glass. He was breathing oddly, in irregular, gulping spasms, as if he had to order his lungs to do that normally autonomic function. She waited, watching, then saw his fingers clench around the base of the glass in his hands.

"I . . . had to leave. They almost got you. . . ."

His voice sounded lacerated, as if torn from him, yet strangely vague, as if coming from a great distance through heavy fog. She knew then that he hadn't really absorbed what she'd told him in the hallway. She leaned forward, concentrating on him intently as she repeated firmly, "It's over, Chase. Granger is dead. So is his organization. There's no one left."

He raised his eyes then, and the disbelief mingled with growing hope in the green depths was heart-wrenching in its intensity. "You . . . you're sure?"

"I'm sure. He died of cancer. Of the colon. Poetic justice."

Her thinly disguised black humor seemed to rouse him a little. She waited, holding her breath as she watched his face, willing him to believe her; wishing she had the file that

Chuck, as he'd asked her to call him, had sent. She would show him all the clippings and make him believe her.

She thought of the picture in that file, of the man who had become the personification of evil for her, and of his harried-looking wife, with a sullen-looking young man beside her—more innocent victims, she supposed, although how innocent anyone who lived with the likes of Granger could be, she wasn't certain. Thought of the accounts of the trial, and a few horrible, stark black-and-white photos of Chase and the "murder" scene, along with the article about his supposed death. It still gave her chills to think about how close they had come to being true.

He seemed to absorb the truth slowly, an odd expression on his face. She watched his eyes as the hollow look left them and the vivid life began to flicker once more.

"You're sure? He's really dead?"

"Yes. And his evil with him."

The light in his eyes caught and flared. "Stevie," he whispered, reaching for her.

Joy leapt in her. "Yes," she said. "Oh, God, I've missed you!"

He pulled her to him, his arms going around her so tightly she could barely breathe; it still wasn't enough.

"I've dreamed of touching you again, every night, for so long...." he said huskily.

With a joyous little cry she was raining wet kisses on his cheek, his jaw, his neck. Then they were clawing at each other's clothes, hungry hands searching, seeking, igniting into searing flame the embers that had never faded, never gone out despite the cold, dark hell they'd endured since he'd gone.

They made love again and again, never quite making it to the bedroom before the need became too great, and he had to bury himself in her again. They were insatiable, rediscovering all the secret places, the special ways of touching. At last, naked and spent, they toppled onto the bed, adrift in that warm sea of completion neither had ever forgotten. He wondered how he had survived without her.

"I love you, Stevie." He pulled her to him tightly. She hugged him back, holding him close as exhaustion claimed him and he drifted into sleep.

In the hour before dawn she watched him wake up, the green eyes a little bleary as the dark lashes lifted. He smiled at her softly, sleepily, then startled her as his eyes shot completely open and he lifted his head sharply. He grabbed her, pulled her to him roughly.

"God, Stevie, do you know how many times I dreamed of this? Of waking up to you, only to find out when I did wake up that it was just a dream? I hated to go to sleep at night, because waking up was hell. Waking up was the nightmare."

"Want to trade nightmares?" she whispered. "Try knowing you were living in hell, and knowing it was for no reason. And not being able to find you to end it. Just knowing you were out there, somewhere, not knowing you were free, not knowing it was over...." She reached up and brushed back his tousled hair with a gentle touch of her fingers.

"Stevie, I...didn't realize." He hugged her tighter. "You had the worst of it, didn't you?"

She laughed. "You can say that? You lost your work, your family, even your name. Speaking of which," she said, suddenly shy, "I don't know if I can adjust to that. John, I mean."

"Don't," he said shortly, fervently. She raised a brow at him. "I'm not the same man I was then. I don't feel like that man anymore. I'll go back to Cameron, but—" he grinned at her "—I've gotten used to Chase. I think I'll keep it."

"Chase Cameron." Stevie tried it out tentatively, savoring it with her tongue.

"That's why," he said. When she looked at him quizzically, he explained. "Because of the way you say it. Just like that. Or when you're pleased with me. Even when—" the grin again "—you're mad at me. But most of all," he said, his voice dropping to a whisper, "I won't give up the way you say it when I'm deep inside you and your nails are digging into my back and you—"

He finished with a husky whisper in her ear that began it all again. It was a need that seemed to feed on itself, and instead of being slaked by each joining was increased to a fever pitch neither of them could deny. That it was the same for her was a gift he treasured beyond anything in his life—even, he realized with some shock, the gift of his release from hell. The thought stunned him, but he knew the truth of it; if not for the danger to her, he would stayed in that tormented abyss if it had been the only way to have her.

She was caressing him now, tracing the rapidly expanding length of him with slender fingers, her head pillowed on his chest, where she couldn't help but hear the hammer strokes of his heart. She lifted her head, her blue eyes alight with the dancing glow that had haunted his nights for so long.

He sucked in his breath at the piercing shaft of heat that stabbed through him at that look. She began to move, slowly, sinuously, her hands stroking, caressing, her mouth leaving sizzling trails of fire over his tingling flesh. And every time he reached for her, she pushed him back with a breathy little laugh.

"No. Let me."

She was driving him crazy. She cradled his aching flesh in her hands, coaxing it to throbbing fullness while she trailed her tongue across his chest, flicking teasingly at his flat, male nipples, then found that old, loved path that had once been a scar. She reveled in every groan that broke from him, each one spurring her on.

Stevie's spirit, so battered and worn of late, was soaring. She had feared never to have this again, never to know this soul-searing passion, this all-consuming fire. Any shyness she'd ever felt was banished by the joy of this reunion, and she responded to his every move, his every sound. This was her salute, her answer to the night of sweet, precious love he had given her before he'd left her.

"Stevie," he said thickly, "stop. If you don't, I—"

"You want me to stop?"

"Yes." He quivered beneath her as she moved again. "No," he gasped.

"Well, then," she whispered teasingly, "I guess I'll just have to decide."

She moved then, freeing him from the silken grasp of her fingers, smiling in ancient female satisfaction at his small sound of protest. She knelt between his legs as he lay sprawled before her, a sheen of sweat on his lean body, that hot, avid gleam lighting his eyes. He was here, she thought joyously, and nothing could hurt him again. Without a word, she bent to him and caressed him eagerly, lovingly, with her lips.

Chase cried out at the searing wet heat of her mouth on him. Her first caresses were tentative, but she learned fast, and soon he was gasping, groaning her name over and over. His hands tightened into fists, around wads of the sheet beneath him, and his head was tossing on the pillow.

"Please, Stevie!"

He was going to burst; he was swollen beyond release; he was coming apart. He bucked beneath her teasing mouth, every muscle taut with strain, every ounce of his being centered on what she was doing to him. He was beyond caring about holding back, beyond anything except the thudding beat of his heart and the sweet, hot touch of her mouth.

Stevie rejoiced in every cry that tore from his throat, every convulsive jerk of his body. With every move, every touch, she exultantly welcomed him home. She loved the feel of him, the taste of him, and wondered that she had ever hesitated to show him like this.

Chase's head shot back, digging into the pillow, the cords of his neck standing out vividly. A harsh, strangled cry ripped from him, a guttural shout of pleasure nearing agony, and he made a final upward thrust of his hips.

Stevie felt it happen for him as she never had before, felt him erupt into blazing, pulsing spurts of heat and shattering release. He was shuddering, tremors rippling through him, shaking his powerful frame as she carefully timed the last, lingering caress of her mouth.

When it was over, he lay limp and drained before her. She felt none of the sense of feminine power she had felt earlier, only an overpowering love and a sense of humble awe that this strong, courageous man trusted her so very much, trusted her with his own vulnerability in the most naked and exposed moments possible to any human being.

He murmured something as she moved up to lie beside him, but she hushed him.

"There's only one thing I want to say," she whispered. "You wouldn't take it before. Will you now?"

He knew what she meant. His eyes darkened with a remembered pain, but in the face of her love, in the warmth of the joy that lit her eyes, it couldn't take root. He nodded slowly.

"I love you. I did that night, and I never stopped."

"I know," he said hoarsely. "I knew it then. I thought if I didn't let you say the words... It didn't help."

"It doesn't matter anymore. Nothing does, except that you're here and it's over. The darkness is over."

He shook his head in slow wonder. All the questions that had been lost in the hot sweetness of the firestorm that had swept them came tumbling back.

"How? How did you know? I was... so careful."

"I know." She reached to turn on the bedside lamp; he needed answers now, and she knew this was going to take awhile. "Chuck Frazier says you're too damn good at this."

"Chuck? You talked to him?"

"Yes. He's been... quite nice, actually, considering how I treated him and right in his own office."

"His own... That's where you went?" He was staring at her. "To Seattle?"

She thought the question odd, but only said, "I had to. I..."

She paused, seeing the change in his eyes when he mentioned his hometown, seeing that he was realizing all the ramifications of this, that at last he could be reunited with the family he'd left for their own sake. The glow that lit his green eyes made every effort she'd made seem like a very small price.

"Why did you go, Stevie?" His voice was soft with wonder.

"I guess it made me feel like I was doing something, made me feel less helpless."

"But how did you know?" he repeated.

"The drawing," she said simply.

"The house?" he asked, bewildered.

"Sean had the idea," she said, and explained about their discovery and her decision to go to Seattle.

"You did all that . . ." he began in a shaky voice.

"I had to. Even if I . . . never found you again, I had to understand."

"Stevie," he said hoarsely, "I had to do it."

"I know."

He shuddered. "I'll never forget lying there on the pavement, helpless, watching that boy die, just for being close to me on the street. I didn't even know him."

"I know. Chuck sent me the article. And the pictures."

"The night of your accident . . . all I could think of was that the next time they wouldn't miss you. And if anything happened to you because of me, I—

"Chase, stop," she pleaded. "I understand. You had no choice, under the circumstances. You didn't know my accident really was an accident. You left to protect me."

He looked at her, his face twisting into a pained grimace. "So I put us both through hell for nothing."

"You didn't know!" she cried. "And I couldn't find you to tell you." She took a breath and steadied her voice. "I wish you'd read a paper now and then," she said with a creditable try at lightness. At his puzzled look, she told him about the ads she'd placed. "But I was afraid that you'd . . . gone too far, that you'd left California."

"I did."

She stared at him, and his lips quirked into a rueful smile.

"I made it as far as New Mexico. To one of those little desert towns along Interstate 10. I got off to get gas at the last gas station for miles. And got right back on going the other way."

"Why?"

He shrugged, a little sheepishly. "I couldn't stand it. Couldn't leave you. Not completely, I mean. Besides, I didn't have any guarantee that if I was gone they'd leave you alone. And if I was here, at least I could keep an eye on you, maybe stop them." He gave a harsh little laugh. "I'd learned by then what to look for."

"You were...watching me?" So that was what he'd meant. He'd known she'd gone somewhere, but not where.

"Always. I had enough money that I didn't have to work, so I figured I could make sure you were okay, for a while, at least. Until I was sure they thought I was gone, sure that they thought we weren't...connected anymore and wouldn't try again. I was down the street every day when you went to work, and I was in the parking lot across the street from Walker and Dunn every day when you left." He lowered his eyes. "I was there the day the newspaper took the picture of you, for the story about the award. That's how I knew you'd won."

"You were there? Every day?"

He managed a slightly wry smile. "I was until one of the people in the building came out and told me if I didn't quit hanging around he was going to call the cops."

"I wish he had," Stevie said fervently, her heart twisting at the thought of him having been so close all that time.

"You do?"

"If he had, it might have been over then. They were looking for you." She explained how she had enlisted the aid of Dave Barton.

"You never gave up, did you?" His voice was hushed.

"I couldn't." She studied him for a moment. "And Chuck wouldn't have, but he'd tried so hard to find you before...."

"I was sorry about that. We'd gotten to be pretty good friends. I knew he'd take some heat for it."

"How did you do it? He never said."

Chase shrugged. "I just started taking walks outside the clinic. I was supposed to, anyway. Walk a lot, I mean. After a while they got used to it and let me go alone. Even packed me a lunch. And I kind of let them think I was in worse shape than I really was. Then one day I stuffed what little I had in my pockets and just kept walking."

"And wound up in San Diego?"

"Not at first. But I didn't feel safe until I'd come about as far south as I could."

He began to tell her then of those days when he'd first arrived, when he'd tried so hard to cut himself off from everyone and everything, keeping his possessions to the minimum, expecting at any moment to have to take to his heels again.

"But I hadn't counted on you," he said softly. "You made me want..." He trailed off.

"Your name," she said slowly. "When I asked you, you said 'it seemed appropriate at the time.'"

He chuckled dryly. "Yeah. Not only did Chase seem appropriate, but it was my grandfather's last name. He was a contractor, but he could have been an architect if he'd had the money to go to school. He's the one who made me want to be one myself. And Sullivan was from Louis Sullivan. He was an architect at the turn of the century, one of the founders of modern architecture. Frank Lloyd Wright worked with him."

"You can go back to your work now," she said, her eyes warm and bright with brimming, joyous tears.

That look of realization entered his eyes again, and Stevie knew he had only begun to grapple with all the possibilities that had been given back to him.

"The pictures Chuck had..." he began slowly. "Is that how you knew? That I was...John Cameron?" He said the name as if it felt strange on his lips.

"That was the... tangible proof," Stevie said, knowing the time had come. She took a deep breath. "But I already knew."

"How?"

"Cassie," she said simply.

He went stark white, staring at her. "What?"

"She's the living, breathing, female image of you."

"You ... saw her?" he choked out.

Stevie nodded. "I...wanted to wait to tell you. Until I was sure you believed me. That it was over, I mean."

"My God."

"I saw your mother, too. But that was before I saw Cassie, so I didn't know then."

"How...are they?"

"Fine. Except they've never gotten over losing you. Your mother is very bitter. Justifiably bitter." She lowered her eyes uncomfortably.

"Stevie?"

She didn't answer. She was wrestling with a decision she'd made that day in Seattle, a decision she wasn't at all sure had been the right one.

"What is it?" Chase prodded. She lifted her head.

"I...tried to decide, after I found out who you were, what to do. I knew I could go to your family and tell them you were alive, but I wasn't sure they'd believe me. And I was afraid that, even if they did, it would only hurt them more to raise their hopes and then have to tell them I...didn't know where you were. That you didn't even know you were safe."

She sighed, lowering her eyes once more. "So I didn't tell them. I knew I'd keep trying to find you, but if even Chuck, with all his resources, couldn't, I didn't have much hope. I just couldn't see putting them through that hell.... They'd already lost you once."

"So you would spare this family you didn't even know, but not yourself," he said softly.

He was watching her lowered head with eyes that were bright and warm for the first time in months. He felt as if he'd stepped out of a deep freeze into the California sun, the door opened by this slender, fiery woman before him. A woman who had more courage and nerve than anyone else he'd ever known. A woman he loved more than he'd ever thought himself capable of loving anyone.

"It's over," he breathed, as if he still couldn't quite believe it.

"Yes. God, I wish you'd known. All those months of hell...."

"Months?" He went suddenly still.

"Yes. Didn't I say? Granger died last summer. About the time we..."

She trailed off, not so much because she was embarrassed to say that it had been about the time they had become lovers, but because he was staring at her so oddly. And even as she watched, she saw the glow that had been rekindled in his eyes waver.

"You're sure of that?" he asked hoarsely.

Her brow furrowed as she looked at him. "Yes. Chuck said so . . . and he sent me the newspaper reports. . . ."

Her voice faltered, then trailed off altogether as Chase went pale. She gave a sharp, pained little cry when she saw that grim, haunted look steal back into his eyes.

"What is it? Chase, please, what is it?"

"If Granger's been dead since then . . . it's not over," he said dully, in a voice that was so weary it frightened her almost as much as the words themselves.

"What do you mean?" she gasped, her voice barely a whisper. "Why isn't it over?"

He gaze lifted, hollow, staring green eyes meeting terrified blue ones.

"Because somebody tried to kill me the day I came back."

Chapter 11

"What are you saying?" Stevie's voice was tiny.

"The day I came back, when I finally quit running away after you nearly got killed..." She made a small sound of protest, but he brushed her off. "The day I came back," he repeated bitterly, "thinking I could somehow protect you, they came after me again. Just a few weeks ago. Long after you say Granger died."

"No," Stevie choked out. "You must be wrong."

"I wish I was." Chase let out a weary sigh as he sat up.

"But...he's dead!" She cried out in protest, moving in a jerky little motion to sit beside him. "He's *been* dead!"

Chase lifted a hand to run it through the tangle of his hair. He looked at the clock on the nightstand, at the glow of the lamp, anywhere but at Stevie. Yet he could see her as clearly as if he were staring straight at her, could see her pale, shocked face and the way she was clutching the sheet in front of her with a white-knuckled hand.

"Chase—"

His head snapped around then. "I'm not wrong, Stevie. That guy who came after me meant business. If I hadn't been on the bike and gotten away between a couple of buildings, he would have had me."

She shook her head in numbed protest. "Maybe...maybe it was just a reckless driver, like my accident—"

"That wasn't an accident. And neither was this. He had a gun."

Her gasp was muffled, and her eyes went wide with fear. For him, he realized with a little shock. She had come within a hair-breadth of losing her own life because of him, yet she was frightened for him. And if he stayed with her, she might not be as lucky again.

These hours had been stolen, as had all his hours with her. He had thought, for this beautiful interlude, that it was truly done, that the nightmare was over. And it should have been, with Granger dead.

His hand went to the back of his neck, rubbing muscles that were suddenly tense. It was a feeling he'd grown so used to that only now, when it had returned, did he realize it had, for these brief promising hours, been gone.

"But he's dead," Stevie said again in the tiny, shocked voice of disbelief. "I don't understand."

"I don't either."

He swung out of bed and walked to the window. He lifted the heavy hotel black-out drape and looked at the gray dawn light. After a moment he let the curtain drop again. He had to face it. Granger's pack hadn't given up the hunt, even though their leader was dead.

"Maybe all of his hounds didn't get the word. Or maybe he paid them to keep going after he died." He gave a harsh, mirthless chuckle. "Maybe he put it in his will. Maybe it will just go on forever."

"Chase, no!"

She scrambled out of the bed and ran to him, throwing her arms around him. She felt him stiffen, felt him try to draw back. She looked up at him; the withdrawal she'd felt in his body was mirrored in his eyes, and she knew what he was thinking.

"No! Don't even think it! You're not going to leave again!"

"Stevie—"

"No!" She released him then, backing up a step. Heedless of her nudity, she looked at him levelly, her delicate chin jutting out determinedly, her eyes bright with resolve. "I'm not losing you again."

"Stevie, I have to. They'll try for you again—"

"No." She glared at him stubbornly, barely sparing a thought for the realization that her accident had been anything but. "If you leave, I'll come after you. If they found you, then so can I."

He shuddered with the effort of denying the urge to say, Yes, come with me. We'll find a place where even Granger's hounds can't find us. Just the two of us. . . .

"No. Somebody still wants me dead. You won't be safe as long as I'm around."

"What makes you think I'll be safe if you go?"

He stared at her.

"They obviously know you're alive. And they know about me, Chase. What's to stop them from using me to get to you?"

"But if I go, if they think we...split up, they'll leave you alone."

Chuck Frazier's image suddenly popped into her mind, his eyes solemn and utterly serious as he labeled Chase a hero.

"They know better, Chase. They know you, the kind of man you are. If you hadn't been that kind of man, this would never have started. They know you wouldn't let someone else be hurt because of you if you can stop it. And they'll use that against you. That's why you came back, isn't it? Because you were afraid for me."

He knew she was right. It had been at the core of his fear ever since he'd realized they'd found him again. He'd done the one thing he'd sworn never to do: he'd put someone else in danger. To them she was a lever to use against him. And if he left, they would use her to bring him back.

He didn't want to think about that. But he had to. He had to plan. He would have to find someplace for her to hide. Once he was sure she was safe, he would leave. He would surface somewhere else, somewhere far from her, where it would be clear Stevie no longer had anything to do with him. Somewhere where it would be easy for the claws that stretched out even in death to reach him....

For the first time in his life, for the first time since his ordeal had begun, he felt the urge to give up. Just let them do it, he thought numbly. Just let it be over. Quit fighting, quit running. Then Stevie would be truly safe. And maybe only then.

He looked so odd, Stevie thought. Not just tense, or desolated by the discovery that he'd been cast back into hell again. Not just drained, but utterly weary. Defeated. And...resigned. She paled suddenly.

"You're thinking of letting them find you, aren't you?"

His startled look told her how accurate her guess had been.

"No, damn it! You're not going to let them win, not after all this!"

Something flickered in the green depths of his eyes, and Stevie knew suddenly that winning and losing had nothing to do with it. Nor did his weariness. The one and only reason was her. He was going to give himself up to his bloodthirsty pursuers so that she would be safe.

For just one moment, Stevie trembled under the realization. If she'd had any doubts that he loved her as much as she loved him, they vanished now. And for one awe-inspiring moment, she knew that if the circumstances were reversed, she would do the same.

Not, she thought on a sudden burst of anger, that she was about to let *him* do anything so stupid. Sometimes a woman just had to grab a man by his silly sense of honor and shake him into common sense, she told herself.

"No, thank you," she said, her cool tone disguising the quivering inside. "I'm not accepting any sacrifices this week."

His eyes widened.

"You're not in this alone anymore, Chase. I'm sorry if you don't like it, but there's nothing you can do about it."

"Stevie, no. If anything happened to you—"

"It's just as likely to happen if you go. Maybe more."

She reached out and took his hands. He closed his eyes and let out a long, tired breath.

"You've been alone for so long," she whispered. "Please, Chase."

A shudder rippled through him. Then he moved suddenly, pulling her into his arms.

"There's got to be something we can do." Her voice was as determined as her tiny chin.

"Like run?" he said hoarsely. "And keep running? That's no kind of life for you."

She laid her cheek against his chest. "There's got to be something," she insisted. "Or someone who could help."

"I wish . . ."

He trailed off, unable to put into words how much he wanted that golden future he'd had a glimpse of bare minutes ago. It had been his for those precious hours in her arms, only to be snatched away again, and that had destroyed the last of his resilience. He held her desperately, and she felt him shudder again.

Stevie knew how close to the edge he was. Even heroes have breaking points, she thought as she held him tightly. And he *was* a hero, just as Chuck had said.

"Chuck," she said suddenly.

"What?"

She pulled back to look up at him. "Chuck," she repeated. "He'll help."

"Chuck Frazier?"

She nodded eagerly. "He will. I know it. He felt so badly when you got hurt, I think he'd do just about anything to atone. Call him."

"What can he do?" he asked gently, hating to put a damper on her enthusiasm.

"I don't know, but something. Maybe he knows something about why they're still after you. Or who it is. He has to help. They owe it to you!"

"Stevie—"

"Call him. Please."

"He can't do anything from Seattle."

"Maybe he can. Promise you'll call him?"

She was trying so hard, he thought, trying to hide her fear even though he could feel it in the tiny quivers that rippled through her. It had been a long time since he'd had the courage to even try to act as if there was hope, as if something could be done. His voice was quiet as he tried to let her down gently.

"Even if he wanted to help—"

"Just try. It can't make things any worse, can it? And he wanted to know, anyway, if I found you again."

"I don't think—"

"Please?"

He let out a quick breath. How could he say no to her? How could he ever say no to her? And he supposed she was right; it couldn't make things any worse. "All right. I'll call him."

She hugged him fiercely. "Everything will be all right. You'll see."

He smothered a short, sour laugh. "I wish I had your faith in the government," he muttered, but he hugged her back.

"I don't know about the government," she told him, "but I think Chuck would move mountains if he thought it would make up for what happened after what you did for them. If nothing else, you put away the man who killed his partner."

He wanted to hope, but he'd been soaring so high and brought so low in such a short space of time that he didn't dare. He would do as she asked, but he didn't have much faith left, even in the FBI agent who, during the harrowing days of his hospitalization, had become a friend.

Once she had assured herself of his cooperation, Stevie picked up the room-service menu and held it in front of him.

"I can count every rib, so you're going to eat," she said sternly.

"You could use a few pounds yourself," he returned, eyeing her pointedly.

The breakfast they ordered was a quiet meal, Chase forcing himself to eat under Stevie's watchful eye as they sat in the hotel's robes. Neither of them said anything more about what had happened, and in some quirky corner of his mind Chase wished they could just stay here forever, hidden in the safe womb of this room. He couldn't help thinking that the moment they stepped back into the world it would all begin again, and this time Stevie might be the ultimate loser.

She watched him, felt the tension that radiated from him. This was the feeling she'd sensed in him from the beginning, magnified a hundredfold. God, how had he survived like this, day after day, month after month? She'd only known he was still in danger for two hours, and she was already strung so tightly she felt as if she would shatter at the slightest touch. She tried desperately to hang on to at least a surface semblance of calm.

They finished eating, neither having really tasted a thing. When the table had been removed, Stevie glanced at the clock and then looked at him expectantly. With a sigh, he walked to the phone.

Chuck was startled to hear his voice, then chuckled ruefully.

"I should have known," he said. "That sassy little redhead wasn't about to give up until she found you!"

Chase managed a creditable laugh. "No. Not Stevie." He coughed lightly. "Listen, Chuck, I'm sorry about what happened. I know you probably got called on the carpet for it."

"For letting you make us all look like fools?" Chuck laughed. "Actually, that was nothing compared to the dressing down I got from your lady, my friend. She chewed me up one side and down the other. I envy you, and that's not something I say lightly."

"You should," Chase said evenly. "She's one of a kind." He glanced at Stevie. Her eyes were lowered, but the pink tinge of her cheeks told him she'd heard.

"I believe that." Chuck cleared his throat. "I tried to find you, when that bastard died."

"I know. Stevie told me."

"So how does it feel to be free again?"

Chase took a deep breath. "I don't know."

"What?"

"Somebody's still after me."

There was a moment of silence. "I won't ask if you're sure. I know you wouldn't say it if you weren't. What happened?"

In a few short sentences, Chase explained about his encounter with the armed driver.

"Did you get a look at him?"

"No. Just the car. It was dark, and we were moving pretty fast. A black two-door, I think. Or maybe dark blue. New. Maybe a T-bird, but I can't be sure. I—"

He broke off as Stevie made a tiny sound. He turned to look at her where she sat cross-legged on the bed.

"It is a Thunderbird. It's been hanging around the apartments for weeks," she said tautly. "I remember because it always seemed to be in the way, and I'd never seen it around before. And it had a rental car agency bumper sticker on it. I thought it was just a tourist."

Her eyes widened in horror as she realized she might have even seen the man who had tried to murder Chase. And he'd been watching her.

"He was always parked on the street, near the driveway," she said. "Where he could see my door. And he was there last night, when I left. . . ."

"Damn." Chase's jaw clenched. "Chuck—"

"I heard. Is that where he went for you? At the apartment?"

"Yes. I was outside." He heard Stevie's gasp but didn't dare look at her. "I kept my distance after that. I should have stayed away altogether," he finished grimly.

"Look, John, if he knows enough to watch her, then it probably wouldn't make any difference. She might be in more danger if he thought she was alone."

A low, strangled sound escaped Chase despite his effort to bite it back. "More danger? They already tried to kill her once."

"What?"

"She had an accident that wasn't an accident. Just like mine. Hit-and-run, waiting until she got out of the car."

Chase heard the sound of a hissing breath. "Damn," Chuck muttered.

"Yes." Chase had his voice under control again, but the single syllable was somehow more terrible, more appalling, than the choked, smothered sound had been.

"I know, buddy." Chuck's tone was low, soft.

"Oh, yeah?" Nobody could know how this felt, Chase thought. He'd brought this down on her....

"Yeah." Chuck's voice was tight. "You're thinking it's all your fault for getting her into this in the first place. That nothing's worth what you've done to her."

Chase sucked in a short breath at the accuracy of the agent's words.

"I know, because that's exactly how I felt a couple of years ago."

Chase let out the breath on a long sigh. "Sorry. I—"

"Never mind. I understand. I don't understand what the hell is going on. Granger's dead. We broke up his organization."

"All of it?"

"Yes. It's scattered. Including his hit men. Torelli's dead, and Maxwell's in the state pen at Walla Walla."

Chase felt a mild spurt of satisfaction that the man who had run him down was in that cold granite prison. But it didn't answer any of his questions.

"When?" he asked.

"Torelli bought it a couple of months after you took your little walk. We took Maxwell down about two weeks after Granger died."

Chase let out a sharp, compressed breath. "Then neither of them was the prowler, either," he muttered, half to himself.

"What?"

He sighed. "Somebody tried to break into my place. If it wasn't them, it has to be the guy in the car. But who the hell is he? And if Granger's dead, why is he still after me?"

"I don't know," Chuck said, sounding both baffled and angry. "Even if he'd hired somebody else before he died, the contract would be worthless now. After the IRS got through with the estate, there wasn't a two-dollar bill left. No pro is going to make a hit when he knows he's not going to get paid."

"Why doesn't that make me feel better?"

There was a pause; then Chuck spoke rapidly in a decisive tone Chase remembered. "Where are you?"

Chase told him, then gave Chuck the phone number when asked.

"Stay there. Let me do some checking. I'll get back to you by—" Chase heard the rustle as Chuck apparently looked at his watch "—noon."

"What can you find out now, after all this time?"

"Maybe I can figure out who the hell it is."

"Even if you can, what good will that do? Knowing who it is won't stop him, not if Granger's dying didn't."

"At least you might be able to see him coming."

Chase couldn't argue with that.

"Just wait. Please," Chuck said.

"Just sit here? No way."

"You should be relatively safe there. And for God's sake, don't let Stevie go home. If he's watching her, waiting for you, who knows when his patience might run out?"

He didn't have to spell it out; Chase knew the other man had reached the same conclusion Stevie had, the conclusion he hadn't wanted to admit: whoever the would-be killer was, he wouldn't hesitate to grab Stevie and use her as bait. When he spoke, his voice was grim.

"Maybe I'll just make sure he doesn't have to do that."

"Johnny, don't be a fool—"

"It's Chase now. And I've already been a fool. I won't let her pay for what I did."

"No." Stevie's voice was small and tight. He hushed her, but he put his arm around her shoulders.

"Just give me a couple of hours," Chuck implored. "I might be able to turn something up. And if not, at least I can call in some local troops for you. We'll smoke him out somehow."

"Please," Stevie whispered; she'd been close enough to hear Chuck's plea.

"No. There were reporters here last night, and photographers. It will probably hit the papers. He could find out she's here, and from there it wouldn't be hard for him to find this room, even though it's in her brother's name."

"Listen to me, Joh—Chase," Chuck said urgently. "If he did follow her, or you, he'll still be around, waiting. If you move, you'll just tip him off. If he didn't, you're still safe there, for a while. As long as you don't move."

He sensed Chase wavering. "Look, I'll give you the number for an agent I know down there. I'll let him know what's going on. If something goes sour before I get back to you, call him."

"Chuck..."

"I know I messed up once, but—"

"I wasn't thinking that."

"No, I suppose you wouldn't. But let me make up for it anyway."

When he began to rattle off a name and number, Chase reluctantly grabbed the pad and pen the hotel had placed beside the phone and wrote them down.

For a long time after he'd hung up, Chase stared at the phone as if he couldn't quite believe that he'd agreed to Chuck's request. He was so used to being on the run, or getting ready to be, that just sitting here went against every hard-learned instinct he'd developed in the past three years.

And more than that, much more than that, the thought that he had endangered Stevie ate away at him. Only the logic of Chuck's words, and the fear that Stevie might be in more danger if he left, kept him there. But it wasn't enough to keep him calm; he was pacing the room as if it were a cage.

Stevie watched him apprehensively. He was strung so tightly it worried her just to look at him. She couldn't help remembering how he had looked crouched beside her bed that night, every muscle taut, like some wild creature preparing to attack. Or defend.

The thought came to her suddenly, and she had no doubt of its truth. He had been ready to defend her then, just as he was ready to give himself up to the hounds for her sake now. She knew by the way he was pacing, by the tense set of his jaw, by the way he kept running his hand jerkily through his hair, that he was on the edge of breaking his promise to Chuck.

At the same time she knew, without conceit, that there was one sure way to stop him, one sure weapon: herself. And she would use it without hesitation. Wherever he went, she would be there. She would stick to him so closely that he could never risk himself without risking her, as well. She would use his love for her as a weapon to protect him. It was all she had.

It didn't take him long to figure it out. When he began to yank on his jeans, she got to her feet.

"Why don't you...take a shower or something?" He didn't meet her eyes.

"No, thanks," she said coolly.

He started to speak, then stopped. When he pulled on his shirt and reached for his boots, Stevie picked up her dress and shook it out. His gaze shot to her again.

At his look she managed a nonchalant tone. "It's a little out of place for nine in the morning, but I don't have much choice."

"It won't be out of place, because you're not going anywhere."

She stopped, holding the dress in front of her. She drew herself up, meeting his eyes levelly. "Wrong, Mr. Cameron. Where you go, I go."

"Stevie..."

"No, Chase. You promised to wait. If you don't, then neither do I."

"I was just going down to check my bike," he said defensively, carefully neglecting to add that he was going for the revolver that was tucked in the locked compartment be-

neath the seat. At least, he thought gratefully, he'd had the
sense to park a couple of blocks away.

"Fine." She was purposefully cheerful as she fastened the
dress.

"Stevie, don't."

"You don't like the dress?"

Her voice was innocent, but it didn't match the look in her
eyes. Chase stopped, boots in hand, his eyes fastened on her
as he tried to decipher that look.

The dress was just as seductive as it had seemed when he
had turned to see her striding toward him last night. She was
even more enticing, her lips still swollen from his kisses, her
hair tangled from his fingers, her skin showing faint, pink
evidence of his beard-roughened jaw. The sweetness of the
night came rushing back. It tightened his throat, and his
body.

"I love it," he said huskily. "I love you."

"Then do what Chuck asked. Wait."

"And if I don't?" he asked softly.

She lifted her head. "What do you think?"

He studied her for a moment. "You'll be right behind
me." That look he'd seen in her eyes made sense now. It had
been a look of total awareness of what she was doing.

"I love you," she said simply.

"You don't play fair, Holt."

"Neither does he."

Stevie held her breath, waiting. She'd gambled, used the
hold she had on him, knowing it might damage the very
source it sprang from. She didn't care. His safety was more
important to her than anything.

His eyes never left her. She watched them, saw the weariness, the defeat, begin to fade, to be replaced by a growing fierceness that made her pulse begin to race. Then he
dropped the boots and held his arms out to her. She ran to
him, knowing she'd won. When his arms came around her,
she felt like nothing in the world could touch them, nothing could harm them. She clung to the illusion as his mouth
came down on hers.

* * *

Stevie heard the water start, a soft smile curving her mouth. She'd taken her own shower cheerfully, knowing now that he wouldn't leave while she was doing it. Not that she hadn't been tempted when he suggested, with the first smile he managed since a matter of timing had destroyed their fragile paradise, that they explore the large Roman tub together, but one of them had to listen for the phone.

She had again put on the thick, white robe monogrammed with the hotel's logo, and now she rubbed her damp hair with an equally thick towel as she wandered around the room. They would probably, she thought, provide a hair dryer if she asked, but she was reluctant to call even that much attention to them. She'd only insisted on breakfast because it had pained her so to look at his drawn face. But they were safe now, as long as they stayed put. She had to believe that.

She listened to the shower, picturing him beneath the running water. A tiny spurt of heat burst from near her heart and cascaded down to pool somewhere low and deep inside her as she thought about him naked and glistening with water. She remembered the day—ages ago, it seemed now—when she had first imagined him like that. It had been so unexpected that it had startled her. Had she known even then, somehow, on some subconscious level, what he would become to her?

Even if she had, she thought as she sank helplessly down on the edge of the bed, she certainly would never have guessed that the reality of that sleek, wet vision would have the power to bring such an overwhelming, trembling weakness to her knees.

She remembered the time she had shaved him. He had told her once what that had done to him and had admitted a little sheepishly that a great part of his snappish temper then had been because of his effort to fight his response to her.

She smiled again, thinking that she had never really admitted to him that her reaction had been as swift and as intense as his. That, she said to herself, was something she was going to remedy right now. She got to her feet and headed for the bathroom, thinking she would give anything to just be able to sit and watch him shave every morning for the rest of her life.

She was reaching for the door knob when a tap on the outer door turned her around. She took two steps before the fear kicked in, shocking her out of her normal response to the knock.

God, she thought, was this how he'd lived all this time, even the simplest things gaining a horrific significance? Taking a deep breath to steady herself and silently trying to convince herself that no one could have found them, she tiptoed over to the door.

She peered through the peephole, squinting to see into the hotel corridor. She drew back, startled, when all she could see was a huge expanse of flowers. Her first thought was Chase, but she'd been with him every moment and knew he hadn't ordered the exotic arrangement.

The tap came again. She leaned forward to look again, and as the man stepped back from knocking she recognized the uniform of the hotel bellhops. Still she hesitated, only answering through the closed door. "Who is it?"

"Flowers, Miss Holt."

"I can see that," she called. "Who sent them?"

Through the tiny scope she saw him wrestle with the large bouquet as he tugged at the card.

"Walker and Dunn," the young man announced. "It says 'Congratulations.'"

Beth, she thought. Sean must have told her that she would be here. It was nice of her, especially since she'd already given Stevie the confirmation of a tidy raise at the ceremony last night. Instinctively she reached for the door knob, then hesitated again at the last moment.

"Uh, this is really heavy, Miss Holt."

"Oh. Yes, okay."

It would be all right, she thought. She would just open it for a second, not even let him in. She unlocked the door and pulled it open a scant few inches.

"Shall I bring it in?"

"No," she said quickly. "I'll take it, thank you."

It *was* heavy, she thought as she took it from him, admiring the graceful spray of gladiolus and the rich, exotic shape and color of tiger lilies.

"I'm sorry," she told him, realizing she had nothing to tip him with. "I don't have any cash."

"'s okay." He grinned at her. "Always a pleasure to bring flowers to a good-looking lady."

He gave her a jaunty salute before turning to walk away down the hall. In spite of herself, she smiled.

Stevie turned back into the room, trying to balance the heavy vase while she pushed at the door with one slender heel. She felt it begin to swing shut and lowered her foot as her equilibrium began to falter.

She had taken a step before she realized she hadn't heard the door click shut. Quickly she set the vase down on a table and turned back to close it. And couldn't quite smother a sob of shock at the sight of the man who stood in the doorway, a small, deadly smile on his thin lips.

Chapter 12

It took every bit of self-control she could muster not to let her eyes flick toward the bathroom, where the shower still ran steadily. At first she stared at the petulant-looking man in the doorway in order to keep herself from doing just that; then she found herself staring even harder.

She knew him. Not by name, but she knew she'd seen him sometime, somewhere, before. He had that vague familiarity of a person seen and then forgotten. He was young, about twenty, she guessed, with untidy light brown hair that hung in lank strands at the back of his neck. His face was set in lines that seemed oddly harsh, given his apparent youth. His jeans were too long and frayed in the back, where they had dragged on the ground behind his worn but expensive designer tennis shoes. His sweater and jacket had also been expensive, but now they showed signs of age and wear.

"So we meet at last, Miss Holt."

Stevie felt her throat constrict, her last hope that this was a mistake evaporating at the sound of her name. Hoping her inner shuddering wasn't visible, she swallowed tightly and spoke.

"I'm sorry, but I think you're mistaken. Excuse me, please, I'd like to...finish my shower."

She glanced toward the closed bathroom door, praying that it would stay that way.

"Nice try, Miss Holt." A pair of close-set brown eyes, oddly flat and lusterless, moved to glance at the vase on the table. "Do you like the flowers? I picked them out myself."

"You?" Who *was* he? She stared at him, trying desperately to place where she'd seen him. "The card says—"

"I know what it says. I wrote it." Something flashed then in those eyes, something both triumphant and bitter at the same time. "Yes, I know all about you. Clever, not getting the room in your name. But it was easy to just follow him up here."

Stevie felt a shiver ripple up her spine. "Go away."

"I don't think so. I know fate when it hits me. And seeing your name and that pretty picture in the paper this morning, after thinking I'd lost track of you, was fate. Just like guessing that when you didn't come home you might have stayed here, where they gave that big bash for all you happy winners."

He drawled out the last word, letting the biting sarcasm echo in the room. Stevie shivered again, but fought against showing it. She wondered how, if he'd been watching her so closely, he'd lost her, then realized that the black coupe had always been parked in back, by her parking space, not at the front of the building, where Sean had picked her up. Not that it mattered now. "Get out," she snapped.

"I don't think so. I've been waiting for this for a very long time."

If she'd had any doubts that she was face-to-face with the man who meant to murder Chase, they vanished the instant she heard the malignant tone that had crept into his voice. Instinctively she gauged the distance between the intruder and the door, wondering if she could shove him outside and get it closed before he could stop her.

As if he'd read her thoughts, he half turned and slammed the door shut behind him. As he moved, Stevie whirled and ran for the phone. She had the receiver in her hand when it was yanked away and her wrist was caught in a painful grip.

"Nice try," he repeated. "But this is going to be a very private party. I've—"

As he broke off, his gaze whipping toward the bathroom door, Stevie's heart quailed. The shower had stopped.

"Well, well," he said with a chuckle that was so malevolent it made her shiver again. "It seems this is going to be easy, after all." The murky brown eyes narrowed. "He's still here, isn't he?"

"No."

The grip on her wrist tightened until she wondered that the bones didn't snap.

"Loyal, aren't you?" He gave a harsh, bitter laugh. "Well, so am I. And I'm going to prove it."

"Who are you?" Stevie whispered, her voice taut with pain as her wrist ached beneath his clamplike hold.

Something flickered in those cold eyes, but before he could speak, the door Stevie had been so tautly aware of swung open.

"Stevie, what was—"

Chase stopped, his hands frozen at the snap of the jeans he'd pulled on, his gaze flicking from Stevie to the man who held her arm, and then to the lethal-looking .45 caliber automatic pistol that had appeared in the man's other hand. For the briefest second Stevie saw fear flash in the green eyes, fear she had seen once before. Fear for her.

"Hello, Cameron." The exaggerated politeness was laced with a savage undertone that was vicious in its intensity. Stevie felt a tingling relief as her captor released her wrist, and she hastily backed away from him, toward Chase.

Chase's brow furrowed as he stared at the younger man. Then his eyes widened, and Stevie knew he had done what she'd been unable to; he'd figured out who the man was. And, more than that, she saw the sudden understanding that had leapt into the green depths of his eyes. He not only knew who, he knew why.

"I see you remember me."

The voice was even harsher, more strident.

"I remember."

Chase crossed his arms over his bare chest and leaned against the doorjamb as casually as if the deadly weapon hadn't been trained on his midsection. The sheer casualness of the movement seemed to infuriate the man.

"Always, the cool one, aren't you, Cameron? Well, no more. I've waited a long time for this," the intruder said again.

Stevie stifled a tiny cry as she saw his hand tighten around the gun. "Why?" she cried. "Granger's dead—"

"Stevie!" Chase snapped, cutting her off. The brown gaze that fastened on her now was alight with a fanatical glow that made dread balloon inside her.

"So you do know." His voice was soft, but the tone was as hard and as cold as the Arctic ice pack.

"She doesn't know anything," Chase said sharply. "I'm who you want, Granger. Let her go."

Granger? A ripple of shock vibrated through Stevie as an image suddenly formed in her mind, a slightly blurry newsprint photo from the file Chuck Frazier had sent her. A stocky older man, his thin, strained-looking wife and a gangly, lank-haired teenager with a sullen expression. A teenager who hadn't changed much in the years since that picture was taken. Granger's son.

She could hear Chuck's voice as clearly as if he were there, talking of the elder Granger's death. "And his son left the state a few months ago." To come after Chase, she thought numbly.

"I'd say she knows a lot," Granger said, studying her expression. "I'd say she even knows you killed my father."

"No." Stevie's voice was harsh.

"Yes! My father died in that damn cell, wasted away to nothing, because of him!"

"Your father was a murderer," Chase said venomously, trying to divert the man's attention from Stevie. "He got what was coming to him."

"Shut up!" Granger whirled, once more training the gleaming weapon on Chase's bare midsection. His eyes were cold, vicious. "You bastard. The only pleasure my father had in that cell was knowing you'd paid for what you did. But I knew when I saw those ads in the paper, using that stinking name those reporters hung on him, that you were still alive.''

Stevie gasped. "You...saw the ads?" God, had she done this, brought this down on them with her efforts to find him?

"Of course," he spat out. "They were in every damn paper in Washington.''

She swallowed tightly. Not her ads, Chuck's. Somehow it didn't make her feel much better.

"Thought you'd run far enough, didn't you, Cameron?" He swung his gaze back to Chase. "But I found you again. It took awhile, but a lot of people owed my father favors. People in a lot of places. They didn't want to pay up, but I made them.''

"Nick, this isn't going to bring him back."

"I know that," Granger snapped. "That's why I swore on his grave that I'd see you in hell.''

Stevie made a tiny sound of protest. Chase's jaw tightened.

"Let her go, Nick. It's me you want. She has nothing to do with this. She's an innocent bystander.''

"Innocent?" Nick Granger's voice rose to a shrill pitch. "Oh, no, Cameron, I'm not letting her go." An avid gleam brightened his brown eyes. "I'm letting you go.''

Chase stared at him. "What?"

An unholy grin split the angular face. "I thought you'd like that." His tone was proud, full of self-congratulation. "Before, I only wanted to get her out of the way. Almost did, that night with the car. But then I thought of something better. Much better. So I waited, watching her place. I knew you'd come back, once you realized you'd left her hanging out to dry. Heroes like you always do.''

"Granger—"

"You're going to know how I felt, Cameron. She's innocent? Well, so was my mother.''

"Your...mother?"

"She had nothing to do with anything my father did. But she died anyway. They took away everything, our home, our money, everything. Because of you. She killed herself when she couldn't face the humiliation any longer. I couldn't help her. Just like you won't be able to help *her*."

He gestured toward Stevie with the hand that was clenched around the gun. She trembled, despite herself. Chase straightened, his face pale.

"No," he whispered harshly. The haunted look Stevie so hated was cheerful next to the expression that had entered his eyes now.

"Yes." Granger's grin became a satisfied smile. "You'll live the rest of your life knowing that she died, and died hard, because of you." The smile became a leer. "And you're going to watch, Cameron. Just like I had to watch my father. And I'll make sure it's an interesting show. I'm going to enjoy it. And her. She's beautiful, isn't she?"

Stevie gasped, and in the second when Granger glanced at her, Chase lunged. He sent the smaller man flying, but Granger kept his grip on the weapon. He brought it down sharply, and Stevie heard the dull thud as it hit Chase's neck. In the moment when he instinctively recoiled from the pain, Granger wriggled free and scrambled to his feet. Wrath distorted his face as he cocked and leveled the gun at Chase.

"You try that again and you're dead! And you—" he whirled on Stevie, who was edging toward the door "—don't move!"

He grabbed her arm and shoved her into a chair beside the table holding the flowers that had betrayed their location. She tore her gaze away from the deadly, seemingly bottomless bore of the automatic pistol and looked worriedly at Chase. He was up, his eyes fastened unwaveringly on Nick Granger. The haunted look was gone, replaced by a fury so strong it seemed to radiate from him in waves.

She saw his fists clench, could almost feel him tense. That feral image of him crouched beside her bed came to her again, and she knew what he was going to do.

No, she pleaded silently. *He'll kill you.*

She saw the moment when he gathered himself to attack again. Desperately she tried to think of something to distract Granger, anything that would keep him from firing that deadly gun. She cursed her sluggish brain. There had to be something she could do. . . .

The phone rang.

It was much too normal a sound to have such a startling effect, but they all jumped and stared at the instrument on the nightstand as if it were some bizarre gadget they'd never seen before.

Chuck, Stevie thought, a tiny surge of hope rising in her. But it died as she realized that the phone would just ring, unanswered, and Chuck would never know what had happened until it was too late. Again.

By the time the second ring faded away, Granger recovered himself and strode across the room. He reached for the cord as if to yank it out of the wall.

"It's probably her brother," Chase said suddenly, unexpectedly. "We're supposed to meet him for lunch."

Stevie managed to mask her look of surprise before Granger cast a look at her over his shoulder. The ringing continued.

"He'll probably show up here if she doesn't answer."

Granger's gaze flicked to Chase, then back to her. Stevie gathered her wits.

"It's true. He's very. . . protective."

Granger made an odd, hissing sound. "Answer it," he snapped at her. "Get rid of him. And remember, I'll be right here, listening."

Oh, God, help me, Stevie thought as she shakily crossed the room. She took a deep breath as she reached for the phone and forced herself not to recoil violently when Granger's hand came down over hers and forced her wrist back to angle the receiver so he could hear.

"Hello." Her voice was flat, but steady.

"Stevie?"

Chuck. Stevie stopped the sharp intake of the breath she instinctively wanted to take. Think, Holt.

"Hello, Sean," she said quickly, grateful that Chuck had progressed past calling her Ms. Holt.

"Stevie, this is—"

"I'm sorry, Sean, but...something's come up. We won't be able to meet you for lunch."

"Oh?"

It was the tone she'd hoped for, prayed for: suspicion. She tried to ignore Granger's hand clamping down fiercely over hers, crushing her fingers against the hard plastic of the receiver. She turned her eyes away from him, hating the feel of him so close. She swallowed tightly as Granger nudged her with the cold metal barrel of the gun. Her gaze fell on the notepad by the phone, marked with the bold strokes of Chase's writing. A name.

"I'm sorry. I know your friend Brian is coming here just to see us. Tell him we hope to meet him very soon."

Please, Chuck, she prayed into the moment of silence that followed.

"I...see. Yes, I'll tell him. Brian will be looking forward to it." Another pause. "I understand you've already met his son?"

He knew. Stevie barely managed to suppress a shiver. "Yes. Just recently." The gun jabbed her this time, painfully, adamantly, "I have to go now, Sean."

"I understand." A note of firm promise came into the young agent's voice. "I'll be seeing you soon."

"Yes. Goodbye."

She held on to the phone, listening to the click of the disconnect, then the return of the dial tone. She couldn't seem to let go, and finally Granger yanked the receiver out of her rigid fingers. Her gaze went to Chase, and she sucked in a breath at the glowing look of knowledge and salute in his eyes. He knew it had been Chuck, she realized. And knew what she had done.

"Very nice, honey," Granger said silkily. Stevie cringed at the falsely sweet tone. "You do as well for me, and maybe I'll change my mind about killing you."

Stevie shuddered. "I'd rather be dead," she spat out.

Granger backhanded her sharply across the mouth. Stevie swallowed a cry of pain. Chase leapt forward, stopping only when Granger jerked the gun around and aimed it at Stevie.

"You try anything, she's dead."

He strong-armed Stevie back into the chair, then reached into his pocket and drew out a length of nylon cord. He crossed the room to Chase.

"Turn around. Put your hands behind you. And just remember, if you make one move I don't like, it's her I'll shoot, not you."

Jaw clenched, Chase obeyed. Granger tied his wrists tightly together, then backed up a step. Chase turned around again, but before he had completed the motion, Granger drew back his arm and sent his fist flying forward. Chase tried to dodge, but the blow still caught him on the ribs and sent him stumbling against the wall.

Stevie was on her feet in an instant. She launched herself at Granger, fingers curled as if to claw the life out of him. She looked like the wildcat Chase had once called her, and never had she looked more beautiful to him. Then Granger heard her movement and turned.

"Stevie, no!"

Chase's shout came just as Granger jammed the gun up against the side of his head. The barrel gouged into his skin. Chase never moved; his eyes were fastened on Stevie.

"It won't take much to make me change my mind," Granger warned savagely. "I'll kill him right now."

Stevie stopped, staring at the gun pressed to Chase's temple.

"If either one of you tries anything stupid again, I'll kill the other one. Sit down."

Stevie dropped, trembling, back down into the chair. Without even turning around, Granger rammed an elbow deep into Chase's belly. Stevie heard the gasp as the air rushed out and saw him double over. Granger raised his arm again. Chase tried to ward it off by kicking at the gangly man's knees.

"I told you what would happen if you did anything stupid," Granger growled, pointing the gun at Stevie.

Chase, shackled more effectively by the threat to Stevie than the cord that held him, backed up to the wall, knowing what was coming. Granger hit him again, harder, then again, and a muffled grunt of pain escaped as Chase sagged against the wall, then slipped down to the floor, hands trapped uselessly behind him.

"You rotten coward," Stevie ground out.

Granger spun around. "Still feeling feisty? I'll take care of that real soon. You won't have *any* spirit left when I get through with you," he promised, then went on to tell her in lurid detail exactly what he planned to do to her.

Stevie tried to shut out the flow of vicious, filthy words. Her gaze went to Chase. He was struggling to get his feet under him, gasping for breath. She saw the rage in his eyes, tempered only by his fear for her.

Then Granger moved, running a hand along the neckline of Stevie's robe. The backs of his fingers brushed her skin, and she flinched. Granger laughed.

"Damn...you...Granger...leave her...alone!"

Chase's voice was harsh, and the words came out between his gulps for air.

"I'm only getting started, Cameron. And you're going to watch. You'll have a lot of memories to live with after she's dead. Just like I remember coming home and finding my mother dead on the floor."

His hand slid lower, his fingers reaching beneath the collar of the robe to touch the upper curve of her breast. Stevie slapped his hand away and tried to get out of the chair. He shoved her back.

Chase made it to his feet. "You touch her again," he choked out, "and there won't be a place on this earth where you can hide. I'll find you."

"Then perhaps I'll just have to kill you, too." Granger smiled lewdly. "Afterward, of course."

He reached down for the tie to Stevie's robe and yanked it loose. The thick terry cloth fell open, baring the inner swell of her breasts. Granger murmured something and reached out to touch her. Stevie clawed at him, her nails leaving four rows of angry red marks down the back of his hand.

"You bitch!" he shouted, jumping back.

In that instant Chase launched himself, arms still twisted painfully behind him, pushing off from the wall with a fierce thrust of one leg. Head down, he hammered into Granger's abdomen, driving him backward.

They went down together with a thud that rattled the walls. The cocked gun fired under the convulsive clutching of Granger's fingers. The round spent itself uselessly in the far wall, but the sound galvanized Stevie. She leapt to her feet, dodging Granger's flailing legs as he tried to rid himself of Chase's muscled weight.

She heard the blows raining down on Chase's body as Granger tried to throw him off. Little grunts of pain escaped him, driving her harder.

She saw the arm that held the weapon begin to curve upward, the chrome barrel angling toward Chase's head. She kicked out at that hand, but her bare feet had little effect. Then Granger began to gain leverage against Chase's fettered body, and she saw him begin to squirm free. Suddenly he'd done it and was aiming the lethal piece of metal.

Desperately she looked around. She grabbed for the nearest thing she found that could be used as a weapon. In between one breath and the next, heedless of the mess she was creating, she brought it down hard on the back of Granger's head.

The oddly hollow thud echoed as Granger collapsed. Chase bucked beneath him, trying to throw off the dead weight. Stevie grabbed Granger's shoulder, tugging at him until Chase was able to scramble free.

He was breathing hard, taking in air in large gulps as he sat up. Stevie, with fingers that were trembling, moved behind him to pick at the rope that bound him. She suppressed a tiny moan when she saw the trickle of blood where the cord had gouged his flesh.

At last she had it done, and the moment his hands were free he twisted around to pull her into his arms.

"God, Stevie, I'm so sorry."

"I don't care," she choked out, her emotions out of control now that he was safe. "It's not your fault. Just tell me you're all right."

"I'm fine. Thanks to you."

"Why did you try that?" Stevie couldn't stop the sob that broke from her. "I thought he was going to kill you."

"I didn't think about it. All I could see was his hands on you." He pressed his lips to her hair. "You took one hell of a chance yourself." He looked around at the chaos on the floor. "Is that how he got in?"

Stevie looked at the scattered flowers, the wet carpet and the heavy vase she had used on Granger's skull. She nodded, biting her lip. "He sent them, then followed the bellhop who delivered them." She shuddered. "God, if I hadn't been so stupid . . ."

"Hush. You couldn't have known." He tried to smile, but it was more like a grimace. "Besides, they wound up saving us in the end."

"It seems . . . appropriate, I guess. To use it on hi-im." She hiccuped in the middle of the word as she tried to swallow another sob. Chase tightened his hold on her, pulling her close, and felt the tiny ripple that went through her when she gave up the battle against her tears.

She was really crying now, her cheek pressed to the bare skin of his chest. He lifted a hand to smooth her hair, murmuring softly.

"It's okay, Stevie. It's over now. You did it, Stevie. You saved us both."

A hammering at the door made them both jump. For a moment terror leapt in Stevie's heart; was it beginning again, just when they thought it was over?

She felt Chase stiffen; then he released her and reached for the gun that lay under the unconscious Granger's outflung hand. He picked it up, ejected the spent shell casing and chambered another round. Stevie wondered somewhat inanely if he had always known about guns, or if that was just one more way his life had changed since he'd been cast into hell.

The hammering came again, then a male voice calling out her name.

Chase got somewhat unsteadily to his feet. He swayed for a moment, shook his head, then stuck the pistol in his waistband. Reflexively rubbing at his raw wrists, he padded quietly toward the door. Stevie wasn't about to be even that far apart from him, and she followed closely. On the way she retied her robe with a shudder and wiped her damp cheeks.

He peered through the peephole but shook his head when she looked the question at him; he didn't recognize whoever it was. When he opened his mouth to speak, she lifted a finger to his lips and hushed him.

"They're asking for me. Let me answer. Just in case."

He hesitated, then nodded, just as the pounding came once more.

"Ms. Holt, are you there?" the man called out again.

She took a deep breath. "Who are you?"

"I'm from the hotel, Ms. Holt. We have an urgent message for you."

Stevie had lost what faith she had in her own judgment. "So call me with it," she said, a little sharply.

"It's about that...package you were expecting. From your friend up north."

Stevie's breath caught. "What friend?"

"Chuck."

Her gaze went to Chase, the question clear in her eyes. Did they dare trust him? Chase let out a compressed breath, then backed away from the door. He flattened himself against the wall beside the door, then pulled out the gun. He released the safety, settled it in one hand braced by the other, then nodded to her. It took every bit of nerve she had to open that door.

He was older than Chuck, around forty, with graying hair and a pair of wire-rimmed glasses. More importantly, he was alone.

"Who are you?"

"My name's Brian," he said, trying to see past her into the room. "Brian Morgan."

The name matched. Stevie caught a glimpse of movement to her left and realized Chase had nodded at her. Her eyes carefully straight ahead, Stevie stepped back as if inviting him in. He didn't move, and Chase mouthed some words at her.

"It's quite all right, Mr. Morgan," she said. "Everything's under control now."

He took one step, and then Chase was behind him, yanking him into the room, twisting his arm up into the small of his back and pressing the gun to his head. Chase looked like a man who had been pushed to the edge and wouldn't need much to send him over.

"Don't move. You've got about two seconds to prove you're who you say you are," he grated out. His voice sounded like he looked. He'd been threatened, beaten, and he'd had to watch while that slime had touched Stevie. He'd had enough, and he didn't try to hide it.

The man's eyes flicked over the unconscious figure on the floor, the empty vase beside him and Stevie's dishevelled appearance.

"Mr. Cameron, I presume?" he said, with creditable calm considering the weapon digging into his neck just below his ear. "My ID is in my front jacket pocket."

"Keep your hands where they are. Stevie?"

She reached gingerly inside the jacket, freezing when she saw the leather of a shoulder holster.

"He has a gun," she said, amazed that she sounded so cool.

"Of course I do. Chuck said you were trapped with a killer." His eyes went to the man sprawled on the floor. "Apparently he underestimated you. And I gather it's not the first time."

Chase ignored the compliment. "Get it," he told Stevie.

She took the gun cautiously, holding it with two fingers. She set it down carefully on the table, then reached for the pocket he'd indicated. A thin leather case was inside, and she lifted it out.

"It looks real to me," she said doubtfully. "And it does say that's his name."

Chase looked at the ID as she held open the case for him to see. Still he hesitated. They had reached the point of no return, and he wasn't sure enough of anything to risk Stevie again. She'd already gone through too much for him. Far too much.

"I don't blame you for being careful," Morgan said. "I remember what happened to you."

"You remember?" Suspicion still laced his voice.

"I heard about it enough. Every time I saw Chuck and we went out for a drink. He'd have a couple, then he'd get to talking, and I knew it was only a matter of time before he'd get around to it. You were the one that ate at him. We all have one, but I've never seen anybody take it as hard as Chuck. He said it wouldn't be so bad if he hadn't gotten to like you so damn much."

"Chuck . . . said that?"

He nodded. "He said to remind you of the night he skunked you in five straight games of gin rummy."

With a sudden exhalation Chase released Morgan's arm and lowered the gun. Stevie nearly cried out her relief.

Unruffled, Morgan glanced at the now-groaning figure on the floor. "Nick Granger, I presume."

Chase nodded. "I should have guessed. But I remembered him as just a kid at the trial."

"He was. But his father did a hell of a job indoctrinating him, it seems. When he knew he was dying, and that the IRS would probably get everything, he realized the pros he hired would quit as soon as they figured out they weren't going to get paid."

"So he went to work on his son."

"Yeah. Hell of a legacy, huh?" As Granger began to stir, Morgan walked over to him. "Guess I'll take him off your hands now." He called over his shoulder, and two gray-suited young men came in, curiosity flickering in their eyes, although they said nothing.

"Thanks," Chase said, rather fiercely.

"And call Chuck, will you? He'll be wondering."

"I will."

Chase shifted his gaze to Stevie. His eyes were clear and vividly green, utterly free of shadows. She ran to him.

"Is it really over?" she whispered, her voice quivering.

"It's over, Stevie. Really over."

She hugged him fiercely, and he didn't even care that she could feel him trembling.

Epilogue

As she got out of her new car and started up the hill, Stevie saw Charlie Starr waving at her with a gloved hand. She waved back, but her gaze lingered barely a moment on him. Then all her attention was riveted on the tall, leanly muscular figure walking a high, heavy beam as gracefully and easily as if it were a sidewalk.

He was shirtless, his tanned skin glistening with sweat under the springtime California sun, his muscles flexing and moving with sinuous grace as he lifted the planks he was carrying to the man farther up. He turned back then, and Stevie's eyes traced the lines of his tautly muscled chest, the ridged abdomen, and lingered lovingly on the path of dark hair that began at his navel and trailed downward to disappear below the waistband of his low-slung jeans.

Then he began to walk back. With his movements, a golden flash shot from the middle of his chest, and her eyes went to the medallion he wore. The disk was about an inch and a quarter in diameter, suspended on a heavy gold chain. Etched into the glowing metal was, unmistakably, the house in the picture. The artist had captured its soaring lines, the height of the cliff, even the restless ocean below, with a detail amazing for so small a space.

She had had it made for him, telling him the original was much too precious to her to give back. The look on his face when he saw it, and the way his fingers shook slightly as he lifted it out of the velvet-lined Pirate's Cove box, had told her that he understood.

He saw her then, and grabbing a smaller crossbeam, he swung down to the ground in one smooth motion.

"Well," he told her with a grin, "we may just make it in time for my family to descend on us this summer."

She laughed. "Good. I want to see them again. I've had about enough of mine hovering over us."

"Your mother has . . . toned it down a bit."

"Because you intimidate the heck out of her." Stevie grinned at him. "Although I did hear her bragging the other day about you really being an architect and opening up your new office here."

Chase smiled wryly; some things, it seemed, would never change. But Stevie had changed, he realized.

"It doesn't bother you anymore, does it?" he asked softly.

Stevie knew immediately what he meant. "No," she agreed, "it doesn't. My mother may never change, but it doesn't matter anymore. Not as long as I have you."

She meant it. In the days when she had been so desperately searching, when all she had been able to think about was the hell Chase was living, her priorities had shifted greatly; nasty comments from her mother now and then were barely worth bothering about.

"Well, if it's any consolation, *my* mother thinks you walk on water."

Stevie giggled. "I like her, too. I'm looking forward to their visit. And I have an appointment set up with a modeling agency for that lovely sister of yours."

He rolled his eyes. He'd recently seen for himself the startling resemblance Cassie bore to him, and it embarrassed him when Stevie mentioned how pretty she was.

Stevie read his thoughts easily. "She *is* lovely," she teased.

"She's supposed to be. She's a girl."

Stevie smiled at his discomfiture. She reached out with her left hand, the hand that bore the glittering gold and rich, deep emerald of the ring he'd presented to her in a box identical to the one that had held his medallion. She'd told him that she preferred the green stone to any diamonds. Chase green, she called it, because it matched his eyes, and the comment never failed to make him blush.

She touched the golden disk that lay against his chest. He never removed it, and just thinking of how it felt, warmed from his body and sliding over hers as he made love to her, finished what looking at him had begun, the rousing of that aching need that seemed always just below the surface.

"It's not Cassie's fault she looks like her gorgeous, sexy, hunk of a brother." Her voice was husky, silky, and hunger glowed in her eyes.

"You know," he said softly, "if you keep showing up here and looking at me like that, this house is never going to get built."

"I can't help it," she said simply.

He closed his eyes and groaned against the surging of his body; she brought him to the flash point faster than he'd ever thought possible.

They stood there, on the bluff overlooking the ocean, with the frame of the house rising behind them. Even in this bare-bones form, the soaring shape of it was clear, the shape mirrored on the golden disk that rested on his chest. She ran a slender finger over that gleaming circle, then turned to look at the growing structure. And then up at the man who had dreamed it.

"'Safe... and free,'" she whispered, remembering the words she had said to him that day so long ago.

"Because of you," he said huskily. "I love you, Mrs. Cameron."

"And I love you, Mr. Cameron," she replied, her hand pressed flat against his chest, her fingertips touching the circle of gold. Again it caught the sunlight, flaring, sending out bright golden sparks, as if announcing to the world that this was one place where darkness had been banished forever.

* * * * *

SILHOUETTE·INTIMATE·MOMENTS®

COMING NEXT MONTH

#405 PROBABLE CAUSE—Marilyn Pappano

Strictly-by-the-book FBI agent Thad McNally had never gotten over his love for Lindsey Phillips. So when the case that had torn them apart was reopened, he didn't hesitate—he went to see her. But things got complicated when he realized that her life—as well as their love—was in danger.

#406 THE MAN NEXT DOOR—Alexandra Sellers

Hot on the trail of an international smuggling ring, police officer Sunny Delancey's low profile was nearly compromised when a mischievous cat got her entangled with the infamous Jock Prentiss. Yet being front-page news proved to be an advantage Sunny couldn't pass up, especially since being considered this hunk's latest lover was no hardship!

#407 TAKING SIDES—Lucy Hamilton

Determined to clear her father's reputation, faithful daughter Hope Carruthers confronted Sean Boudreaux, the only man who could set the record straight. Yet when searching for the truth demanded working closely with sexy Sean, Hope's heart discovered a different sort of truth altogether.

#408 ANGEL ON MY SHOULDER—Ann Williams

Cynical Will Alexander had no idea who the cupcake with the big blue eyes was—she claimed to be Cassandra, his guardian angel—but there was no way *anyone*, not even a woman as enticing as Cassandra, would stop him from getting revenge against his enemy. But he hadn't counted on Cassandra's heavenly means of persuasion....

AVAILABLE THIS MONTH: